The Other

By Troy Young

Troy Young

ISBN: 978-1-7770603-0-5

The Other

Contents

On Cape Breton speech (in It Came From The Sea):

Cape Breton has a local dialect. Actually, several regional dialects. My parents are from Cape Breton, and I have been exposed to these speech patterns and accents for a long time, even slipping into them myself when I have been there for even a few hours. They are influenced by Scottish Gaelic, Irish Gaelic and Acadian French.

In the story, the residents from the fictional Gallou Cove speak with an extreme version of the accent, while other residents from different parts of the island will be more muted. A 'd' sound will often replace a 'th'; you'll see the words dat, dis, den substituted for that, this and then or the 'h' will get dropped (they would not pronounce thinking as dinking; instead they'd say tinking). The words 'right' or 'some' will be used in place of the word 'very'. The use of the phrase b'y (pronounced bye; short for boy) is common, as are phrases with religious connotations (Jesus (or Jaysus), Mary and Joseph). If you are trying to picture what it sounds like in your head, you can drag out the vowels (it can sound like a lazy form of speech).

If you want to learn more, you can look up the Dictionary of Cape Breton English, which has an expansive overview of the speech patterns of Cape Breton.

It Came From The Sea

The early morning sun crested the eastern horizon. Gallou Cove, Cape Breton Island, was home to three hundred souls, nestled in small single-storey homes dotting around the rocky shores, south of Louisbourg Harbour, with the reconstructed fortress and town of the same name.

Mary-Margaret McKeegan was up early walking her golden retriever, Benny; she liked to get up before most others, both to watch the sunrise, and because the deserted beach meant she could let Benny off his leash. Come down later, and she'd run into some busybody who would give her the standard lecture of Benny being off-leash, and how he'd be 'pollutin' the sand with his turds' even though Mary-Margaret was conscientious about picking up after him.

Mary-Margaret had moved to Gallou Cove twenty years ago, but in many ways was still considered an outsider. The thing she liked best about town was nothing ever happened there, and nothing ever changed. Until this morning anyway.

Benny was ahead of her, and he started to bark at something on the beach. Mary-Margaret was too far away to make it out, but something dark lay across the sand. *Probably a basking shark,* she thought to herself. While it happened infrequently, these carcasses sometimes washed ashore.

"Oh, Benny, what have you found there, eh, boy? What is it? Huh, boy, whatchoo got there? What...oh." Mary-Margaret stopped and stared. Whatever it was, it was no basking shark.

Unlike a lot of things that wash ashore, this was still fresh. It looked like a squid, with a long cylindrical body and six tentacles: four smaller ones and two longer ones that ended in sharp stingers. Its body was armoured, like a giant lobster with a

1

green and blue mottled appearance. But the most disturbing thing was the massive, shark-like maw that split the armoured body midway up, filled with sharp, jagged teeth, and the single large fish's eye perched above it. Looking at the creature with its alien-like features caused her to feel sick.

"Benny, heel, heel!" she yelled. The dog came to her side, and she leashed him. Then she took out her phone and began to take pictures.

Mary-Margaret took Benny, and they left the beach and the disturbing creature behind. She headed into town and tied Benny in front of the Shoreline Cafe and went inside.

"Mornin', Mary-Margaret," said Hazel Tutty, the owner of the Shoreline. Hazel was already pouring Mary-Margaret her customary cup of coffee.

"Morning Hazel," she said, sitting on one stool at the counter. "Saw something right strange on the beach this morning. Something has washed up there."

"What was it?" asked Hazel, placing a scone with some butter and jam on a side plate in front of Mary-Margaret.

"I don't rightly know," she said. "But I took some photos on my phone." She pulled out the phone and allowed Hazel to scroll through them.

"Jaysus, Mary and Joseph girl, what in de hell is dat?" Hazel said, wide-eyed looking at the photos. "I ain't never seen nothing like dat before in me life."

"Me neither. Right disturbing, it was. Freaked out poor Benny."

"It's freaking me out just looking at de photos. Hey Cecil, you ever seen anything like dis before?"

Cecil Walker, the self-styled mayor of the town, seemed to know everything there was to know about everything, at least in his mind, anyway. He wasn't really the mayor, as Gallou Cove was too small to have a mayor, but he called himself that anyway. As usual, he was holding court that morning at the Shoreline, and he came over at Hazel's call.

"Hazel, Mary-Margaret, whatcha got dere?" he said, sauntering over and looking at the pictures. "Lard thunderin' Jaysus, dat's goddamn ugly. I ain't never seen nothing like dat before. I wonder if any of de boys dat work de boats have ever seen its like. How big was it? Hard to tell from the photos."

"It was thirty feet if it was an inch," said Mary-Margaret. "Should we call someone to come and look at it?"

"Who'd we call?" said Cecil. "If de boys won't know what it is, no one will."

"We could call up to Eskasoni, to de RCMP detachment dere?" said Hazel.

"Why? Did de thing break into your home or something? Why'd de police care about something like dis?"

"Well, I don't know Cecil, but someone needs to know. At least we're gonna want to get dat ting off de beach."

"We can get a couple of boys with boats to drag it back out to sea where it came from den," said Cecil.

"Why do we want to make this our worry?" said Mary-Margaret. "I think Hazel's right, call the RCMP and even if it's not something they will deal with, at least let them figure out what they should do."

"We don't need no outsiders coming into town and getting involved with our business. Let me round up a coupla fellers, and we'll take care of it. Let's go look at dis ting." Cecil motioned for a few of the patrons in the Shoreline to follow.

Mary-Margaret and Benny led the small gathering to the beach where the carcass still lay where she found it. The residents stared at this unknown thing laying on their beach. Cecil gave a low whistle when he saw it. "Dem pictures, dey didn't do it no justice."

"What do you tink we should do, Mayor?" asked Burns, one of Cecil's hangers-on. "I don't tink we should put it back out to sea. Someone needs to see dis."

"I think you're right, b'y, I think you're right. Dis ting...it's unnatural innit?" declared Cecil. "It's strange. Just looking at it... it's giving me a headache, you know? I tink dat de damn things radioactive or something. I'll bet dem goddamn Yankees have been testin' nukes underwater and created a goddamn monster. Like dat Creature from de Black Lagoon. You can't trust dose damn 'Muricans."

"Let's not be gettin' hasty, now," said Mary-Margaret. "I'm sure someone will know something about it. Maybe we could get some marine biologist up from Dalhousie University to tell us what it is?"

"And I'm tellin' ya, dere ain't no fancy educated marine biologist dat's going to know any more about dis den de fellers dat work de boats all day long. If it's out dere in dat ocean, dey've seen it. Let's wait until Mike or Wally or one of de other fellers gets in, and we asks dem."

Not knowing what else to do, they went to the Shoreline. "I put in a call to de Mounties," Hazel told them when they got there.

"You did what now, woman?" asked Cecil.

"I said I put in a call to de Mounties."

"I thought we decided we'd handle dis ourselves?"

"Just because dese fools call you Mayor doesn't make it so, Cecil Walker. De Mounties said dey'd send someone dis afternoon to look at it."

#

At the detachment of the Royal Canadian Mounted Police in Eskasoni, the call was handled with the expected level of seriousness that such requests deserved.

"Hey, who wants to go look at a sea monster?" the staff sergeant chuckled.

"A sea monster? Where?" asked a constable.

"In Gallou Cove."

"Pass," said the constable. "I don't want to drive down there."

"It's like an hour away. You got something else that needs doing?" asked the sergeant.

"I don't want to go, that's all."

"Well, I guess you shouldn't have spoken up then, should you have, smartass?"

"Ah, don't make me go! Please, Sarge!"

"Make him go where?" said Corporal Joe Mills as he entered the detachment.

"Gallou Cove. We got a call about a sea monster."

Joe shrugged. "I'll go."

"Really?" said the constable.

4

"Sure thing. It's a nice day out, and a drive to the shore is better than whatever else the Sarge might make me do. I've never seen a sea monster, either."

"That's a good point. I'll go, Sarge," said the constable.

"You had your chance. All right, Millsy, go check it out."

Joe Mills drove to the town and got his first glimpse of Gallou Cove. It was a typical small coastal town with brightly painted tiny houses dotting the rocky shore. The main street had as many boarded-up shops as open ones. There was a convenience store (that still had VHS tapes available for rent), a hair salon (complete with faded photos of hairstyles from thirty years ago hanging in the window) and his destination, the Shoreline Cafe.

The Corporal parked his car in front of the cafe. He took one last look at the computer screen, making sure the details matched the ones he had transcribed in his casebook. A good officer kept proper notes.

The bell above the door tinkled as he entered. Joe pulled out his case book and read from it, even though he had already committed everything to memory. "Excuse me, is there a Hazel Tutty here?"

"Dat'd be me, darlin'. I be de one dat made de call about de sea monster dat washed up de way," said Hazel. "It must have been a long drive for you; can I getcha something, luv?"

"No, ma'am, I'm fine. What can you tell me about this unidentified organic mass found on the beach this morning?"

"You mean de sea monster? Well, I hasn't seen it. I had to stay in de cafe. Mary-Margaret, she's de one dat found it. Well, her and Benny. I can ring her if you'd like, and she can tell you what she found."

"No need, Hazel, I can tell de officer alls he needs to know. Mayor Cecil Walker," Cecil strode forward and thrust out his hand, which Joe took after a glance at it. "Ise seen de beast with me very own eyes. Tis nothin' like I've ever seen in me life. We're waiting for de boys to get back in on deir boats to sees if deys knows what it is." Cecil looked at Corporal Mills shrewdly. "What d'ou say your name was? And where you from?"

"I'm Corporal Mills, and I'm from the Eskasoni detachment."

5

"Youse not from Eskasoni, b'y. Where d'ou come from?"

This wasn't the first time this question had been asked of Joe. "I'm from Fredericton originally, but I've been policing these parts the last ten years."

"You see dat, Hazel? I told youse not to call. Not only do dey send us a mainlander, but he's not even from within de province!"

"Oh, g'way would you, Cecil. It doesn't matter where de officer is from; he's here to help. Don't mind Cecil, Officer Mills. He likes to tink he's more important dan he is."

"It's fine, ma'am, and it's Corporal, not Officer. Now, Mr. Walker," ignoring the honorific that Cecil had given himself. "You said you saw this unidentified organic mass? What did it look like?"

"I'm gonna call Mary-Margaret," said Hazel. "She should be here. It was her discovery, after all."

"Well, Corporal, as I said, I've never seen anything like it ever, and I've celebrated seventy years on dis here planet, all of it right here in Gallou Cove. Not a ting happens dat Ise don't know about it, you see? Dis thing, it was as long as a fishing boat, see, long and tube-like, like a squid, with tentacles and a lobster body and a big shark's mouth."

"Uh-huh," said Joe, jotting this all down and glancing to see if Cecil was pulling his leg, but the earnestness on Cecil's face told him that Cecil was telling the truth. "Maybe I should see this myself. Hazel? Is this..." he looked at his notes. "Mary-Margaret and Benny meeting us here, or on the beach?"

"Mary-Margaret is going to meet us here. She'll probably leave Benny at home."

"I will want to get a statement from Benny."

"Dat's fine, but all you're likely to get outta Benny is 'woof'," laughed Hazel.

"Benny is a dog," said Joe, scratching Benny's name out of his notes. He struggled to think of a relevant question to ask, but couldn't think of anything. Joe figured it would be a stinking, rotting pile of flesh and he'd have to call the municipality to send a bulldozer to get it off the beach. Nothing more to it; might as well wait until Mary-Margaret showed.

He didn't have to wait long. Mary-Margaret soon arrived. "Corporal Mills, this is Mary-Margaret," said Hazel, introducing her to the RCMP officer.

"Ma'am."

"Pleased to meet you, Corporal. I assume you'll have some questions?"

"A few, but I need to assess if there is anything to be done with it," said Joe. "Most likely, it will be something for the municipality to come to clean up."

"Oh, dat's rich. I can see dem municipality boys right messing up de beach as dey play around in de sand with it," said Cecil. "Good for nothing, de municipality is, b'y."

"Shush now, Cecil," said Hazel. "Why don't you get outta me hair and go with Mary-Margaret and de Corporal to see de ting? Make yourself useful for once."

Cecil grumbled but held open the door for Joe and Mary-Margaret, and the three of them filed out of the Shoreline.

"So, you were out walking your dog when you came across this unidentified organic mass?" Joe asked as they made their way to the beach.

"Oh, yes. I take Benny out early morning before anyone else is out there. We were out, and Benny found it."

"Are you sure it wasn't a big pile of seaweed?"

"I never seen seaweed with an eye or a mouthful of teeth," said Mary-Margaret.

"Ah, dat's right, I forgot about dat eye. Bigger dan a hubcap it was," said Cecil.

Joe could see the beach ahead. A small crowd had gathered there; news of the discovery had attracted an audience. They crossed the sand, and he excused himself as he pushed through the gathering and caught sight of the creature for the first time. He knew this was not something for the municipality to handle.

It was as Cecil had described: a lobster-squid-shark hybrid with a single, starring dead eye. The smell coming off of it was unbelievable. It wasn't the smell of decaying organic matter; it was something else. Being near it, looking at it, was unsettling. He took out his phone and started to take pictures.

"All right, I need everyone to step back. We don't know what this is or if it's dangerous, so please keep going back, back,

back." Joe spread his arms wide and walked towards the group, getting them to shuffle backwards. After fifty feet, Joe stopped. "No one comes any closer than this line, understand?" he said, drawing a line about fifteen feet long in the sand. He needed to get police tape and stakes to cordon off the area from his cruiser. "Cecil," Joe said. "Do me a favour and make sure no one gets any closer. I have to go back to my car." Joe figured that making Cecil feel important would work to his advantage, and he was right.

"Youse all heard de Mountie," said Cecil, puffing out his chest and hiking up his blue jeans under his prodigious belly. "Keep it clear. Dis here is an official investigation, and we can't have none of youse messing up de scene."

Joe laughed to himself as he made it back to his cruiser. He opened the door and sat in the car, his left leg still out on the ground, and he reached for the radio. "Dispatch, it's Mills. Can you patch me through to the staff sergeant, please?" There was a pause as they made the connection. "Sarge, Millsy. This thing, it's strange. We will need an expert in on this."

"What is it?"

"Hell if I know, that's why we need the expert. I think it might be an undiscovered species. We've got a genuine scientific discovery on our hands here. I will secure the site."

"All right, I'll call Dal; they'll send someone. They won't get there until tomorrow afternoon, though."

"That's fine. I guess I'll be on this case for a few days then?"

"At least until the researcher decides it's time to get it off the beach, yeah."

"All right. I won't bother to come into the detachment then. I'll check in from here in the morning."

"Roger that. Let me know if things change. Out."

Joe opened his trunk and got out the caution tape and the stakes. He made his way back to the beach and staked out space around the creature.

"Thanks, Cecil, for keeping everyone back," said Joe.

Cecil smiled. "Happy to help. So, what's de next step?"

"Well, I think we may have an important scientific discovery. We've got a call into Dalhousie, asked if they could send a marine biologist to look at it. If it is something new, maybe they'll name it after Gallou?"

"Wouldn't dat be something?" said Cecil. He'd be in his glory talking about this for the next couple of days to anyone who would listen.

"I'm heading out, but I'll be back in the morning. It would be a big help if you could organize a little watch, you know, to have someone keep their eyes on it until I get back. We want nothing to happen to it before the researcher gets here."

"Consider it done Corporal; you can count on me," said Cecil. "I'll gets a bunch of fellas, and we'll spend de night here on de beach, keeping our eye on it for ya."

Joe smiled and headed back to his home. The next morning when he arrived back on the scene, he found evidence of a large bonfire, beer bottles strewn around the area and a few men asleep in lawn chairs. Cecil was up and awake.

"Sorrys about de mess dere; not to worry, we'll clean it all up," said Cecil as Joe walked over.

"Sure," said Joe. He had gotten word a Dr. Adele Kramer would arrive around noon. It was over a four-and-a-half-hour drive from Halifax to here. "We have to secure this until the researcher gets here."

As Cecil went to rouse his buddies and clean the beach, Joe stood looking at the creature from a distance. He didn't want to be any closer to its disturbing presence than necessary. While he was there, he noted something peculiar. Nothing was coming close to the creature. No birds were pecking at it, no crabs nibbling on it, no insect alighting upon it. Everything was giving it a wide berth. Very unusual.

"So's, I spoke to Mike and Wally and a few of de boys dat work de boats and dey ain't never seen nothing like dis before. It's like straight outta dat sci-fi or something," said Cecil. "I doubt your fancy marine biologist is going to know what it is either."

"Maybe not. They'll make some notes and then haul it away. This thing will be over in a few days."

"Oh, d'ou think?" said Cecil, hoping that this little adventure would last a little longer. "What in de hell is dis here now?" he said, looking past Joe towards the town.

Joe turned around to see a news crew coming towards them. "Deys from de CBC," said Burns, running ahead of the crew. "Hazel called dem."

"Ah, dat gossipy woman, can't keep nuthin' to herself," said Cecil. "Why'd she go and do dat for?"

"Maybe you'll get on TV," said Joe, smiling at Cecil.

"Wait, d'you think so?"

"They will want to ask people about it. You're the mayor, aren't you?" Joe chuckled. "We'd better go greet them."

Joe, Cecil and Mary-Margaret were all interviewed. Joe and Mary-Margaret's interviews were concise and to the point. Cecil's interview was a rambling affair that touched upon things unrelated to the creature, railing against the government, the Americans and the sad state of the Toronto Blue Jays.

"I tink dat went well," said Cecil.

Everyone headed back to the Shoreline Cafe to wait for Dr. Adele Kramer. She showed up later than expected at half-past one.

"Dr. Kramer?" asked Joe.

"Yes. And I suppose you are Corporal Mills?"

"Call me Joe."

"Ok, Joe. And you can call me Adele." Adele was in her early 30s and had her hair pulled back into a functional ponytail, held in place by her Dalhousie University cap. "Where is our globster?"

"It's pronounced lobster, miss. I'da tought a marine biologist would know dat," scoffed Cecil.

"A globster is a term used to describe an unidentified organic mass that washes ashore. Given that no one knew what it was and asked that I come here to check it out, I believe the term applies," Adele said.

"Where ya from?" asked Cecil.

"From Dalhousie."

"Dat's not what I meant, miss. I mean, where your people from?"

"I'm from Victoria originally. Not that it should matter."

"BC! "

"Oh, g'way wouldja? At least she's from an island." Hazel said as she shoed Cecil away. "Miss, jeet yet? Ise can whip something up right quick for you if you'd like."

"Sorry, 'jeet'?"

"It means 'did you eat.' It takes a bit to get used to the local colloquialisms, but you'll pick it up quick," said Joe.

"Dat's what I asked her, in plain English. So, jeet?"

"I haven't yet, no. But first I'd like to see that globster."

"I can take you there," said Joe. Cecil followed them down.

They strode down the path to the beach. The crowd was growing.

"Dere's a buncha fellas I ain't never seen before," said Cecil. "Word's getting around, I guess."

"I heard a report on the radio as I drove here," said Adele. "Every fifteen minutes. There was lots of speculation about the sea monster that washed ashore. People have such vivid imaginations. It will draw lots of interested people to your town."

"Did anyone share with you the pictures we took?" asked Joe.

"No."

"The term 'sea monster' might not be that much of a stretch of the imagination."

"I've seen many things washed up on a lot of different shores. They always look stranger than you'd expect. Decomposition can change what you're looking at, making it seem more alien than it is."

"Well, I'd hate to see what this will look like when it decomposes," said Joe.

They pushed through the final people crowding around the creature and Adele got her first view. She stopped dead in her tracks. "What in the hell is that?"

"That's our globster."

Adele climbed under the police tape and knelt beside it. "What a stench," she said. "I can smell it starting to decompose, but there is something else there too. I can't put my finger on it. It's making me lightheaded."

"You'll get dat way just looking at it," said Cecil. "So, what d'ou tink it is den?"

"Well, it is exhibiting a variety of characteristics. I'd say it is some hybrid of Architeuthis, Nephropsidae and Carcharodon Carcharias, but I don't see how that is possible. I cannot classify its genus."

"Arch-a what now? What were dose words you used? Not all of us went in for dat fancy book learnin', you know. Put it in terms a non-egghead can understand."

"A hybrid of a giant squid, lobster and great white shark."

"Well, Jaysus, Mary and Joseph, we didn't need no marine biologist to come here and tell us dat. We'd figured dat much out by ourselves."

"I will need to inspect it. This creature is unlike anything I or anyone else I think has ever seen."

"Do we have an unidentified species on our hands?" asked Joe.

Adele was staring at the creature. "We know so little about the oceans; new things are discovered in them all the time. We can assume that this is not something that anyone has classified before." She stood and walked around the carcass. "I've got a colleague in the Zoology Department at Miskatonic University in Arkham, Massachusetts, who has been studying several weird sea creatures found near the towns of Innsmouth and Kingsport. I will take some pictures and draft some notes and send them to him. He probably hasn't seen anything like this either; he'll want to come and look at it himself."

"So, can we assist you?"

"I want to get this thing off the beach. I will dissect it to get a look at what it looks like on the inside. It's the only way we'll figure things out. This beach is too open; even if I erected a tent over it, I'm worried that it will speed up decomposition. How long has it been here?"

"Someone discovered it yesterday morning."

"Hmm. That would explain the limited decomposition, but I would expect this thing to be covered in insects or partially eaten by crabs."

"I noted that too," said Joe. "Birds are avoiding it."

"Is there anywhere we can take this thing? And a way to move it if there is? A whale this size would be about seven or eight tons, but with that exoskeleton, it could weigh more. Figure at least ten tons."

"Well, George has a Caterpillar backhoe dat weighs more dan dat. And he's got his big flatbed dat he uses to haul it around. As for where we can put dis ting, well, we could put in de old fish packing plant. Tings built out on de pier. It's been locked up since it shut ten years back, but it's plenty big. Youse could store twenty of dese tings in it. We might even get de 'frigerator back on in dere. Old Eddie, he's a right wizard with 'lectricity. If anyone can get dat place working again for youse, it'd be Eddie."

"Who owns the fish plant? We'd need permission to go in there," said Joe.

"Bah, dey'd gone bankrupt and de bank I tink owns it or something. Old Veronica, she used to work in de office dere; she probably still has de keys on account dat woman never throws anything out."

"Keys or not, we can't break in and use the place without permission. It's trespassing, and there will be insurance and liability issues. We must find out and ask to use it."

"Bah, youse law and order types spoil all de fun. And here I was thinkin' we was starting to get along."

It wasn't hard to track down the owner of the fish plant. Before he died, Mary-Margaret's husband Herb had purchased the property for next to nothing from the bank. He had it in his head to refurbish the building and the accompanying pier to turn the little town into an artist community with studio and gallery space. His plans for the plant died with him. "How'se come I didn't know about dat?" said Cecil after Hazel had told them Mary-Margaret owned it.

"It's not like we need to ask you permission before we do something in dis town, you know," she sniffed.

"Yeah, but..."

"Don't you 'yeah, but' me, Cecil Walker. I'm down to my last nerve, and you're on it!"

Mary-Margaret let them use it. "I don't know where the keys are." But as Cecil had said, old Veronica, who had worked in the front office, still had a set hanging on the keyrings by her front door so that they could get inside.

Someone had stripped the place bare. All the front offices were empty, and the back where they processed the fish was cold and dank. "Back in de day when dis here plant was running, dis place was like one big 'frigerator," said Cecil. "You could drop 'er down to thurty-nine degrees Fahrenheit in about thurty minutes."

"What's that in Celsius?" asked Joe.

"I don't know, I never abide by dat metric system. Government conspiracy dat is. Just like chemtrails and daylight savings time."

"It's about four degrees Celsius," said Adele. "That will do."

Eddie worked on restoring power, hoping the refrigerators still worked after lying dormant for ten years. Joe decided he did not want to hang around and watch this happen. It was better if he had no official knowledge of this. He went down to the creature.

George Rantwell refused to help for anything less than two hundred dollars. This was an issue since no official body had provided a budget for dealing with this carcass. Adele forked over the two hundred, seeing as she wanted to move this process along. "I'll figure out a way to pass the costs on to the university," she shrugged.

George almost got the flatbed stuck in the sand on a few occasions, but he managed to get it positioned close to the creature. They debated how to get it onto the flatbed. George thought they could dig small shallow holes under the beast to thread straps and lift it in the air, but Adele said no to that plan. "The carcass might snap in half under the strain of the weight," she said.

They decided they would try to drag it onto the flatbed, hoping that the hardened carapace would protect it. George used the backhoe to pull the creature from the sand, scraping it up the steel ramp. They got it on mostly intact; One of the long tentacles, one with a stinger, was ripped off. George used the backhoe to scoop it and place it on the flatbed beside the rest.

It pained Cecil that he couldn't be in two places at once. As much as he wanted to watch the move, he knew they had to get the refrigerators back online.

"Eddie! How's it goin', b'y?"

"Keep yer shirt on," said Eddie, trying to hook up the old panel to the wire outside. With no way to turn off the power, not without calling the electric company and having to go through the official rigmarole, he was running it live. The old panel was sparking in a few places. From time to time, as he attached the wires together, he would jump and curse as he received a shock. He yelled back to Cecil: "Give 'er a flip!"

Cecil flipped the big switch on the side to the refrigeration unit. The old machine groaned as it came to life, but soon it was humming along, and the temperature was dropping.

The operation took four hours; an hour and a half to load the specimen onto the flatbed and two and a half to get it down the street to the old fish plant. By now, over a thousand people gathered on the beach. Cars choked off the road through town. Hazel was run off her feet as the Shoreline overflowed with customers.

"I ain't never seen anything like dis in Gallou Cove," said Cecil, wide-eyed as they backed the flatbed into the fish plant. The carcass slid off and onto the floor with a loud crunch.

"Where'd all dese people come from?" asked Eddie.

"They all want to see the sea monster, I guess," said Joe. "Never underestimate the power of radio."

"It's also tearing up Twitter and Instagram," said Mary-Margaret, showing them her phone. "Hashtag galloucove and hashtag seamonster are both trending. Lots of people talking about how they want to come to see the sea monster. They got some good shots too," she pulled up a picture of a young woman in a beanie and sunglasses standing in front, flashing a peace sign and making a duck face. "This woman here, she's a world traveller; she's got over two million followers."

"What de hell is an Instagram?" asked a confused Cecil.

"We got this thing inside. Now, what?" asked Joe.

"It's been a long day. Let's shut it down for the night and work on it first thing in the morning," said Adele. "I might need to get a circular saw to cut through the exoskeleton. I'm not going to learn much until I open it."

"Where are you staying?" asked Joe.

"The nearest hotel was in Sydney," she said. "That's forty minutes from here, so I got an Airbnb in Louisbourg instead. I think I'll head over there; this town's getting crowded, and it looks like it will take some time getting out of here."

"Yeah, I'll call in some help," said Joe. "If for nothing else but traffic control."

"Airbnb, huh? Dat's an idea," said Eddie.

#

Joe showed up at the fish plant early the next morning, a tray of coffee in his hand. Steam rose off the hot coffee in the cold air of the refrigerated room. Adele had beaten him there and was already at work. "I brought you some coffee," he said. "I don't know how you take it, but there are sugar and creamers for you."

"Thanks."

"The smell isn't improving, that's for sure." The thing was unnerving. Joe felt there was a buzzing in his head at the edge of his consciousness, and it made him dizzy.

"Yeah, I thought I'd get used to it. No such luck. It's making it difficult to focus."

"Making any headway?"

"This exoskeleton is tough. I wrecked the first two saw blades I used on it. Cecil sent Burns to Sydney to the Canadian Tire there to get a diamond-tipped blade." She shrugged. "If that doesn't work, maybe I'll hit it with a sledgehammer or something."

"Get a giant lobster cracker," joked Joe. "There's probably a novelty one somewhere."

Adele laughed. "I'll poke around in its mouth and check out these tentacles while I wait," she said. "The teeth, they're nasty. Bigger than a great white."

"It's a lot bigger than a great white shark."

"Yeah, I measured it. It's thirty-three feet long. That's thirteen feet longer than the largest great white. Its maw is fifty percent bigger, so that's not surprising." She shuddered. "I wouldn't want to run into this thing out in the ocean."

"How do you think it moves?" asked Joe. "It doesn't have a tail."

"I assume it propels itself like a squid does, a form of rudimentary jet propulsion. Now a squid," she began to walk and point at the tentacles. "It has eight smaller tentacles and two longer ones. It uses the longer ones to catch prey and the smaller ones to hold it in place as their beak tears into whatever they caught. This only has four of the smaller ones, and with those stingers, I don't think this thing uses the longer ones to catch prey."

"You think those stingers are poisonous?"

"Venomous. If it injects a toxin, it's venomous. If it's something you consume, it's poisonous. And that is my assumption, yes. I will dissect the big tentacle that fell off, assuming the venom production would be in the main body, but some form of the delivery system should be easy to find. There could be traces of venom that I can get analyzed."

"You able to do that here?"

"No," she admitted. "I have neither the tools nor the know-how to analyze the toxin. I'll have to send it back to the university. What's the mood in town?"

"Getting busier all the time. The locals have started to rent out their extra rooms, charging people to set up tents on their property. Pictures of this thing have gone viral, and we got news crews coming in. The government is sending someone in from the Department of Fisheries and Oceans to handle the requests. They've gotten calls about this from as far away as Sweden and Japan. The biggest thing that's ever happened to Gallou Cove, that's for sure."

"Well, that's great. Once the government gets here, they'll bring in their own people. They haven't sent in an order for me to cease, have they?"

"Not that I know of," said Joe.

"Good," said Adele, pulling out her phone and turning it off. "And now the university can't get to me either. When will they get here?"

"Tomorrow."

"Looks like I'm burning the midnight oil then. I want to get as advanced as I can on my research before someone stops me."

17

"You sure they'll do that?"

She shrugged again. "They might allow me to collaborate, but I'll not risk it. I'll assume the worst-case scenario."

"I'll leave you to your work, then. The detachment sent a few constables; I've got two maintaining order with the traffic situation, and I have one stopping people from coming out onto the pier to get to the plant. So far, people are respectful, but those who missed getting a glimpse of this thing on the beach will try to get out to the pier to see it."

"Thanks," she said. Joe left.

There wasn't much to do but visit the Shoreline Cafe. It was standing room only. Cecil was sitting in the corner, regaling several visitors on the sea monster. "Dat damn ting, just to cast your eyes on it, will make you feel all weird inside. And de stink, b'y, enough to choke you. Never seen nothin' like it. No one has."

Joe shook his head and suppressed a laugh; Cecil was enjoying the attention. He walked to the crowded counter and overheard Eddie talking to another resident. "I puts me back room up on de Airbnb, you see," he was saying. "All dese people in town lookin' for a place to stay, I might as well make a few bucks, right? I'm getting forty bucks a night for it."

"Old Andy is getting sixty for dat room above his garage."

"Dat old place? It's a dump. Does it have a bathroom?"

"He's got dat old outhouse out back."

"What? Jaysus, b'y, I'm getting hosed! I gotta find a way to get dat fella to leave so I can put up de rate!"

This time Joe laughed out loud. He got Hazel's attention. Exasperated, strands of her hair had fallen out of their bobby pins. "God love ya, Corporal, what can I get for ya? It might be quite de wait; I'm getting run off me feet here."

"That's okay, Hazel. I don't mind a wait. Why don't you have any help?"

"I called me sister to come down from New Waterford; she'll be here later dis afternoon. 'Til den, it's just me."

"What's the easiest thing for you to get me? I don't want to add to your worries."

"A bowl of clam chowder, coming up."

18

Without a place to sit, Joe took the bowl outside onto the street. The constables helped maintain order. While he was standing there, he noticed Burns coming back with supplies in a Canadian Tire bag. Joe gave him a nod.

"Hey dere, Corporal. Dis is crazy," he gestured at the traffic. "Kennington Cove Road be backed up all de way to Louisbourg. Took me an hour to get here from dere. It's like de whole island is down dis way to see dis ting."

"Enjoy it while it lasts," said Joe. "I figure someone will move it out of here in a few days."

"Enjoy it? Hazel's doing a good business because of dis, but for de rest of us, it's a right pain in de arse." Burns hurried away to take the saw blades to Adele.

Joe radioed into the detachment to update them. Then he went to check on Adele. When he got there, the smell of the creature mixed with the metallic smell of a burned-out circular saw.

"Oh, good. I could use your help," said Adele. "The diamond-tipped blades worked, but I'm afraid this old saw couldn't handle the task. I owe Eddie a new saw." Joe could see the breached carapace; a line ran the length of the torso, with only the last two feet still intact. "I want to pry this open. See if you and Burns can insert those crowbars into it and pry it apart."

Burns had stayed to watch. He passed a crowbar to Joe, and they both stuck their tool into the gap and worked the gap wider along the entire length. It let go with a loud crack; black liquid gushed out, and the stench grew stronger.

"This is unlike anything I have ever seen," said Adele, looking at the exposed insides. She closed her eyes and shook her head. "I can't even...I..." she leaned over and emptied the contents of her stomach. This, coupled with the odour and intense vertigo he was feeling from looking inside the creature, caused Joe to vomit as well; Burns followed suit.

The world was spinning for Joe. They had to get out of the fish plant. He reached out and grabbed hold of both Burns and Adele and steered them to the door, and pushed them out into the fresh air. The three lay on the pier gulping in air.

"Jaysus, what in de hell?" spit out Burns. "What did dat ting do to us?"

"That thing is a biohazard," said Joe. "I'm shutting this down until the government types get here. Let them figure it out."

"No! You can't!" gasped Adele. "This is an undiscovered creature. The research into it could be invaluable. Let me continue!"

"You were in there. That thing overwhelmed us when we cracked it open, and we don't know why. The government guys will drape this building in a tent and use hazmat suits to protect themselves and others. It's not safe in that building with the creature in its current state. My responsibility is to keep the people in this town safe, and that includes you, whether or not you want me to."

"You can't do this!"

"Last time I checked, I can. I'm the authority in this town, and until someone with higher authority than me says otherwise, this is a closed site." Joe looked at her. "I'm sorry, but I have no choice."

"What if I got some protective gear? Could I go back in then?"

"You have a hazmat suit back in your car?"

"No."

"Do you know where to get one?"

"Back at the university. But that would take five hours to get it here. And they don't let you walk out of the building with them. Someone will want to know why I need it and I can't tell them that. I'm sure they'd tell me the same thing you are; stand down until the government gets here."

"You're not going back in. I'm sorry."

"Well, I don't know where to get one of dose fancy suits," said Burns. "But what about some SCUBA gear? Or maybe even better, one of dem rigs dat firefighters wear? Would dat work?"

"I suppose," said Joe. "It would at least give a person protection from whatever airborne toxin that thing is giving off. It's not quite the same as a hazmat suit."

"Can you get me one?" asked Adele.

"Ise can sure try. Me cousin in Louisbourg is in de Fire Department, see. He might get us one or two on de sly. And someone in town is bound to have some SCUBA gear. Cecil would know."

"Would you let me go back in if we got some of this gear?" Adele asked Joe.

"If we can, then I'll let you go in. But we need at least two sets because I'll be there with you. If something goes wrong and one of us is overwhelmed, the other person is there to help. And I'd prefer the fire gear over SCUBA; the fire gear is rated for hazardous environments."

"And you'd have no problem with them getting gear from the Fire Department?"

"I'll put in a call to the Chief myself. I'd like them to be on-site to administer first aid; they can also hose us off when we get out of there in case there are any contaminants on us."

"Thank you," sighed Adele.

"If you find something new and exciting, name it after me," smiled Joe.

"I was dere too, remember," said Burns. "And it was my idea to use fire suits!"

"I'll put you both as co-researchers," laughed Adele.

Joe went back to his cruiser and placed a call into the Fire Chief in Louisbourg. The Chief agreed to help. "My boys would love to be dere," she said. "We've heard de news about dat monster; we want to see it up close. But I have two conditions. First, if we get a call, we got to bug out of dere. Which brings me to my second one; your boys will have to keep a lane clear in town. We need to vacate if called, and I will not navigate dat traffic. If you can't assure me we can get out of dere with no issue, we will not take part."

"Fair enough," said Joe. "When can you get here?"

"We'll be dere in thirty."

Joe coordinated with his constables to keep the main road clear of traffic and then went back to relate to Adele that the Fire Department would soon be there. Cecil and Mary-Margaret were both on the pier.

"Fire Department is on its way."

"Thank you," said a relieved Adele. "I have some theories about the creature I need to confirm."

"Like what?"

21

"That is not a carbon-based life form."

"Sorry? Explain that to me."

"All life on Earth is carbon-based. It is the basic structure, and metabolism uses carbon compounds for their functioning, water as a solvent, needs oxygen, creates waste, etc."

"So, everything poops?" said Mary-Margaret.

"In a manner of speaking, yes, at least concerning animal life. Carbon is so abundant that all life we have studied uses it as a key component. There are theories that alternatives could exist."

"Oh, like in Star Trek?" asked Cecil.

"Wait, are you using science fiction as a basis of your theory?"

"Not just science fiction, no. There have been theories that on other planets, ones that have a different chemical structure from Earth if life were to form there, it would need different chemical compounds to survive. Like Titan, Saturn's moon, there is liquid methane in abundance. The theory is life there would use methane instead of water as its basis, making the whole basic structure different. Given the strong smell we encountered, I believe we have a life form that uses a different chemical structure, such as ammonia or methane. In concentrated amounts, it could have negative effects on us."

"What are you saying?" asked Joe.

"I don't think this thing is from our planet."

"We got an alien on our hands?" asked Cecil.

"Maybe. I don't know for sure. I need to inspect it to confirm my theory. And I can't confirm it here. This fish plant isn't a laboratory. I'll see if my hypothesis is still valid and requires further testing."

"If you thought this town was full of people now, wait until the rumours start we have an alien in here," said Joe. "This needs to stay between the four of us. No one else needs to know." Everyone turned to look at Cecil.

"What?" he said.

"He means keep your big mouth shut," said Mary-Margaret. "Don't go running around blabbing to everyone about the alien."

"I feel dat accusation unfairly targets me."

"Maybe," said Joe. "But I'd feel better if you stayed here on the pier with us for now."

"What? I was about to go back to de Shoreline for a cuppa," said Cecil.

"You was going back to start flapping your gums," said Mary-Margaret. "You want to keep sticking your nose into everything, well sometimes it's going to bite you. I'm with the Corporal; I think you need to stay right here with us."

"You can't do dat to me!"

"Well, I can order you into quarantine," said Joe. "I can say you pose a public health risk since you've been exposed to some unknown substance here at the pier. Or you could stay close by."

"Besides Cecil," said Mary-Margaret. "You might miss out on something. Think of the story you'll be able to tell, you being right here and all when the good doctor made her discovery. You were one of a very select few on hand to witness it."

"Because if you leave, I won't let you back here," said Joe.

Cecil was mulling this all over. The lure of telling everyone in the Shoreline about an alien was pulling at him, but the chance to be on hand was too hard to pass up. The TV fellas might want to interview him again. "All right, I'll stay put."

The Fire Department showed up a brief time later. The Chief introduced herself. "Linda Deveaux. Is dis the ting?" She looked in through the door. "Damn, dat is sure strange."

"That it is. That's why Dr. Kramer wants to get a close look at it," said Joe. "I'm Corporal Mills, and it's good of you to do this."

"As I said on de phone, we want to see it for ourselves. I will give you access to two SCBAs."

"SCBAs?" asked Adele.

"Self Contained Breathing Apparatus. Like SCUBA, but without de underwater designation. Dese are not what you should use; de ones designed for environmental hazards have full-body protection to keep you away from contaminants. But I take it dere is a sense of urgency. And do you feel it is safe, Dr. Kramer?"

"I do. I don't believe we are at risk of contamination; we need access to fresh air."

23

"I will give you a full set of fire gear. It will give you an extra protective layer, and we can hose you off, just in case."

"Thanks."

"Our full facemasks have built-in radios, so if we need to extract you, we'll hear you. I will request we tether you so we can drag you out if dere is an incident. We can also talk to you. Remember, our first duty is to de people of our district. We get a call, and we have to leave, no lingering. If we call you, you need to drop everything and exit de building. We clear?"

"Crystal."

"So, who is going in with you?"

"I am," said Joe.

"Ok, we'll match you with two sets dat should fit and den brief you on deir use."

Joe and Adele got measured by two of the firefighters and helped into their gear while Mary-Margaret and Cecil stood off to the side and watched.

"You've got about thirty-five minutes of compressed air as long as you don't exert yourself. Exertion causes you to use de air faster. Dere is a big gauge to keep your eye on dat shows you how much time you have left, but we'll watch dat for you out here, so you don't need to use it. We'll give you a head's up when we tink de air is getting low, and we can swap out de tanks for you. Now pull on your hoods." Joe and Adele pulled on the hoods that covered their heads. The hood had a clear face shield built into it. Chief Deveaux held her radio to her mouth. "You hear me?" came her voice over the speakers built into the hood.

"Loud and clear," said Joe. Adele gave a thumbs up.

"You're good to go den."

Adele and Joe went back in. Heading over to the creature, they noticed the insides were asymmetrical. Joe still felt a sense of vertigo looking at it.

"This doesn't look like anything I've ever seen," said Adele. "Does it look like it's moving? Not moving like you would expect it to move, but shifting? Like part of it is there but when you stare, it's not there?"

"Yes. I couldn't have defined it, but I knew something was wrong with what I was looking at it. But now you say that, that's it."

"It's like our brain is trying to make sense of what it's seeing, but it can't."

"It's making me dizzy."

"Well, don't puke again. I can't imagine it would be enjoyable in these masks to do that."

"Not to mention we don't want to clean dem out," came Chief Deveaux's voice over the speakers.

"Oh yeah, I forgot you were listening," said Adele.

"What do you want to do?"

"I'll take some tissue samples, samples of its blood, standard stuff. I can't test it until we get back to a proper lab. But I'll also take some pictures of the insides too. At the limited glance we've had, I can't identify its heart, or its brain or any organs. It may look like a squid or a lobster from the outside, but on the inside, it shares none of these characteristics. And now that we have it broken open, I'll explore the venom sac; I cut open the tentacle that fell off earlier before Burns got back with the saw blades. I found the delivery system, but there was no venom. The composition might shed some light, so I'll want a sample of that, too."

"I guess we better get to work then because it seems like you have a lot you want to do. Is there anything I can help with?"

"You can take some pictures. My camera is over there," she pointed to a collapsible table they had set up. Joe grabbed the camera and started to take pictures of the insides while she broke out a scalpel and tried to inspect the creature.

"I must be doing something wrong," he said. "How do I show the picture I took?"

"It should show up," she said.

"Nothing but a black screen."

Adele took the camera from him. "It should be working. It's all set properly." She double-checked that the lens cap was off. Then she turned to Joe. "Smile," she said as she raised the camera and snapped his picture. "Look." It displayed his image in the fire gear.

Raising the camera again, Adele snapped some pictures of the inside of the creature. When she checked the screen, it was still black. "This is weird," she said. She stepped back and took a picture of the entire creature. When she looked this time, the exterior of the beast and the fish plant were all visible, but it blacked the internal parts out. "Ok, this is starting to freak me out."

"Starting?" said Joe. "I've been freaked out for a while."

"You got your phone? See if you can take a picture with it."

Joe pulled out his phone, but the results were the same. "You said that our brain was trying to make sense of what it was seeing but couldn't. Could the camera be doing the same? Maybe their processors can't focus on it?"

"That makes no sense at all!"

"You're trying to make some sense of this thing?"

"There are static scientific principles. While it can trick our minds, the camera shouldn't be tricked. It's a matter of capturing refracted light and converting it to a file. No reason it shouldn't capture the inside of this creature."

"And yet, it's not."

"And that's what makes no sense!" she said.

"What about film? Do you tink a camera using film would work?" came Chief Deveaux's voice in their ears.

"I don't know," said Adele. "These cameras should work. I can't document what it is I'm seeing."

"Can you draw it?" asked Joe.

"Can you?"

When Joe looked at the insides, he found his mind couldn't focus, and he started to feel vertigo again. He had to close his eyes. "No, because I can't focus."

"It seems the closer to the exoskeleton, the less distorted my vision gets. I can focus on things there, at least for ten seconds. I can try to spend my time starting on the outer edges and work my way in until I can't concentrate anymore."

Adele secured samples of internal matter, plus chips from the exoskeleton. She took samples from the large and the small tentacles and siphoned some of what she assumed was its blood, storing the samples in a refrigerated biohazard container. They had to swap their air tanks twice during this process.

"Hey, I think I've located the venom sac," she said to Joe. Adele was looking in the hole where the tentacle had torn away. "It's inside this breach, right against the exoskeleton."

"Now that you've located it, what are you going to do with it?"

"I will extract some," she said, going over to her kit and taking out a large syringe. "If I insert this needle, I should be able to puncture the sac without harming its integrity and remove some toxins."

"Keep your eye on her Corporal," said Chief Deveaux. "First sign of anything wrong, get out."

Joe could see Adele rolling her eyes. "I know what I'm doing," she mouthed, but not out loud so it wouldn't get picked up by their radios.

She pushed the needle into the sac. Things went wrong at once. The needle smoked and disintegrated, and liquid started to spurt out of the hole in the pouch which was becoming a small tear. "It's not venom, it's acid!" yelled Adele. Acid splashed onto her thick protective clothing, which started to smoke.

"Pull dem out! Now!" came Chief Deveaux's voice over their headsets. They got yanked off their feet and dragged across the floor towards the door. "Spray dem."

"Wait!" said Adele, pulling off the firefighter's coat and throwing it on the ground. The sleeve where the acid had hit had burned clean away.

"I'm ok," she said. "But I didn't want you spraying me with acid still on me. Adding water to acid can be dangerous, and I couldn't be sure it would dilute it. I've never seen acid work that fast."

"Good call. Now spray dem." The firefighters turned the hose on both of them. Without the protective jacket, Adele got soaked.

Joe and Adele pulled off their hoods. "What kind of creature uses acid?" asked the Chief.

"It's rare, but some insects and lizards do," said Adele. "There are a few sea creatures that use it too, like the cuttlefish or sea cucumber. This thing reminds me of a cuttlefish; they are related to squid, and they can have an outer shell."

"Why didn't you mention them when you first saw it?" asked Joe.

"The largest cuttlefish is less than two feet long, and they are not found in the Americas," she said. "The North Atlantic is too cold for them."

"So, could this be an ancient form of a cuttlefish, like a prehistoric version?"

"Well, except for the non-carbon-based life and the fact we can't look at its insides without getting dizzy, sure. We are no closer to figuring out what this is, and it's nothing like we've seen before. While similar to things we can identify, it's too unique. I need to get my samples and get them analyzed."

The Chief's radio went off. "Dat will have to wait, I'm afraid. Dat's a call; we need to go. I need you to get out of your gear, now."

The two firefighters that helped them get into their gear helped them get out of it. They stowed the equipment, and the truck left, its sirens blaring and its lights flashing.

"I don't suppose you will let me go back in there to secure my samples?" Adele looked at Joe.

"Not a chance," he said. "Not unless the Fire Department comes back."

"Yeah, I didn't think so," she sighed.

"It's too dangerous," he said.

"I know, but I don't have to like it. I hope the Fire Department returns before the government guys get here."

"The Department of Fisheries and Oceans will probably confiscate them all, anyway."

"Yeah, I know." She sat on the pier. "I hoped that if I got far enough into it, they'd have no choice but to keep me on."

"They still might."

"I don't think so. I'm sure someone will kick this up the ladder. They'll want to keep this under wraps."

"And how will they do that? It's been on the news now. Do you know how many photos are all over the Internet already? Everyone knows it's here."

"Yes, but they don't know what it is. The government will say it is a rare form of squid. I've heard rumours of strange things washed up over the years, and they always get explained away. They feel it will cause a panic or something."

"Well, dis has been quite de night and all, lots of excitement b'y. It's been crazy. You still tink Ise needs to be here?" asked Cecil. They'd almost forgotten that he and Mary-Margaret were on the pier with all the excitement.

"I want to see if the Fire Department comes back, so a little while longer, Cecil."

"Jaysus, b'y, my back teeth are swimmin'. I gots to go take a leak!"

"Well, don't do it around here," said Mary-Margaret. "I don't need to see that."

"Oh g'way, wouldja? I'm going to go piss off de edge of de pier." Cecil turned away from them and started to walk past the fish plant, down to the end of the dock. He rounded the corner at the end and disappeared out of sight.

The evening's events were hard on poor Cecil. He was bored. Cecil needed people, and he had seen little to tell others. He wished he'd left, to hell with what the Corporal said. Undoing his trousers, he relieved himself off the edge of the pier into the sea.

The moon was almost full and high in the sky. Cecil was gazing out across the water, the moonlight making it dazzling for being almost...he glanced at his watch; it was almost midnight. He zipped up and adjusted himself and turned to head back to the others when he noticed something out of the corner of his eye.

He turned back to face the sea. Something wasn't right. He'd lived by the shore all his life, and he'd never seen the sea act like this. The water, instead of coming towards the beach, was receding. An eerie stillness was in the air. He squinted and looked out; the ocean began to foam and boil.

"Hey, guys, something right funny is going on," he yelled. "You need to come sees dis."

Turning back again to focus on the sea, he noted the water beginning to rush back in, a six-foot-high wall of water. The pier was fifteen feet above the sea level, so Cecil was not in danger. Not from the water, anyway. Then he saw it. A form began to rise out of the water, its immense bulk becoming clear. Its long cylindrical body towered sixty feet above him, a hideous stench assaulting his nose. It froze Cecil in fear. A large eye, above a

29

large mouth, and as big as a Buick, stared at him. His mind began to unravel, and he tried to scream, but nothing came out.

He didn't feel the stinger or the acid eating through his body. His mind had shut down, except for a vague knowledge of being lifted high in the air before being tossed into the gaping maw.

Back on the pier, alerted by Cecil's yell, Joe, Adele and Mary-Margaret had turned to make their way down the dock towards him. They froze when they saw Cecil's form, pierced and attached to a tentacle, lifted high into the air and thrown into the darkness. They couldn't see anything more than a vague shape, but they heard the mouth gnashing together.

"Run!" yelled Joe. He grabbed Mary-Margaret by the arm and pulled her off the pier back towards the land. Adele turned and sprinted past them.

They kept running as fast as they could, not looking behind them, desperate to get up the path towards town. They heard a massive crash as something heaved itself into the pier and the fish plant. It obliterated the pier; the sound of splintering wood and a great splash as the whole structure dropped into the sea. Turning around at this, they saw a large indistinct shape slipping into the waves, leaving nothing but destruction behind it.

The noise attracted attention from town. People were rushing to see what happened. There was nothing but splintered wood lashing against the shore; all that remained of the pier and fish plant. The seas returned to normal, while the bright moon cast its glow upon them, giving the scene an eerie feel.

#

Next day the government showed up in force; the army, the Department of Fisheries and Oceans and other unidentified units. Everyone who was not a resident of Gallou Cove was ordered to leave the town. Corporal Joe Mills and Dr. Adele Kramer were subjected to an extensive debrief. The road to Gallou Cove was blocked off; traffic had to divert an hour out of their way to bypass the area. They cordoned off the beach from where they found the creature to the remains of the fish plant; the army had put up a chain-link fence and covered it with an opaque cloth, blocking the view while soldiers patrolled the perimeter.

Joe and Adele were housed in a trailer brought in, along with other trailers, to accommodate the significant number of government employees who had taken over the town. They forced all the businesses to close; the town was effectively under martial law.

Two days after the events at the pier, Joe ran into Adele on the street outside the now-closed Shoreline Cafe.

"Hey," said Joe.

"Hey," said Adele, her hands thrust into her pockets. She stood in front of him for a few moments, using her foot to play with a rock on the ground.

"I saw on the CBC they are calling this a freak tsunami that wrecked the old abandoned pier," said Joe. "The story mentioned that one resident was missing and believed killed by the wave."

"Yeah, I saw that." She looked at him. "I don't see how people will buy that."

"People will believe what you tell them. There will be conspiracy theories about sea monsters."

"And this time they'll be right," she laughed. "I wonder how many conspiracy theories are true?"

"Turning into a flat earther on me?"

"No. It's just...you wonder how many things get brushed aside. There are a ton of pictures of this thing..."

"They announced that it was a rare squid that washed up on shore," said Joe. "They had not identified it since it was larger than these specimens grow to be."

"And people will buy it, won't they?"

"People find comfort in things they can understand. Dumb it down, and people will believe almost anything."

The door to the Shoreline opened, and Hazel appeared. "Oh, Dr. Kramer, Corporal Mills. I didn't realize youse was still in town. Did you hear?"

"Hear what?" asked Joe.

"All us residents, dey's expropriated our property. De entire town," she said. "Giving us all five hunnerd thousand dollars for our places. Most of dese shacks around here, why you'd be lucky to get forty or fifty thousand for dem. Everyone feels like dey

31

won de lottery or somethin'. Dey gave me an extra hunnerd thousand on account of me losing my business."

"Really?" asked Adele.

"If you agree to be out in two days, deys paying for all your moving expenses, too. Dat's why it's so quiet in town; everybody's packing to leave."

"Where will you go?" asked Joe.

"Well, I will stay wit me sister in New Waterford to start. Den, I'll see. But me cafe days is over; I'm retired. Maybe I'll go on a cruise," smiled Hazel. "I ain't never been off de island before; time to see a bit of de world, I suppose. It was a right shame about Cecil though. We should have listened to him when he said drag dat ting back out to sea. He'd have never left Gallou Cove, though, no matter how much money dey'd offered him."

"Did he have a family?"

"Not a proper family, dear. But to him, everybody in town was his family. He had his faults, but his heart was always in de right place." She wiped away a tear.

They heard a bark and looked up to see Mary-Margaret and Benny walking towards them. "Howdy," she said as an enthusiastic Benny sniffed them all. "You getting ready to leave, Hazel?"

"Yes, I am. I had a few personal items I needed to get out of de cafe and to give it one last look over before I go."

"Where are you off to?" asked Adele.

"Well, I'm not sure. Not only do I have the money that the government gave us, but Herb and I were far from poor. And he had a big insurance policy on the fish plant too, so financially I won't have to worry about anything. I might go look for a place in Florida."

"Dat far away, huh?"

"If I can't stay here in Gallou Cove, well, I might as well be somewhere warm."

"Did they talk to you about what happened at the fish plant?" asked Joe.

"They did. I'm sure they asked me the same questions they asked you. I told them I didn't see much. We had our backs to it, and we only saw something massive slipping back into the sea."

"That's what I told them," said Joe.

"Well, it's the truth," said Adele.

"Well, I better get home and finish packing," said Hazel. "Mary-Margaret, if I don't gets a chance to see you before I go, I want to say goodbye." The two ladies hugged, and their eyes were moist. Hazel trundled off back towards her house.

"I should be getting back to things too. You'd be surprised how quickly you can get things done when you are properly motivated. Dr. Kramer, Corporal Mills, thank you for everything. I wish things had turned out different." Mary-Margaret glanced back toward the sea. "But all things considered, at least many people are way further ahead than they were yesterday. Silver linings, I suppose. Poor Cecil, though," she sighed. "At least they identified him by name as the resident that was washed out to sea; he'd have liked that." She turned and left the two of them alone.

"So, what's happening to you?" asked Adele.

"I got a surprise transfer," said Joe. "Back to your old stomping grounds. They are transferring me to Victoria, effective immediately. My wife isn't happy, and she'd be less happy if she found out everyone here was getting half a million dollars to move. But hey, I'm replacing one beautiful island for another, so that's not bad. They could have sent me to the Northwest Territories."

"Still, it's about as far away from here as they could get you," said Adele. "And getting rid of everyone in town; they want the people far away."

"I understand the road they've closed, it's a permanent closure. Already working on a bypass. You will get nowhere near this place."

"I checked Google Maps this morning. They have already removed Gallou Cove from it. Unless you have an old paper map, you won't even find it."

"Seems excessive."

"Maybe. They must know more than we do."

"So, you going back to Halifax?"

"Yes, and no. I'm going back to Halifax, but not back to the university. They offered me a job."

"Who did?"

"The Department of Fisheries and Oceans. I'm the new Director of Oceanic Abnormalities."

"What does that job entail?"

"I don't know. They never said," said Adele. "And when I tried to look it up online, it doesn't exist. I don't know whether this is a new position or..."

"So, why are you taking it?"

"It's a huge upgrade in salary: benefits, full pension, access to a state-of-the-art lab and a team of people reporting to me. And I'll never have to write another grant proposal again. It was too good to turn down."

"Buying your silence, are they?"

"Seems like that, yeah. I'm surprised they didn't offer you more."

"I already work for the government, I guess. They needed to compel everyone else to do what they wanted while they could order me to go."

"Still doesn't seem right."

"I learned a long time ago life wasn't fair. I'll get over it. So," Joe looked at her. "What do you think that was?"

"I don't know. I lost all my samples and my notes when it destroyed the pier. We lost the specimen. So, we'll never figure it out."

"And the thing that attacked the pier?"

"My theory is it was a mother looking for her lost child. What we had was a baby." She looked out over the water. "I said there is so much about the oceans we don't know. I'm not sure if we want to know. There are things best left undisturbed."

"Well, on that happy thought," said Joe. "I think it's time I get going. I've spent enough time away from home. Victoria might be a nice change of pace after this." He held out his hand to her. "Pleased to meet you, Dr. Kramer."

"You as well, Corporal Mills, even if you were a real pain in the ass at times," she smiled at him.

"Actually, it's now Inspector Mills."

"Inspector? That's an upgrade in rank."

"Three upgrades. It's not like I'm not getting anything out of this."

She laughed at him. "Enjoy British Columbia, Inspector Mills."

"I hope so," he said, opening the door to his cruiser. "Enjoy discovering your oceanic abnormalities."

"I think I will."

Troy Young

It Slumbers Beneath The Ice

Dr. Adele Kramer sat in her new office. After the events at Gallou Cove, she had expected a reprimand, placed on a blacklist that would deny her future government grants, something negative. Instead, the government had offered a job: Director of Oceanic Abnormalities.

The job description was light on specifics. When she tried to research the job, the position did not exist on any of the department web sites. She reported to the Assistant Deputy Minister of the Department of Fisheries and Oceans for the Atlantic region: he had met with her, but he could answer none of her inquiries. The offer came with a significant raise in salary from her research position. And with full benefits and pension (and negating the need to write another grant proposal ever again), she accepted.

Adele moved into this office a week ago, but apart from being welcomed, she had nothing to do.

"Can't beat that view," she said, gazing out over Halifax Harbour. Her office was huge, newly renovated and complete with a new laboratory with everything a researcher could want. Strangely, there were no other occupied offices in her wing. Even the desk set aside for her assistant was empty; no one had been assigned to her yet. To get to her wing, she had to traverse a construction zone where other renovations were ongoing; in five days, she had yet to see a single worker.

The not knowing was getting to her. Dr. Kramer showed up on time every morning to her empty office. Her phone never rang, nor did she receive any emails. When she pressed the Assistant Deputy Minister, he only gave her vague replies. "Your position is important," said the latest response. "But, we filled it earlier than we intended, and I am sorry to say the support networks are not in place. We hope to rectify this as soon as possible. Until then, we ask you to be patient; you will receive a full description of your intended role here with the Department of Fisheries and Oceans, and your work will begin soon." Her last phone call had been abrupt. She suspected the ADM didn't know what to tell her.

It was Friday, the end of her first week on the job, and she was watching Fuller House on Netflix and nursing her second cup of coffee, the frustration of doing nothing wearing on her when she heard a sound. Someone had moved aside the plastic tarp that sealed off the construction site at the end of the hall. Being alone at the end of this massive building, distant from anyone, the sound of an unknown intruder raised fears in her. She grabbed her cell phone off her desk and picked up her keys, holding them in her right hand. "Hello?" she said, hiding the quiver in her voice from the person coming down the hall.

"Hello," came the answering voice. Dr. Kramer peeked out of her office. A handsome man stood in her laboratory, his white teeth in stark contrast with his dark complexion. He held his hands out in a gesture of openness. "Nice set up you have here. State-of-the-art. I hope you are finding everything."

"Excuse me, but do I know you?"

"Not if I've done my job right," the stranger smiled at her. "But you will get to know me. We'll be working together."

"Why wasn't I told about this? I have had no notice that someone would be here today. Why was I not involved in hiring who reports to me?"

"Because I don't report to you. You report to me."

"I report to the Assistant Deputy Minister of the Atlantic region of the Department of Fisheries and Oceans."

"On paper, sure. In reality? No. Go ahead, call him. See what he says."

"You stay right there." Dr. Kramer closed the door behind her and clicked the lock. She did not trust the man standing in her lab. Picking up the phone, she hit the speed dial button to connect her to her boss.

She heard a ring over the receiver of her phone. A ring answered out in the hallway. "Hello, Dr. Kramer," came the stranger's voice over the line, echoed in the hall. "Please, unlock your door, and I'll explain the situation to you."

Adele slammed the receiver and went to the door. She unlocked it and threw it open. "You have five minutes to explain to me what is going on. If I don't like your answers, I'm out of here."

The strange man smiled at her again. "Understandable. I would have been here sooner, but I was detained in Ottawa. Apologies for having kept you waiting, and for not clarifying things for you earlier, but once you have heard everything I have to say, I am certain that this will be of no consequence to you. May I come in?"

Adele backed into her office, not taking her eyes off of him. She sat in her chair as her unknown guest sat opposite her.

"My name is Harjit Singh. This is the trickiest part of introductions because I don't exist. Not in the traditional sense as far as the government is concerned. You won't find my name or position on an organizational chart. I report to the Clerk of the Privy Council and the Prime Minister himself."

"I don't understand."

"No one does at first. But bear with me. Like me, the department I'm responsible for again doesn't exist in a normal sense. It would be impossible to run something of any size off the government accounts, so most of our employees find homes in other departments."

"Like in the Department of Fisheries and Oceans?"

Harjit smiled. "You catch on quick, Dr. Kramer. Or may I call you Adele?"

"You can, for the next-" she looked at her watch. "Three and a half minutes. You are running out of time, and you haven't compelled me yet."

"Adele, I read the report on the Gallou Cove incident. Your assumptions impressed me. Most people, confronted with something unknown on the scale of what you saw, try to find logical reasons to explain it. Our minds have trouble dealing with certain things, so they default to what they are comfortable with."

"Like saying the creature was a rare form of squid?"

"Bingo. Despite people having seen it and photos going viral across social media, give them a mundane solution, and they'll believe."

"And you write off those who don't buy into that explanation as kooks and conspiracy theorists."

"Again, you understand. Researchers try to link to something familiar. You only had the chance to spend one day studying it."

"I spent my first day trying to get the thing off the beach and into a space where we could preserve it. The old refrigerated fish plant fit the bill."

"You made the assumption it was...otherworldly?"

"It didn't fit into any of the parameters of life as we classify it. What else could it be?"

"But I understand you came to that conclusion even before you cracked open its exoskeleton."

"I did."

"Most wouldn't. That stood out the most about you. That's why we are sitting here." Harjit looked at his watch. "I see my five minutes are up. You can pack up your things if you wish, and I'll head back to Ottawa. Or we can continue. Your call."

Adele looked at him. Harjit sat implacable, a bemused look on his face. "I'll let you finish. You still haven't sold me, but you've intrigued me enough for you to continue. But you need to pick it up if you will convince me to stay."

"You're lying," Harjit smiled at her. "You've decided, and now you're attempting to regain control; I get it. But I assure you you will not regret this decision. You're curious about what was in Gallou Cove. Why did the government act so fast to isolate the town? What do we know? These things have been killing you."

"You going to tell me, or continue to be obtuse?"

Harjit laughed. "You're feisty; I like that. I need people that think differently, that what they presume they comprehend doesn't prevent them from finding out the truth. People that take risks, that challenge authority..."

"Even your own?"

This elicited a smile. "To a point, yes. I need independent thinkers, people that can take control of a situation. Someone that agrees with me is not the person I need in the field. You are my eyes and ears; I need people who think in ways similar to me, but who use their own judgment."

"What was that thing in Gallou Cove?"

"I don't know."

"So why secure the area? Why the radical step of expropriating the town and forcing everyone to move?"

"Because we don't know what we're dealing with."

"What do you know?"

"Not as much as we need."

"You can't tell me anything?"

His smile faltered. "I was like you once. I was young and naïve. But then... I saw something. I continued to encounter and discover similar things. There are things on this planet that don't belong. Things we can't comprehend. Our job is to make sense of it."

"Why do I believe you aren't telling me everything?"

"If I told you everything, you'd think I was crazy."

"Are you?"

"I'm not..that...crazy. You can't do what I do and not have the job affect you. You have been affected by what you witnessed in Gallou Cove, haven't you? The nightmares still happening?"

Adele stiffened. "How did you know about the nightmares? I told no one I had them."

"The nightmares come with the territory. I recruit people with the temperament I need, and they must have encountered something. Only those exposed are invited to my team. I won't put someone into these situations unless they have."

"Exposed to what?"

"I don't know."

"You're a bit of an asshole."

41

"I resent that," he said with mock indignation. "I'm more than a bit. But we'll get along fine."

"I don't know..."

"You do. You believe what you encountered in Gallou Cove isn't unique. It's not. And that scares you, and I don't blame you for being scared. Things...things have been slumbering for years, maybe thousands of years. When I say I don't have answers, it's because I can't prove anything, but I have theories. I want you to observe, to learn so I can visualize the problem through your eyes, to see if you confirm my hypothesis."

"Why do you need a marine biologist?"

"I don't. I need people who have attention to detail and push boundaries; that's what I mean by thinking and acting like me. I want to hear your observations in your own words, and I'll tell you some in return, but not everything; you'll tailor your report to match what you believe I want to hear if I do. As time goes by, we'll develop a level of trust and understanding, and you'll align with my thinking. Until then, I want your judgment."

Adele shook her head. This was crazy. She couldn't believe she hadn't left at the five-minute mark. But she needed to understand. The Gallou Cove specimen, and the thing that came for it, she couldn't shake them. They were unnatural, and she feared what it portended.

"So far, I've been sitting with nothing to do. Do you have something for me?" Adele asked him.

"I take you're staying?" Harjit said with a sly smile.

"You know I am."

"Good," he said, reaching into the jacket pocket of his suit. "Because I already booked your flight. I can take you to the airport. You have time to catch your plane."

"Airport? Where am I going? I must go home and pack, and it would help to know where you're sending me."

"We'll provide you with everything you need, don't worry." He slid the ticket towards her; Ottawa was her destination.

"What's in Ottawa?"

"Nothing. There aren't any direct flights between Halifax and Iqaluit; you must go through Ottawa."

"I'm going to Iqaluit? Nunavut?"

"You're going through Iqaluit, yes. But your final destination is further north of that."

She narrowed her eyes. "How much further north am I going?"

"Two thousand kilometres further. Are you familiar with Alert? It's the most northernmost permanent settlement on the planet. Your destination is two hours west of Alert."

"So, I'm going to the edge of the Canadian Arctic. Why?"

Harjit gave her a wan smile. "You'll find out when you get there. Remember, climate change is putting life on this planet at risk."

"It's causing an increase in severe weather, threatening our means of food production and putting our coastal cities in danger. I agree with you."

Harjit chuckled. "I wish that was the extent. Go to Alert. You'll understand what I mean."

#

Harjit accompanied her to the Halifax airport in the back of a black limousine with government plates.

"Are you coming to Ottawa with me?" she asked.

"No. I have business that requires my attention. You aren't the only asset I manage."

"How big is your department?"

"It fluctuates. The department has a high turnover rate."

"Why? What am I getting into here? Is the job dangerous?"

"You were in Gallou Cove. What did you encounter? And I don't mean with the specimen. What happened? What happened to Cecil Walker?"

"Something...ate him."

"You will come across many somethings. Now," he smiled a disturbing smile. "Not all of them will try to eat you. Some will turn your mind to mush."

"What are you doing? Are you trying to get me to tell you to stop the car and let me out?"

"That's exactly what I'm trying to do. I only want people on my team willing to sacrifice things to get the job done. It sounds melodramatic, but you and I, and people like us, we are all that stands between humanity and total annihilation. You should be second-guessing this. What I'm telling you is insane. You sat in an empty office for a week with no contact, no direction from anyone. If you hadn't been asking questions and contemplating quitting, I would have left you in that office and had you reassigned somewhere next week. Anyone content to sit and do nothing isn't welcome on my team."

"How do you know I was thinking of quitting?"

"You were talking to yourself in the office. Leave someone alone long enough, and they'll talk to themselves."

"Is my office bugged? Have you been spying on me?"

"I know the government does many stupid things, but sticking you in an empty office for a week with no direction is a stretch, even for the most dysfunctional bureaucracy."

"This was a test? You have been spying on me!"

"Yes. I needed to evaluate you to find if you were suffering any long-term effects after your contact with the creature. Be thankful you didn't lay eyes on the mother; the consequences could have been devastating. Listen, if you had not gone to Gallou Cove, you'd be sitting at Dalhousie doing your research and wondering where you'd get your next project funding from. A layer got peeled back for you. Your life will never be the same. It's why I knew of the nightmares. I told you it comes with the territory. Those of us who have encountered- I call it 'The Other' for lack of a better term, we suffer from them. We are dealing with powers and things beyond our ability to comprehend. Our weak minds can't handle it, not long-term. This is part of the reason for the turnover rate. But I know those of us touched by The Other, we don't shake the effects. If you go home, if you walk away from this, your mind will keep reaching out, trying to make sense of everything. The nightmares will get worse, and you'll develop other conditions. The best way to overcome the symptoms is what you'll be doing, confronting The Other. I don't know why, but as you continue to engage The Other, the less pronounced the symptoms get. I wouldn't be surprised if the nightmares stopped in a few days."

"Why? This makes little sense!"

"You're right; it doesn't. None of this does. But that's what happens. If you do nothing, your mind consumes itself. Left to your own devices, you'd be a vegetable in six months. Your mind, in an attempt to limit the damage, will shut itself off. Engage The Other, and you might continue to function normally for years."

"This is insane."

"Sanity is overrated."

"And the people in Gallou Cove? The entire town and others saw the creature, and many got close to it."

"Most will be fine. But you cracked the specimen open, which exposed you to things they weren't."

"Corporal Joe Mills and a local named Burns were with me when I cracked the exoskeleton open. What will become of them?"

"I've been in contact with Mr. Mills. We had a similar conversation yesterday. As for Burns, he wouldn't be much use to my organization or me."

"So, he gets left to turn vegetative?"

"We're watching him. He might not be affected. From the report I gather, he was there for the initial exposure to the interior of the creature, correct?"

"Yes."

"You, he and Mr. Mills were overcome, so you left the vicinity. Only you and Mr. Mills returned later for more in-depth study and exposure?"

"Again, yes."

"Burns' exposure then was minimal. Any adverse effects should be minor. He might have trouble sleeping, develop a psychosis; we'll intervene if he poses a danger to himself or others. Any future care he might need, we'll cover."

"And Joe? How is he?"

"He's having nightmares, same as you."

"But he received a transfer to Victoria? A promotion?"

"And you were hired to work for the Department of Fisheries and Oceans." Harjit picked at a piece of fluff on his pant leg. "His skills are better suited elsewhere. You're a special find. There's no one on my team with the knowledge of the sea you have. The Other, it's everywhere. I've got half a dozen cases open, from Newfoundland to Vancouver Island. I've never had one as far north as Alert, though. You're breaking new ground."

Adele stared out the window, watching a plane coming for a landing; they were approaching the airport. This was insane. At the airport, she should hail a cab and go home. And yet, she wouldn't. Something had happened in Gallou Cove. Something clicked in her mind. Harjit was right; she doubted she could shake it. The nightmares were getting worse. By confronting this... Other... would it lessen them or not? Was it true? She needed to face the issue.

"Should the driver turn around?" asked Harjit. "Last chance."

"No, I'll go. If the danger is as pronounced as you say, I need to help. I have no choice."

"Thank you." He nodded. "My first encounter with The Other was six years ago. I was working in Fort McMurray on the oil sands. Me and a few guys in my crew, we encountered something late one night. The entity seeped into the ground in front of us. Like someone poured water into sand that soaked in, but the ground was frozen solid. Didn't leave a trace. We questioned what we witnessed; it was incomprehensible. Then a few days later, one guy, he just snapped. He killed his wife and two kids. He ranted about the darkness. Kept saying the darkness told him to kill them. He wasn't at fault; it was the darkness. Two days after that, I got a visit from the government, and received the same pitch I gave you."

"What happened to the guys with you?"

Harjit shook his head. "They're gone now. Whatever we encountered that night changed us. I use this as part of my motivation to keep going. This isn't unique to Canada; I have colleagues around the world, doing something similar for their governments, too. Its been going on for centuries, but in the past decade, things have gotten worse. I told you things are waking. We need to stop them from doing so and eliminate those that have awakened. If we don't, well..." his voice trailed off. "I don't want to contemplate that outcome." The car pulled up into the Departures area of the airport. "Two guys will meet you in Iqaluit; they are not mine, but they've encountered The Other and don't realize what has happened to them. Don't tell them what I've told you and try to limit anyone else from helping you; we need to limit exposure. Good luck."

Adele got out of the car and watched him drive away. She looked at her ticket. "I guess I'm going to Nunavut."

#

The plane landed in Nunavut around the time she would have arrived home from work. The flight was under two hours from Halifax to Ottawa, a short layover and another three hours north.

When she had landed in Ottawa, a woman met her and handed over a new suitcase, a heavy parka and her ticket to Iqaluit. "What's this for?" asked Adele. "It's April."

"I was told to meet Dr. Adele Kramer at the airport and to give her these things. Sorry," the woman shrugged.

Adele was happy to have the parka. The pilot had announced it was a blustery minus ten Celsius or fourteen degrees Fahrenheit in Iqaluit. She deplaned and had to walk across the tarmac to the terminal.

Entering the welcome warmth of the building, she looked at the interior. Modern and new, but small. The airport had five gates, two luggage carousels, a gift shop and a lounge. She headed over to the carousel designated for her flight.

Her plane had been full, so one hundred and fifty people jostled around the carousel to pick up their bags. All Adele could remember about her luggage was it was red. She'd accepted the bag three hours ago and seen it only once. She only realized which bag was hers after it had passed three times. With her bag secured, Adele wondered what to do next. Harjit said two men would meet her.

"Dr. Adele Kramer, could you please come to the tourist information desk? I repeat Dr. Adele Kramer to the tourist information desk, please; your party is waiting for you here."

Glancing at the directional signs, she followed the arrow to the tourist desk. Two men were standing by it; the taller one had his blond hair pulled back into a ponytail and leaned on the counter, making small talk with the woman staffing the desk.

The other was an Inuit man wearing the uniform of a Canadian Army Ranger.

"Are you Dr. Kramer?" the soldier asked as she approached, a smile splitting his face. She nodded. "I'm Sergeant Pete Ivalu, Canadian Rangers. Welcome to Nunavut."

"Hey, and I'm Scott Brennan, with Indigenous and Northern Affairs Canada. Pleased to meet you," said the taller man, extending his hand. Adele gave the hand a shake.

"Dr. Adele Kramer, Department of Fisheries and Oceans. Call me Adele."

"And you can call me Sergeant Ivalu." The soldier smiled at her again, even bigger than before. "I kid. Call me Pete."

"Thanks, Pete. Sorry, I'm strung out. I didn't know I was even coming up here until my boss showed up in my office this morning and said I was going to Nunavut."

"Where you based out of?" asked Scott.

"Halifax."

"Well, that's a hell of a commute," he said. "Let me help you with your bag."

"No, I'm fine, I can manage, thanks. Get me to where I'm staying. I want a decent meal, a hot shower, and to lie down. It's been one hell of a day."

"We can take you," said Pete. "And we'll be back for you bright and early. Our plane leaves at seven a.m."

"Seven a.m.? You've got to be kidding."

"Nope. We're hitching a ride on an air force transport that's flying to Alert."

"We'll fill you in on things on the flight up," said Scott. "Get your rest tonight."

Scott drove his pickup truck over to the hotel where he and Pete bade her goodnight and reminded her they would be by at six-fifteen to get her. Adele checked in, went to the hotel restaurant, had her shower, and fell asleep.

#

"Alert is a tiny place, home to sixty-two people," said Pete over the engine noise of the C-130 aircraft. "We will regroup with members in my unit, and then we'll move on to where we're going. Can you ride a snowmobile?"

"I've never driven one."

Pete waved his hand dismissively. "No worries, it's easy to learn. The place is remote, and we have no other way to get there."

"And where are we going? I was told the destination was west of Alert, nothing more. I'm not even sure what I'm doing here."

"I've been to our destination and seen it with my own eyes, and I don't even understand what the hell it is," said Scott. "Why are they sending someone from Fisheries and Oceans? The people that decide these things are way above my pay grade, I'm afraid. They told us you were coming, and we should support you, and you were in charge of this operation. We'd hoped you would know more about it."

"This is my first week on the job and my first assignment. My orders were to meet two guys in Iqaluit and head north. This isn't a marine phenomenon I'm coming to investigate?"

"Partially. Tomorrow we'll visit an abandoned village," said Pete. "The village is further north than my people live, though. We have an oral tradition, so we've been passing stories down for generations. We have a story of a lost tribe. The tribe shunned contact with others. I'm not as up on my folklore as I should be; my grandmother would be so disappointed in me." Again, with a huge smile.

"Why am I visiting an abandoned village?"

"Right," said Scott. "Why?"

"It only became abandoned in the last few weeks. In the 1980s, the government discovered a previously unknown clan. Isolated as they were from any groups for hundreds of years, the isolation made them develop a distinct culture, different from other Inuit. Genetically, they may be Inuit, but culturally, they are unique."

"The government has been leaving them alone but keeping their eye on things from a distance in case they ever needed help. The sea ice is receding, and things are happening due to climate change, so they wanted to make sure nothing happened to them."

49

"But something did happen to them," said Scott. "Three weeks ago, one of our planes did a fly-by and noticed no activity at the site."

"They called the Rangers, and my unit checked things out."

"I was with them. My job is to act as a relationship specialist between the federal government and the various Indigenous groups up here."

"What did you find?" asked Adele.

"They abandoned the village," said Pete. "The villagers bugged out. No signs of violence. They were just gone."

"No one knows where they went. It's not like they left a forwarding address," said Scott.

"There is something you're not telling me."

Pete and Scott hesitated before replying. "Our superiors instructed us not to tell you, but to let you discover for yourself," said Pete. "You'll find out tomorrow."

"Things are pretty messed up," said Scott. "I've been to the village, and it was unlike anything I've seen."

"Come on, guys, give me something here. I didn't get flown four thousand kilometres from my home with no notice to visit an empty village."

"We didn't say the village was empty," said Pete. "We said the villagers abandoned it. That's a subtle difference."

"Now we're splitting hairs here."

"They left something," said Scott. "That's what they told us to show you."

"They left something? What does that mean?"

"They built something. A shrine or something similar. We're saying more than we should," said Pete, looking at Scott. Scott shrugged.

"This shrine, is this the partially marine-related thing?"

"Not exactly," said Scott.

"Not exactly? What is that supposed to mean? I'm more confused than before you started to tell me."

"All I can add is that we are to rendezvous with a Coast Guard icebreaker," said Pete.

"Coast Guard? Don't they fall under Fisheries and Oceans?" asked Scott. "Adele, are you with the Coast Guard?"

"Coast Guard? No, I'm a biologist who specializes in marine life."

Scott threw up his hands. "Terrific. I don't know what we witnessed, but it had nothing to do with marine life. Why am I still here? My job was to liaise with them, but if they're gone, who do I liaise with?"

"Did just the two of you see this shrine?"

"Yes," said Pete. "Scott and I entered the village proper; the rest of my men set up along the perimeter."

"Let's follow the same protocol when we arrive," she said, remembering Harjit's direction to limit the number of people exposed. "I only want the three of us on this." Both men nodded in agreement. "That's settled then. I'll wait and see for myself."

#

They landed in Alert; members of Pete's squad were waiting for them, swelling the populace of the tiny outpost. The plan was to leave the next morning.

"The strange thing about this village is it seems to have been permanent," said Pete over dinner. "This goes against our culture. For generations, my people were semi-nomadic, changing camps to follow our food sources. We'd have the same spots we'd return to every season. This village was inhabited for generations. The villagers built huts out of stone."

"And how's this strange? I'm sorry I'm not well versed in our indigenous cultures," said Adele.

"The Inuit travelled seasonally to follow our food sources. An earlier culture, called the Dorset, made permanent residences out of stone and lived further north, but if I remember, they abandoned that way of life a thousand years ago as the climate became colder and the game moved south. I'm sorry, but I'm not an anthropologist, so I may be wrong on some of what I'm telling you."

"I'm confident we don't need the specifics, just the general idea of what's happening. They lived in isolation from other Inuit for a thousand years then?"

"That's my guess. How they survived in these conditions, I can't say."

"Maybe we'll find out tomorrow?"

Scott laughed. "We won't find anything that will shed light on their history. Besides, the things in the shrine will occupy your energy; you won't care about figuring out how they survived." He lowered his voice to a whisper. "You'll be glad they disappeared. We're better off with them gone."

"Scott!" chided Pete.

"It's true, man. You were in that place. You saw it, the same as me. It's messed up. How can people live like that? Do you want my opinion? This is a waste of time. We should blow up that shrine and forget they even existed."

"Blow up the shrine? Why?"

"Wait until you get there. No reason to keep it intact. It would be better if the shrine were to disappear." Scott closed his eyes and shuddered. "Maybe then the nightmares would stop."

"Nightmares?" This piqued Adele's interest.

Scott looked sheepish. "Yeah. Ever since we were entered the shrine, I've been having these weird dreams. I can't stop dreaming about what I saw. But it's disjointed, a jumble of thoughts and random images."

"Pete, are you having nightmares too?"

"Not as bad as Scott described, but my dreams have been unsettled."

They are experiencing things as Harjit implied. She'd had another Gallou Cove nightmare last night, but the dream had been less intense, less fearful. Harjit had said once you confronted the... The Other... your mind created a barrier. If that were true, she'd devote her energies to this investigation, if only to get the dreams to stop.

"I guess I'll see for myself tomorrow."

"I still don't know why you're here," said Scott. "Unless you're not telling us something."

Adele hesitated before responding. "You have your orders to keep things from me until I see it myself. I have my orders, too. We'll see what happens tomorrow." She got up from the table. "Goodnight, gentlemen. We'll take this up in the morning."

#

The next morning came, and the sun was glinting off the snow. Pete's squad of fourteen soldiers were waiting on their snowmobiles at the edge of the town. Adele got a quick rundown on how to operate the machine; it was like a jet ski, of which she had many hours of experience. A few test runs around town, and they were ready to depart.

When they got to the village, Adele was miserable.

"Show me what you've found. The sooner we do this, the quicker we can return to Alert."

Pete stationed his men around the perimeter, and he, Scott and Adele made their way into the village. Little stone huts, eleven of them, set haphazardly across the plain.

"Go investigate the huts if you want, but there is nothing there. They are simple structures and are devoid of any ornamentation and housed four to six people per hut. The detritus left behind is useless," said Pete. "What you want to inspect is the shrine."

He led them towards the centre of the village where a separate structure sat apart from the huts — made of stone and whale bones and taller than the other buildings, but not more significant in diameter. "They carved their way through the permafrost and hollowed out space underground. Something else that sets them apart from other Inuit." They paused at the entrance.

"I'm not going in," said Scott. "I don't need to go through that again. Why did I come back here? You guys go check it out."

"Our job was to bring her here."

"And we did. She's here. Nothing was said about me going back inside that thing."

Pete gave Scott a withering glare before turning to Adele. "I guess it's just the two of us. You ready for this?"

"I am. It's why I'm here, right?"

They took out flashlights and entered the darkened interior. Whalebones acted as a framework to support the stone edifice which loomed fifteen feet high inside. A spiral set of stairs carved into the frozen ground dominated the floor, further backed with whalebone. Pete led the way.

The light from their flashlights pierced the darkness as they entered the underground cavern, glinting off the white objects scattered across the floor. Adele stiffened.

"They're bones. Human bones."

"They've been placing their dead here. At least I hope that's the reason. But check out the walls."

Adele walked over to the wall and shone her flashlight on it. Dark red images and writing appeared. She started to experience the same disquieting feelings and dizziness she had while dissecting the specimen in Gallou Cove. "What is this?"

"Your guess is as good as mine. Pre-contact Inuit spoke Inuktitut, which was strictly oral. We didn't develop a written form until after European missionaries got here. Where this tribe would have learned to write, I can't say. The language is not Inuktitut. I do not understand what any of it says."

"The alphabet seems to be Arabic. I recognize the letters, but the writing is gibberish. This pattern, 'Ph'nglui mglw'nafh Cthulhu R'lyeh wgah'nagl fhtagn' gets repeated many times. It makes no sense."

"There are pictograms too. Look." Pete pointed at one in particular. It showed people in boats hunting a whale. "This is reminiscent of Inuit pictograms, showing people doing everyday things. But this one is a mystery."

Adele inspected the pictogram Pete indicated. People gathered on the edge of the sea and appeared to be pushing a whale carcass into the water. In the water, far below was a figure surrounded by something. "Does this appear to be ice? An iceberg?"

"It could be. I can't say for sure. The figure looks like nothing I've seen."

"What are they doing with the whale? Does your culture include disposing of whales into the ocean?"

"We hunt whale to survive, not to throw away."

"I didn't think so. It looks like a sacrifice."

"My people worshipped the power of nature. Our shamans tried to appease the nature spirits when we thought they were angry. Sometimes they made sacrifices, but I never heard of an entire whale sacrificed."

"That still doesn't explain this figure trapped in the ice."

"None of this makes any sense to me."

"How much time were you in here? Did you get a look at everything?"

"No. We didn't stay long. Long enough to become disturbed, but not long enough to make sense of what was here. These words and pictures make you off balance. We got headaches and wondered if something environmental was causing them. I expected they'd send someone to test the site for substances."

"The symptoms are not caused by the environment. The pictures and the words are the source. I've experienced these same feelings before, but they were around a creature of unknown origin. That's why my boss sent me here; to confirm a connection."

"A connection?"

"Yes. There are things we don't understand, and my job is to figure it out."

"You don't work for the Department of Fisheries and Oceans, do you?"

"That's what it says on my business card and pay stub."

"That's not an admission."

"It's my answer, though. How are you holding up? I want to investigate the room as long as I can."

"I'm good. A little unnerving, but I can handle it. Scott's the squeamish one; he's the reason we left."

"Ok," said Adele, taking out her phone. "I will take a video of this. Can you shine your flashlight at the same place as mine to make it as bright as possible? Follow me around as I film this."

"Can do."

Remembering the impossibility to take pictures of the insides of the creature in Gallou Cove, Adele worried that she wouldn't capture images here either. She took a few snapshots; the images were clear. Buoyed by that, she and Pete walked around the walls of the subterranean room while she filmed what they displayed. She photographed the phrase 'Ph'nglui mglw'nafh Cthulhu R'lyeh wgah'nagl fhtagn' because of its repetition in a variety of sizes and angles.

"Look at this," said Adele. On the floor near the wall was a shallow soapstone dish and a rudimentary brush made of whalebone and hair; a red liquid filled the bowl. She shined the light further on the wall, illuminating a pictogram. "Scott said it's not like they left us a forwarding address. He was wrong. They did just that."

The pictogram showed people leaving a grouping of huts surrounding the structure they were in. They were heading towards a cave cut into the side of an ice flow. Embedded in the ice was the same mysterious figure from the sacrificial scene.

"You reckon this is what they set off to find?" asked Pete.

"Just a hypothesis. The villagers left for a reason; this shows a reason. Whatever that thing is, they've gone off to find it. That's where they are."

"Do you want to find them?"

She stared at the figure trapped in the ice. "They aren't important. Maybe Scott is right, and we should forget they even exist. But find them, and we find that. And whatever that is, it's the reason I'm here."

#

"How are we going to track the villagers?" asked Adele when they returned to Alert.

"The Canadian Coast Guard Ship Howard Phillips is due in the region tomorrow," said Pete. "We can get the Coast Guard to use their helicopter to search for any ice caves at the water's surface out on a flow. The cave's got to be near their settlement; whatever is there, it's the reason they stayed put for so long."

"So why move now?" asked Scott. "If, as you suspect, they inhabited this village for at least a thousand years, what would make them leave? If something is in the ice, and that's a big if, why did they only go searching now?"

"That's the mystery," said Adele. She didn't share with them Harjit's belief in slumbering entities waking. This would give credence to his theory, and this could be the likely cause. That would mean the pictograms showed something real, and the villagers were aware; this was no myth to them, but a reality. The entity in the ice was waking and called to them; they responded.

"Suppose the helicopter does a sweep and doesn't find an ice cave; can we put this to rest? Say they disappeared and we don't know where they went? I want to go home and return to doing normal job duties."

"Sure," she said. "If they don't find a cave, we report to our respective bosses that we found nothing here, and we go back to our lives. If they find a cave, though, we have to explore it." Adele was sure a cave would be found.

"Why us?" said Scott. "This is way outside my job description. I'm not an explorer; I have nothing to offer."

"My boss ordered me to include no one else in my investigation. My job is to discover what's here, and they told you to follow my orders. I can't do this alone. I'm sorry, but that's how it is. If you don't like it, you can tender your resignation."

Scott slammed his fist on the table and stood. He left the room without looking at Adele.

"You don't want to do this?" asked Adele, turning to Pete.

"Nope," he said. "But as a soldier, I'm used to following orders. It's not about what I want to do, but what my duty requires me to do. I'll go wherever you tell me."

"That's good. At least I can count on you."

"You can. I want to find where they are. There will be a cave."

"Yeah, I'm sure we'll find one. No way this is coincidental. Something is going on here."

"And I get the sense you know more than you are telling me. That's fine; I'm used to my superiors not telling me everything." Pete got up from the table. "Just try not to get me killed, ok?" He left the room.

Adele massaged her temples and sighed. This mission was insane. Whatever was in the ice, they couldn't allow someone to free it. It was up to them to stop the villagers. But how?

#

The CCGS Howard Phillips entered the region the next day as scheduled. Pete gave them the coordinates for the village and asked them to search for a cave from the air. It didn't take long for the Coast Guard to find a semi-submerged cave entrance. The ship anchored opposite the cave and the helicopter came to Alert to pick them up and bring them to the vessel.

"Dr. Kramer, I'm Captain Armitage; welcome aboard. I understand that I am to offer you whatever support you might need. What do you need?"

"Captain, thank you. Myself, Mr. Brennan and Sergeant Ivalu need to explore the cave your pilots located. We'll need access to one of your rigid-hulled inflatable boats and safety equipment to explore. I'm rated to operate the boat; only the three of us are going."

"Dr. Kramer, are you sure? Caves in the ice can be dangerous places. The cave could be compromised if the ice shifts or calves off a new iceberg. My sailors have experience navigating the ice up here; you should have someone with you."

"Sergeant Ivalu will act in that capacity. I'm not about to put anyone but my team at risk."

"Fair enough. I have given you my concerns and will log that I have done so. I will give you access to the equipment you need. Why is it important to explore this cave?"

Adele shook her head. "I am not at liberty to tell you, Captain. Sorry."

"I figured. Do you need anything else from us?"

Adele paused for a moment, pondering their task. Something Scott had said earlier stuck with her. "Do you have any explosives on board?"

Captain Armitage narrowed his eyes. "We do. Are you trained in their use?"

"Again, I'll defer to Sergeant Ivalu. I'm uncertain we'll need them, but if we do, I'd rather have them with me."

"One of my sailors will confer with him then. You'll want to be underway as soon as possible?"

"Yes. No sense wasting time. We need to know what is happening in the cave."

"I'll have the boat readied for you then. You'll be underway within the hour."

"Thank you, Captain."

The Captain left to direct his sailors to their tasks as Adele returned to Scott and Pete. "Pete, you will liaise with a sailor. Are you trained on how to use explosives?"

"Demolition charges? I've had some basic training in their safety and proper use, but I'm no expert. Why do we need explosives?"

"Something Scott said at the village, how we should blow up the shrine. If the pictogram is true, whatever the ice has imprisoned cannot be freed. We need to do whatever we can to stop that from happening."

"I'm glad someone is listening to me," said Scott. "Let's go blow the thing up and go home."

"That's our worst-case scenario. We might not find anything."

"They found a goddamn cave. Something is trapped in the ice. We all know it." Scott's voice grew distant as he glanced in the cave's direction. "We've known there was something more to this as soon as we entered that goddamn shrine. It was too real."

"And now you have to see for yourself; you need to know, don't you?"

Scott looked at Adele. "Yes. You've seen something similar to this before, haven't you? That's why they sent you."

"I have. My boss sent me to connect the two creatures. Like you, I have nightmares from my experience. He told me to confront them head-on if I wanted them to go away. They haven't disappeared for me yet, but they are getting better."

"If going to the cave will stop the dreams, then let's go explore the goddamn thing. I'm sick of this."

"And you, Pete?"

"I go where I'm told. I'll talk to the sailor and get the explosives. Let's hope we don't need to use them."

#

Adele steered the RHIB towards the cave mouth. Blue streaks were visible in the ice, and the dark hole beckoned to them. She eased the boat through the placid water and into the darkness. Pete turned on the light mounted in the bow, the beam dispelling the dark.

The ice glittered around them as they headed further into the cave, the sounds of the engine echoing throughout the cavern.

The noise banished any hope of stealth. Pete gripped his bolt-action rifle in his hands, scanning ahead. The grim determination of a person who has come to grips with facing a challenge they dreaded was on Scott's face. Adele slowed her breathing.

"Something's up ahead," said Pete. Adele eased back on the throttle, bringing the boat to a stop. Pete tilted the light to illuminate what he had seen.

A group of indigenous kayaks and larger boats were tied along an ice shelf a few feet above the waterline. The mouth of a tunnel cut into the ice could be seen behind them.

Adele pulled the boat alongside the kayaks. No villagers were visible. Pete leaped off the bow and onto the shelf and Scott threw him a line. Pete then drove a spike into the ice and secured the boat in place.

Scott and Adele soon joined Pete on the shelf. "The kayaks confirm our missing clan found its way here," said Scott.

"Yep. And I guess they headed that way," she said, pointing at the tunnel. "Let's go find them."

They strapped crampons to their feet to help them on the ice. Attaching lights to the webbing they donned allowed them to keep their hands free for the ice axes they had brought. Pete slung his rifle over his shoulder.

"We'll leave the explosives on the boat for now. If we find we need them, we'll come back. Let's go," said Adele.

They entered the tunnel, their lights casting a dazzling glow over the icy walls. The passage was wide enough for them to walk single file. The floor was uneven and littered with ice shards.

"This doesn't appear to be natural," said Scott. "A natural fissure in the ice would be smoother."

Pete inspected the nearest wall, running his gloved hand across it. "You're right. Someone has cut their way through the ice. The grooves of their tools are visible."

"Talk about labour intensive," said Adele.

"They brought the whole village with them. Lots of bodies to do the work. And they have been missing for at least three weeks," said Pete.

"Have you ever tried to cut a hole into a frozen lake using an axe?" asked Scott. "That's a beast of a job. I can't imagine how much effort this would have taken."

"There may have been a fault in the ice," said Adele. "Widening a natural fault would be less work. Either way, this requires real motivation. What could they be up to?"

"We'll find out soon enough," said Scott. "But I'm not sure I want to."

They proceeded in silence, getting deeper into the flow. The tunnel continued onwards for hundreds of feet until it opened up into a natural cave.

"These caves are formed by water running through the ice. I suspect Adele was right in that our missing villagers had natural help to get this far. Still doesn't tell us why they are here," said Pete.

"Let's look around. We might find something."

They split up, shining their lights around the floor of the cave. "Oh, god..." said Scott, shining his light on a dark lump. "Guys?" He turned and wretched.

Pete and Adele made their way over to him. Something splattered the icy wall with red. The dark lump was a pile of furs, also stained red. Two skulls smiled back at them.

"What the hell?" said Adele. Pete looked at the pile of furs. Using his ice axe, he prodded and sifted through the furs, uncovering two more skulls: one was the skull of a child.

"What happened to them?" asked Adele.

"They couldn't work," said Pete. "Too old, or sick or young. So they served another purpose."

"That purpose is food! What the fuck is wrong with these people?" shouted Scott.

"That's a probable assessment," said Pete.

"At the risk of sounding culturally insensitive, this isn't common?" asked Adele.

"Cannibalism? No, we're not savages," said Pete, offended. "Eating people is as culturally taboo to us as to you. Cannibalism has happened in the past, but European explorers in the Arctic have succumbed to it as well to prolong their existence. If they ran out of food here, maybe they had no choice."

"I'm sorry, I don't know. I'm trying to make sense of what we're seeing."

"It would explain the bones in the shrine," said Scott. "These guys have resorted to cannibalism in the past."

"So, we've stumbled across an isolated cannibal cult?"

"Seems that way," said Pete.

"What are they trying to get to?"

"Whatever they drew on the walls, I suspect." Adele looked around, afraid to find more remains. "They think it's real, and they hope to find it."

"How did they find out about this cave, huh? What would have brought them here?" asked a panicked Scott. "It's goddamn random to me."

"I don't know, Scott, okay? What do you want from me?"

"Let me get the fuck out of here. We go back and get the explosives, and we bring down the whole damn berg."

"No, we're going forward. We will find them and figure what the hell they are up to. You don't want to continue? Go back to the boat and wait for Pete and me. Your career is over if you do; I'll guarantee that."

"You goddamn bitch!"

"Scott! Settle down, man," said Pete. "I don't want to go in either, but we have to."

"Why? Why do we? I'll be happy to turn around and forget this whole experience."

"You won't, though, because you're already corrupted," sighed Adele. "You've encountered what we call The Other. We don't know what The Other is but left to your own devices, and you'll go insane. The way to stave off the insanity is to keep struggling against it, to search it out. I encountered something similar in Cape Breton and got hired by a secret government department investigating this type of phenomenon. Sorry I didn't tell you; I was under orders. That's why I needed both of you, to not subject anyone else to this."

They stood not speaking for a few minutes, the only sounds echoing through the cave was their agitated breathing. "Were you going to tell us?" asked Pete.

"I don't know. I'm not sure what my boss will do during his debrief of this adventure. He recruited another person who was with me when I had my encounter. He might approach you too. I think he wanted me to observe you in action and wait to hear my recommendation. This is my first assignment, so I'm speculating."

"What would happen to us? You said we'd go insane; how do you know this?" asked Scott.

"I'm new to this too. Two weeks ago, I was as oblivious as you, working as a researcher in Halifax, and now I'm dealing with cannibals in an ice cave in the high Arctic. I'm making this up as I go along. But my boss said that within six months of encountering The Other, subjects that don't strive against it go into a vegetative state. He may have been trying to scare me into working for him, but it could have been one of the few truthful things he said to me. So, we have two choices, neither of which I like. We find out what the hell is going on, or we leave now and wait for insanity to take us."

"Not much of a choice," said Pete. "If you tell me we're leaving, I might disobey that order now that you've told me the alternative. Scott?"

"I'm going with you," he said, resigned. "Let's end this. You should have your gun ready; I don't want to be next on the menu."

Pete nodded and packed away his ice axes and unslung his rifle. He worked the bolt and confirmed a bullet was in the chamber. "I have ten rounds in the clip, and two extra clips for a total of thirty rounds. I hope I don't need to use them."

"Why do they give you a gun like that? As a soldier, shouldn't you have automatic weapons?"

"My gun's not for combat. I use it for hunting; This little baby will bring down a polar bear. Stopping power, not rounds per minute, is the difference between life and death in the Arctic."

"If you're finished discussing the merits of your weapon, let's get going. I don't want to be longer than we need to be," said Adele. "Pete, take point. If they are hostile, and we have ample evidence to suggest they are, do what you have to do."

Without looking around the chamber, they entered another ice tunnel on the far side. This one was smoother and broader as if formed. There was a slight rise which made the way harder to navigate, but their crampons allowed them to find purchase on the slippery floor.

After a few more minutes, Pete raised his hand, signalling them to stop. "Do you hear that?"

Scott and Adele both became quiet. "Is that chanting?" whispered Scott.

"Yes. Pete, do you recognize the language?"

Pete shook his head. "It's not Inuktitut or any spoken indigenous language. I can't make out what they are saying."

"We know where they are now," said Scott. "That's something going our way."

"Let's see if we can't follow the sounds then. We should be able to get close without being noticed. These lights give us away, but I'm not blundering around here in the pitch black."

They started forward again, the distant chanting echoing through the tunnel. The volume increased, telling them they were getting closer. It was impossible to determine how many voices were part of the chant. Without warning, the chanting stopped.

"Oh, oh. Now what?" said Scott, a note of fear in his voice. He clutched his two ice axes.

"Shh, listen," said Adele. They stood there, bracing themselves in the slanted tunnel, trying to hear something in the silence.

"They're coming!" yelled Pete, as the sounds of many feet moving across the ice reached them. Beyond the edge of their lights, they could make out dark shapes heading closer. They made no sounds as they came forward; the first figures came into view.

The tunnel was wider than the first, allowing the villagers to come at them two at a time. Clad in mouldering furs, their eyes wild and their features withered and emaciated, they came like ghosts, silent and staring. The crack of Pete's rifle rang through the narrow passage, followed by the click of him slamming the next round into the chamber. The first cultist dropped, his face exploding in a bloody mist. Pete dropped the second with a shot to the chest. He continued to fire his rifle with expert precision, shooting one projectile after another into the mass of people streaming towards them. The three of them had to dodge the bodies as they slipped down the incline towards them. Pete hugged one wall and Scott the other. Adele avoided the body that slid her way, but then her foot slipped in the added blood that flowed downwards. The next body slammed into her, knocking her over, and carrying her to the bottom of the tunnel. She could hear Pete's rifle continue its deadly work until it stopped making a sound.

Adele scrambled to her feet and started to make her way back towards them. She couldn't see Pete or Scott because of the slope of the tunnel, but she could see their lights. Bodies continued to slide past her, and the river of blood grew. "Pete! Scott!"

From ahead came sounds of a struggle. She could hear Scott roaring in anger, and meaty blows hitting home. Pete cried out in pain. Adele used her ice axe to help pull her up the slope faster. Scott was hitting a body on the ground over and over with his axe while Pete was holding himself up against the far wall. There were no bodies apart from the one that Scott was savaging.

"Scott! It's ok; it's over. Listen to me," she said as she made her way back to them. He gave another angry scream and threw his weapon, his body heaving with the exertion, his face and arms covered in blood.

"They just kept coming. I emptied my clip and tried to change it, but they were on me too fast. I bashed one in the face with the butt of my rifle, but then one got me with a spear, right in the thigh. Scott grabbed him off of me and hit him with his axe."

"Are you going to be ok?" she asked, glancing at Scott, who was trying to get his breathing under control.

"Yeah, he grazed me. He didn't nick an artery. The wound is superficial. Maybe check on Scott."

"Scott? Buddy? You ok?"

Scott slumped against the wall, his breathing rapid. "I am not fucking ok. How could I be ok?"

"I mean, did you get injured? You're covered in blood."

Scott shook his head. "Not mine. It's this fucker's," he prodded the body with his foot. The corpse began to slide, slipping back down the tunnel until they lost it in the darkness.

"How many do you think there were?"

"I took one out with every shot I fired. So that's ten. The guy I bashed in the face makes eleven, and the one that Scott went nuts on makes twelve."

"And back at their village, we estimated between forty to sixty people were living there?"

"Something like that, yeah."

"So that means there might still be twenty to fifty of these bastards still ahead of us," spat Scott in disgust. "Jesus Christ."

"I doubt it," said Pete. "There might be a few still doing an important task ahead, but I think they sent the bulk of their people at us. They were intent on stopping us; you wouldn't split your numbers when dealing with a threat."

"You're talking as if they are acting rational," said Scott.

"I'm inclined to believe Pete, although there could still be more of them ahead. It's too late to back out now. We see this through to the end."

"Or die trying," scoffed Scott.

"If that's what it takes, yeah. Do we have a choice?"

There was only one course of action.

Pete reloaded his gun and moved forward again. Scott, agitated, followed behind him. Adele took up the rear.

The tunnel levelled off and widened. There were no side tunnels, only the one path leading deeper into the ice. It opened up into a cavern.

"We've found the rest, I think," said Pete.

Casting their lights around, they saw the remains of at least thirty people. Blood soaked clothing littered the ground, bones scattered, and uneaten viscera was frozen to the floor.

"Great. Let's go home," said Scott. "I'm so done."

"No, we have to find what they came for. You said it yourself; something's here. They didn't go to all this trouble without a purpose."

"You think the crazy cannibals needed a purpose?"

"Yes," said Pete. "For a thousand years, they stayed in that village. Why leave it now? They didn't do it on a whim."

"There has to be a way out. Look along the walls."

Again they spread out, shining their lights towards the walls.

"You hear that?" asked Scott.

"No, what is it?"

"It's a kind of pinging," said Scott. "It's sharp and steady. Ping. Ping. Ping."

"Pete?"

Pete shook his head. "I do not hear it."

"Stop messing with me, guys. It's there. Ping. Ping. Ping. Like a beacon. It's coming from over here." Scott led them towards a hole that was large enough to crawl through at the back of the cavern. "It's coming from in there."

They hesitated, looking at one another. Pete got on one knee and shined his light inside. "It's a small cave, covered with the same writing as we found back in the village. There is something black in there."

"Do we go in?"

"Whatever they came here for, it's in that cave."

"Yeah, but now I'm here, I'm not feeling so confident."

"I didn't kill a guy with an axe to turn back on the doorstep," said Scott. "I'm going in. The pinging, it's so strong, I don't understand why you can't hear it." Scott crawled into the smaller cave. "You guys should come and see this. It's big."

Pete crawled in after him, and after a moment's hesitation, Adele followed Pete. The same writing and symbols they encountered earlier adorned the walls. The disquieting feeling gripped her heart, stronger than before. She felt dizzy. It disturbed Pete to be in the cave; Scott appeared to be unaffected.

"Look at this thing."

Scott pointed to the back of the cave. There, they had chipped away the ice from something big. It was round and had a resilient and rubbery looking exterior. More of it was visible still trapped in the ice, its dimensions extending beyond their ability to see.

Adele pushed past Scott and Pete to get right beside it. She took off a glove and reached out to touch whatever it was. "I think it's organic."

"What do you mean?"

"I mean that it was alive. It's not mineral."

"A whale?" asked Pete.

"No." She shook her head. Memories of Gallou Cove were coming back. "I've seen something similar. Not in these

67

dimensions or colouring. It's not what I investigated, but it's similar." She studied what she could make out through the ice. Then she realized. "I think it's a head."

"A head?" asked Scott. "Of what?"

"I'm not sure. But look, it's cylindrical. And here," she pointed past the floor. "I think those things look like tentacles. And this part that goes out that way," she indicated. "That looks like a set of shoulders."

"I see it," said Pete. "I think you're right. And those dark patches deeper in the ice, they look like wings."

"Yes. I wasn't sure at first, but those are wings."

"If you're right, this thing is huge," said Scott. "That head has got to be eight feet or more."

"If the proportions are similar to a person, figure this thing to be at least thirty, thirty-five feet tall then in total."

"You think this resembles a person?" chuckled Pete, despite the tension in the cave.

Adele laughed a nervous laugh, too. "No, I don't. This is why they are here. We've found it, whatever it is, and now we have to destroy it."

"You want to destroy it?" asked Scott.

Adele glanced over at him. Scott had a dull, vacant look on his face. "That's why we came, remember? You wanted to blow up the shrine they had built to it. Now you see it, and you've reconsidered?"

Scott smiled dreamily. "They're dead. And this thing..." he shrugged. "It's trapped by the ice. I say we leave it alone and go."

"You said to blow it up."

"That's before I saw it. It's harmless," he said with a dopey smile.

"We came to do a job. Let's get it done," said Pete. "We go back to the boat and get the explosives, set them and blow this thing to hell."

Scott shrugged, his eyes glazed.

"Scott," said Adele, concern entering her tone. "You need to leave. This is affecting you, somehow."

Scott grunted and shook his head side to side. The glaze over his eyes diminished somewhat. "Yeah, I think you're right. Let's blow it up. I want to go home. I'm so drained."

"We all are, buddy. Don't worry, we're almost done here," said Pete. "When we get back to Iqaluit, the first beer is on me, ok?"

Scott nodded and crawled back out of the hole. Adele looked at Pete and then followed Scott.

They made their way back through the ice tunnels. Passing by the site of their fight with the villagers, to the bottom of the incline. There, piled where they stopped, were the bodies of their attackers. Pushing the bodies aside, they cleared a path for their return with the explosives.

The boat was where they left it. Pete climbed into it, his injured leg slowing him. Opening up the crate of explosives, he passed them out to Adele and Scott. "They're inert in this state; they won't be live until we hook them up to the detonator."

"How do we set off the explosives?" asked Scott. He had returned to his usual self now that they were away from the creature in the ice. "Can you do it wirelessly?"

"You can, but I don't trust it in this ice. It's a thousand feet back to that creature. And I don't want to be standing too close when we set off the charges. It's liable to bring the flow crashing down on top of us."

"How are we getting out of here?" asked Adele.

"We set it off from the boat. Throw the switch and gun it for the entrance."

"Why can't we blow it up from outside the ice then?" asked Scott.

"We don't have enough cable to reach. As it is, we will be tight with what they gave us. We can get twenty, thirty feet into the water, but not enough to get to open water. It won't collapse instantly. We should be fine."

"Should?"

"We'll find out, won't we? I believe someone said: 'Or die trying'?"

"I'd rather not if we can avoid it!"

"Scott, don't worry. I trust Pete. He doesn't strike me as someone with a death wish. It's the best plan we have. We have no other options. Let's get this over with."

Pete grabbed a few of the shaped charges and the spool of cable to connect the charges to the detonator. Back into the depths of the ice, they traversed to where the thing lay dormant.

Scott crawled back into the hole, with Adele following him. "Scott? What's wrong?"

Scott was standing still in the middle of the cave with his back to Adele, his head cocked to his right. He didn't respond to her query.

"Scott? Look at me." Adele faced him. His mouth was slack, a drop of drool hanging from his sagging lip. He was staring off into nothing, his eyes with a cloudy expression, oblivious to his surroundings.

"Pete! Get in here, quick. Something's wrong with Scott."

Pete slipped in through the hole and surveyed the scene. "Hey Scott, buddy, what's going on?" Pete came over and gripped Scott's arm. Scott did not acknowledge his presence.

"Get him out. Whatever this monster is giving off, he can't handle it. Maybe take him back to the boat?"

"Will he let us?" Pete pulled on Scott. Scott stumbled but maintained his balance. He allowed Pete to direct him. Adele and Pete helped Scott lower himself in front of the hole. Pete reached back in to grasp Scott's hands to pull him back out into the cavern.

Adele slid out of the hole behind them to find Scott sitting up and shaking his head. Pete was taking a knee beside him, concern etched on his face.

"I'm fine, guys," said Scott. "I don't know what happened. I heard you talking to me, I was aware you were there, but I couldn't move or speak. My body wouldn't respond to me. I've never felt like that before."

"Is there anything else you're feeling now?"

"No," he said, shaking his head. "And the pinging has stopped. Although when I was in that cave, I could hear what sounded similar to mice scurrying in a wall. It was faint and indistinct, but there was scratching at the edge of my consciousness."

"And now? None of that?" asked Adele.

"No, I'm good. Just exhausted."

"You stay out here then," said Pete. "I don't need your help on the charges. You're a liability to us in that state. The first time you entered, your reaction wasn't this strong. I'm not sure if whatever symptoms you have will get even worse a third time."

"I'll stay here," said Scott, propping himself up against the wall. "Conserve my strength."

"We can handle it. Pete? You ready?"

"You bet, boss. Let's lay these charges." Pete slipped back into the hole.

Pete was laying out the charges before him. "These are shaped charges," he said. "They focus their explosive power to weak spots; these will cut through ninety centimetres of concrete. Should make short work of the ice and our friend here."

"And the rest of the flow?"

"I'm not sure. This is big. The explosion might only impact here. Blow up this bastard's head and collapse this cave. It could break a hole above us to the surface. Or, if there are fault lines in the ice, the flow could break up. We won't know until they explode."

"That's comforting."

"Got a better idea?"

"No. Let's get them set."

Pete grouped the charges along the back wall of the cave, closest to the creature. He intended to focus the majority of the explosive power directly at the monster. "I will attach the wires once we're finished here and run it back to the boat. I need to see how much length we have. You stay to make sure the wires stay attached. I'll do one last check when I come back for you and Scott, but I don't want them coming disconnected and winding up halfway back."

"That makes sense. I can stay here, and we can leave Scott where he is. How long do you figure?"

"Fifteen minutes tops for me to rig this, get back to our boat and secure the cable and come back for you."

"You are coming back, right?"

"I resent that. Yes, I'm coming back."

71

"Sorry, but this...thing," she pointed at the creature. "You can't anticipate how it affects people. Look at what it does to Scott."

"I'll be back. I promise. That should do it," Pete said, attaching the wire to the last connector. He spooled out excess cable behind him to give him some slack as he exited through the hole.

Adele stood in the cave alone. Her light played off the words, and the pictograms were staring back at her. She could see 'Ph'nglui mglw'nafh Cthulhu R'lyeh wgah'nagl fhtagn' everywhere. It meant something, but what she could not fathom. It was lonely standing there. The cold pressed in around her. Now that she was not moving, standing still, alone with her thoughts, it took on a malevolent aspect, clawing at her, seeking to strip her of her warmth. She began to shiver.

The crack of Pete's rifle jolted her. "Pete!" she screamed. She got on her knees to crawl out into the cavern, but something made her stop. She paused, her breathing rapid. Adele turned to look at the thing behind her, gazing at the dark rubbery surface exposed from the ice that was trapping the creature.

It opened its yellowed, gummy, eye.

Adele screamed as a crushing wave of pain assaulted her mind. She fell to one knee as it twisted her thoughts. Images came unbidden to her, not memories, but of things unseen. The images shifted. Three pale, dying suns hung over a blasted planet. Stunted humans in furs were prostrating themselves. Sheets of ice moving across the land. Great migrations of people and animals. She drifted through the vastness of space on gossamer wings. Colours she had never seen, and could not recognize. Smells and sensations, dizziness, her insides twisting. A city was rising from a plain. A black bubbling mass of something unknown, but alive. Teeth, biting and gnashing. A massive being at the edge of her ability to see, being served by lesser entities that shared its form. Cyclopean architecture, with shapes devoid of symmetry. Waters rushing in, a city sinking. Darkness. Tearing in the deep recesses of her mind.

Reeling from this psychic assault, she struggled to her feet, fumbling at her belt for the handle of her ice axe. She stumbled closer to the creature. It was shifting and stirring. The surrounding ice was cracking; she could see its massive muscles straining against its captive bonds. She fell against it, her arm pressing into the creature's hide, steadying herself. The eye gazed at her with absolute hatred.

Adele grasped her ice axe and drove the point into the eye.

The thing screamed, audibly and in her mind. The thrust of its consciousness into hers knocked her off her feet. Its pain, its terror, its madness after being trapped in the ice for millennia gripped her. Adele got to her hands and knees and crawled towards the exit.

Scott was crawling towards her.

"Scott! What are you doing? Run! Get out of here!"

Scott stood. He stood before her, his arms held at his side, his head drooping forward. His eyes were bloodshot and unseeing, and his lips pulled back in a snarl. With a guttural grunt, he threw himself at her, his weight knocking her flat.

Adele twisted on the ground, pinned beneath him. Scott's hands gripped the edge of the hood of her parka, forcing her head back painfully. He lurched further upon her, his teeth biting at her, sinking deep into her cheek.

Screaming and struggling against his greater strength and weight, Adele got her left hand on his throat, wrenching his face away from hers, his mouth dripping blood as bits of her flesh fell out. One ice axe was embedded into the creature's eye, and the other was pinned under her. She scrambled with her right hand, looking for anything she could use to get Scott off her, her left hand holding his gnashing mouth at bay. Her fingers found Scott's axe attached to his belt. She grabbed the axe-head and struggled to free it from its holder.

She pulled it partway out, but the awkward angle she was at, coupled with Scott's weight and the constant struggle against him, made it slip from her grasp. It slid the rest of the way out and fell on to the ice beside them.

Adele flailed at Scott, striking him in the face. It had little effect on him. He reared back and then drove his head forward, her arm unable to hold him. His forehead connected with her nose, breaking it. Warm blood threatened to run into her throat, choking her. Her hand slipped off his throat and up onto his chin; she tried to push it back, but the last two fingers slipped into

Scott's mouth. He bit hard, biting through her glove and severing the tips.

She screamed again at this latest indignity and physical pain. Scott shifted to her left, which freed her right side. With him off balance, she pushed him further, but not enough to move him off her. As he adjusted to regain his purchase on her, her hand glanced against the axe where it had fallen. Closing her fingers around the axe head, she swung her hand upwards to connect with the side of Scott's head, driving the point of the axe into his temple.

Scott went limp and slumped to the left. She lay there on her back, gasping, trying to take in oxygen to recover from her exertions. The pain in her cheek, her nose and her severed fingers were great, but it paled to the pain still flooding her mind from the creature which was increasing in agitation. Ice began to crack and fall from the ceiling of the cave as it shifted against its bonds.

Adele shoved Scott's body off of her the rest of the way. She spared a glance at the charges. Most remained in place, their wires still attached. Remembering Pete's gunshot, she crawled out of the cave, intent on finding him.

Once back into the cavern, the psychic screaming in her head abated, allowing her to focus. She regained her feet and headed towards the boat. It was at that moment she realized that her flashlight had fallen off her webbing with her struggle with Scott; it was lying back in the cave.

Unwilling to go back to get the light, she headed into the darkness, trusting her direction and instincts to take her back to the boat. Stumbling forward, she slipped at the top of the tunnel incline and slid downwards, picking up speed until she reached the bodies at the bottom. Crawling over them, she regained her footing and headed off in the direction she thought she needed to go, her arms before her seeking the walls.

Her hands found the wall she sought, and she began to creep along. Soon, she saw a light up ahead, the glow of Pete's light. It was not moving.

"Pete!" she gurgled, her mouth filled with her own blood, flowing from her broken nose and ruined cheek. "Pete!"

"I'm here," he muttered. He was bleeding from a cut above his eye and a deep wound in his side. A cultist lay nearby.

"What happened?"

"We counted twelve, right?" he smiled up at her. "The ten I shot, the one Scott killed and the one I bashed with my gun? Did we count the bodies at the bottom of the tunnel? I think I only stunned the one I bashed. He ambushed me on the way back to the boat." He noticed her wounds. "Jesus, what happened to you? And where is Scott?"

"Scott's dead. He attacked me. That thing, it woke. It attacked my mind, and then Scott struck me. I think he was in its thrall. It called out for help, and he answered. We have to get out of here. We need to blow it up, whether or not we can get out. Can you move?"

"I'm weak from loss of blood, but I can manage. Get me to the boat; we'll bring this place down on it. I hope the wires are still attached to the explosives."

"They are."

Adele reached to help Pete. He got to his feet, wincing in pain, clutching his side. His face was pale and, despite the cold, beaded with sweat. The two of them staggered back the short way to the boat, playing out the remaining wires behind them.

When they got to the cavern with the boats, Pete let out a dejected moan. Their craft had its inflatable sides ripped apart. It rested half-submerged in the icy waters.

"We're not getting out that way. We must use a kayak. Do you think you can manage?"

"No choice. Let me hook up the detonators."

Pete struggled with the detonators but secured the wires. Adele helped him into a kayak before scrambling into one herself. She wasn't confident managing one of the larger boats on her own. The two of them made it twenty feet offshore.

"Here goes nothing," said Pete, slumping in his kayak, pain etched on his face. He stubbed the button on the detonator.

A loud rumbling roar echoed from the tunnel leading towards the creature, followed by a shock wave and the shaking of the entire flow. An ominous cracking sound filled the cavern.

"Pete? We have to move. Now!" Adele began to paddle as fast as her exhausted and wounded body allowed. Pete struggled behind her but inched forward.

The cracking sound grew louder and insistent. Chunks of ice began to fall from the ceiling, splashing into the surrounding water. "We wanted to know how far the explosion would reach. If we had our boat, we'd be out of here by now," said Pete.

"Less talking, more paddling. Can I pull you?"

"No. I will slow you down. Go. Head for the exit."

"I'm not leaving you, Pete."

"Then you'll die for no reason. Get out of here. I'll make my way as fast as I can. One of us should make it out to tell somebody what the hell happened here."

Pete was right. Harjit needed to know. If she stayed, they'd both die. She could make it out, but how could she abandon Pete? "You're not giving up on me, are you?"

"I'd rather not die today," he said through gritted teeth. "Go. I'll be as close behind you as I can."

The rain of ice increased in intensity. Adele pushed her tired muscles to their limits and drove her kayak forward with steady strokes. Pete struggled behind her. Ahead loomed the central cave mouth, the brilliant sunshine of the outside world blazing beyond its edges.

Her body resisting at every stroke, she willed herself forward, and the nose of her kayak shot out into the bright world. Trying to get away from the edge of the flow, she steered her boat towards the icebreaker in the distance.

She turned around to look for Pete. He was labouring hard, and getting closer to the outside, to safety. The point of his kayak was breaking through into the sun when the edge of the cave collapsed, a massive chunk of ice breaking his kayak asunder. Pete slipped under the surface of the icy waters.

"Pete!" she screamed, driving her kayak back towards the now crumbling entrance, the waves created by the collapsing cavern threatening to capsize her boat. She struggled against the effort of the waves to push her back, looking for something near where his craft slipped under the water.

A hand breached the surface fifteen feet from her. She dug in with her paddle, closing the distance. She grabbed the hand and pulled Pete above the surface. He coughed, trying to clear his lungs of the frigid seawater while Adele tried to pull him up onto the top of her kayak. Not strong enough to pull him out of the water with his clothes weighing him down, she held on to him. "You ok?"

"I think so," he said. "I can't believe we did it."

They clung to each other as the boat from the icebreaker approached.

#

Adele sat in the office, waiting. Her broken nose gave her two black eyes. She flexed her hand with the missing fingers, tapping on the desk with her other hand. The damage to her cheek was deep, and a scar would remain. The physical injuries may be more noticeable than her mental scars, but the latter were far deeper.

They had medevacked Pete and her from Alert back to Iqaluit, where they received medical treatment. They kept them separated; she had no word on what Pete's condition was. After two days in the hospital, they cleared her to go and sent her south on a military plane instead of a commercial flight. They took her to Canadian Forces Base Trenton, where she was sitting in an office, waiting for debriefing.

Adele looked out the window to watch planes taking off and landing. The waiting was getting to her.

"You made it back. I hoped you would. I like you, in an appropriate employee-employer way," said Harjit as he entered the office. "I read your notes. So, I was right."

"How did you know? You thought something was trapped in ice. Why were you so sure?"

"I wasn't. A hunch you confirmed. There was a report that gave me the idea. Back in the 1930s, a Dr. William Dyer of Miskatonic University wrote it. That's in Arkham, Massachusetts."

"I am familiar with Miskatonic University. I hoped to share my notes on the Gallou Cove creature with a colleague who works there."

"Small world, eh? Dr. Dyer's report regarded an expedition to Antarctica. He reported on entities he believes were not of this world. Sound familiar?"

"Yes."

"Something was in Antarctica. They may have disturbed it, or it may have been waking up on its own. The reports from the village included things that registered with me. It's why I sent you up to check it out. Dr. Dyer's report made me wonder if there weren't things sleeping in the ice waiting to wake. I'd like to say I hate it when I'm right, but I don't, not a single iota. I love being right, even if it scares the hell out of me."

"So, we found your something, and we blew it up."

"Yes." Harjit opened the file he had before him and thumbed through it. "Captain Armitage reports the sonar on the icebreaker noted something large breaking off from the flow around the time the explosions. It sank to the bottom."

"You think we killed it?"

"These things we've encountered are scary shit, and they are tough, but they aren't immortal. To quote one of my favourite movies, 'If it bleeds, we can kill it.' These things will die."

"Is that Terminator?"

"Predator."

"I always mix up my Schwarzenegger movies."

"You did good work, and you only lost one man. That's a great ratio. This job suits you."

Adele snorted at that, which hurt her nose. "A person dies, and you think I did a great job?"

"Yes. If it had broken free, it would have killed you, the sailors on that boat, and the people in Alert, and then disappeared. Who knows where it would have gone next? Given the alternatives, one person is a great outcome."

"You act as if he was expendable. He was a person. Scott Brennan. He had a family and people that loved him, and he's dead."

"I know who he was. But we're expendable in this conflict, although I'm a little more important than you, I'm afraid."

"There's that charming asshole side coming through again."

Harjit smiled. "I have a reputation to maintain. But you seem to be defending a person who tried to kill you."

"Scott wasn't in his right mind. It was that thing. The thing made Scott a puppet."

"It did. You know how? It had broken Scott's mind. I said The Other leaves an impression on you and confronting it keeps things in check."

"That is central to this whole gig."

"What I did not tell you is that constant exposure leaves you open for more and greater damage. It's a Catch-22; do nothing, and the madness consumes you. Confront it, and you will keep it in check, but expose yourself to more and more, you increase the chances you'll succumb."

"So, we're damned if we do and damned if we don't?"

"The operative word is, we're damned. There is no getting out of this."

Adele stood up to stare at the planes. "I figured as much. There is no going back. I can only keep going forward. How's Pete?" she said, changing the subject.

"Sergeant Ivalu is recovering well. He's still in the hospital, but they tell me that physically, he will make a full recovery."

"And mentally?"

"He's strong, the same as you. He's becoming a part of our team. I gave him the full rundown, the same spiel I gave you, and he agreed to join us."

"Wait, you went to Iqaluit to talk to him?"

"That's right."

"And you didn't stop in to see me?"

"You were fine. I needed to talk to Pete. We were on the same flight back."

"Son of a bitch."

"Now, now. You needed time to decompress, to recover. That was a difficult encounter you had. If you had seen me, it would have been hard for either of us to resist having the conversation we are having now. I was doing you a favour."

"I guess. So now what?"

"Now? Go home to Halifax. Take a few days or even a few weeks off. You need to heal, physically and mentally. I'll call you when I need you."

"You've got something?"

Harjit got up from the desk and closed the file. "I've always got something. This, well, it never ends. I need you to be at your best. I'll call you when I think you're ready." He left.

Adele continued to stare out the window at the planes. "When I'm ready." She nodded. She would be.

It Lives in the Woods

Joe Mills awoke covered in sweat. He did not know where he was. Groggily he looked around, the realization penetrating the fog in his mind.

He was in a small motel that had seen better days on the 400 highway through Muskoka, the cottage paradise north of Toronto. He shouldn't be here. Joe should be house hunting in Victoria, British Columbia.

Throwing back the covers, he struggled to sit up. The crusty shag carpeting scratched at his bare feet as he headed into the bathroom where he pulled the thin plastic covering off a water glass. Turning on the water, he waited for it to get cold; the water got cool but never cold. Giving up, he filled the glass halfway and gulped it down. The water had a swampy taste.

Splashing water on his face, he turned off the tap and blindly reached in the direction of the hand towel. Patting himself dry, he looked up into the mirror. A tired, haggard face almost unrecognizable as his own stared back at him.

The nightmares that began after Gallou Cove had not abated. They were getting worse. He kept seeing the town in his dreams, but a grey stretched version of the town. The residents, the people he had known in the few short days he was in Gallou Cove appeared in them, but they were gaunt and grey with hollowed eyes, their voiceless mouths hanging slack. The specimen they recovered from the beach hung over the scene, emitting a buzzing sound, like bees trapped in a wall. And looming over the entire town was a large shadow. In the dream, he turned to gaze at what was causing the shadow, and he jolted awake before it became visible.

Going back into the bedroom, he glanced at his bed with the damp sheets. He would find no comfort in it. Joe looked at the other bed but knew sleep would not come. He might as well begin his day. The red numbers on the cheap alarm clock said 5:27 am.

Turning back into the bathroom, he turned on the shower. At least the temperature in the shower reached an appropriate level. Joe climbed in and let the hot water caress his tired body and soul.

His life had been a whirlwind in the past ten days. From the call that brought him to Gallou Cove, that fateful night, the quick descent of the government to eradicate the town, his promotion and transfer, to ending up here in this motel; he could barely process the changes. As a reward, or more likely a convenient way to deal with him, he had received a three-rank promotion in the Royal Canadian Mounted Police. This was unheard of and unprecedented. They transferred him from Cape Breton to the other side of the country, to Victoria, six thousand kilometres away.

Joe's wife was not happy about moving. They had put down roots in Cape Breton during the ten years the RCMP had stationed him there, and it was close enough to drive and visit family in Fredericton. Transfers came with the territory, and they had managed ten years in one location. Besides, if you get transferred somewhere, Victoria was about as lovely a place as you could want. And the increase in pay helped to assuage those concerns.

Joe had left his wife to pack up their home while he boarded a plane to head to Victoria, to check-in at his new detachment and to secure temporary accommodations. The first part of the flight from Halifax to Toronto had been without incident, but upon deplaning at Pearson Airport in Toronto, he had been stopped at the gate.

"Inspector Joe Mills?" inquired the security guard. "Could you please come with me? We have a situation we would like your help with."

"What's this about? I have a plane to catch."

"I'm not at liberty to say, but they told me to assure you not to worry about missing your flight. Someone has taken care of everything. Now, if you please?"

Joe followed the guard through the airport and down a quiet corridor behind a security desk. They ushered him into a room in the security centre; from the looks, it was an interrogation room for any passengers flagged as a security risk. The guard closed the door behind him and left Joe alone.

Joe didn't wait long before the door opened, and a smiling man with a dark complexion entered; he was holding a file folder in his hand. "Inspector Mills, please have a seat. We have much to discuss."

The man pointed to the chair opposite him as he pulled out a chair of his own. Joe sat down and leaned forward, crossing his hands in front of him on the table. "Why am I detained? The guard said there was a situation, and you needed my help. I would expect the airport had sufficient security and could call in the Ontario Provincial Police or the local RCMP detachment if needed."

"If the problem was at the airport. It's not. I needed to speak to you. I have a special assignment for you."

"Special assignment? Be more specific. I have a plane to catch and am supposed to check in at my new posting in two days."

"This is your new posting. You're checking in now."

"Excuse me? You're not making any sense. If you don't stop being evasive, I'm leaving."

"You can do that. Leave whenever you want. You won't, however, be reporting to the detachment in Victoria. It's too risky."

"Too risky?"

The man took a page from his folder and slid it across to Joe. "Yes. You are on immediate and indefinite stress leave. Given the trauma you suffered, it would be unwise to allow you to command a detachment. We also need to limit your time around your wife."

Joe grabbed the paper off the table and scanned it. It looked official. He, newly appointed Inspector Joe Mills, was on leave, with pay, until further notice. "What's going on?" he said, getting out of his chair. "Explain, and fast."

The man smiled. "Please sit. What I will tell you might be hard for you to believe. You're not on indefinite leave, more like indefinite secondment. Secondment to me."

"To you? Who the hell are you, and why would I report to you?"

"My name is Harjit Singh, and I don't exist."

"Cut the melodrama."

"Fair enough. I'll get right to it. I head a secret government organization that investigates paranormal activities. We don't show up on the government accounts and my team members ostensibly work for other departments. You will stay on the RCMP payroll, show up in their ranks, but in reality, you're mine."

Joe sat back in the chair. "This is unorthodox."

"Everything we do is unorthodox," said Harjit. "My team is from a variety of backgrounds, with unique skills and talents. Common ground is exposure to The Other."

"The Other?"

"It's a term, nothing more. I needed to call it something. Short for otherworldly."

"What, like aliens?"

"Maybe. I don't know for sure. I know there are things we don't understand, can't comprehend. Things that pose a direct and real threat to humanity. Like that thing you encountered in Gallou Cove."

84

"That's what this is about? I told the government everything."

"You did," said Harjit, picking up the folder in front of him and thumbing through it. "Your powers of observation, your ability to take charge of the situation in the face of the unknown and most of the decisions you made impressed me. You did not shirk from it and did an admirable job."

"A man died. A creature destroyed a town. And you think I did an admirable job?"

"Yes. The outcome could have been worse. That creature in the fish plant, I don't know what it was, but things like it have been showing up for decades, centuries even. We have a significant database of similar occurrences, but they seem to be happening with greater frequency. I'm not sure if we are getting better at finding them, or if something is causing this activity to increase."

"Are you saying this Other has wiped out other towns the same way?"

"No, that was an isolated incident. I have no recollection of a live specimen assaulting the land like that. To come to find what I assume is its child shows a depth of understanding and familial bond that frankly scares me."

"Adele noted that bond too."

"Yes, Dr. Kramer mentioned that in her debrief. I have a spot for her on my team, too; I'm heading to Halifax to speak to her next."

"So, what do you want from me?"

"I need people who can investigate similar occurrences for me. I have half a dozen case files open all over the country. These incidents are not just happening here; I have counterparts around the globe, investigating similar occurrences in their countries. We get together twice a year to compare notes; our parties are legendary."

"You think I am right for this job?"

"I have a limited pool of people to draw from. I only consider those with a documented encounter. Once you are exposed, you are marked. The nightmares, how are you handling them?"

"Nightmares? How did you know about those?"

"Everyone has them after their encounter. I can help you get rid of them. Maybe not entirely, but I can help lessen their frequency and strength."

Joe thought of this for a moment. "How?"

"Our minds have difficulty processing our interaction with The Other. The nightmares will continue, and they will get stronger and worse until your mind shuts down. You may exhibit other tendencies and symptoms that could make you a threat to yourself or others. Therefore we cannot let you assume your role in Victoria and why it is better not to spend too much time alone with your wife."

"You're telling me my life is fucked, then?"

"No. In some inexplicable way, the more you try to confront it, the longer you keep your sanity and functions. I nor anyone else who has studied these outcomes have any idea why this is the case, but the sheer act of resisting The Other by putting yourself in its way seems to keep the symptoms at bay. My first encounter with The Other was six years ago, and I'm able to function as normal. Others, left to their own devices, are catatonic within six months."

"If I do nothing, I'll be a vegetable in six months, if I don't snap before that and kill myself or someone else around me?"

"Not a pleasant picture, I admit, but you have the gist."

"How long can I put this off?"

"That depends. What I'm asking you to do is dangerous. This job will expose you to further psychic assaults. The path to insanity might be hastened, or you might find it helps. The longest documented period between exposure to The Other and succumbing to insanity has been eight years. Others embrace this contact and become willing servants and slaves; some of them have survived decades, but they are twisted, and evil shells to whatever powers are driving them."

"You're coming up on eight years."

"I'm aware. Joe, I'm offering you the best chance you have for a semblance of a life. It's not the one you planned for yourself, but how many of us get to live out our plans? I want my people to know what they are getting into and that they understand the consequences. It's a lot, but I need your answer now or..."

"Or what?"

"I said you couldn't resume your duties, and we won't place your wife in danger."

"Is this a threat?"

Harjit closed the folder and put both hands on the table beside it, not looking Joe in the eye. "You are a threat. My job is to eliminate threats. They will find contraband in your luggage. We'll present evidence of illegal activities you have been a part of for almost a decade. We will arrest you, hold you without bail, and your wife will lose out on your income and your pension."

"You're blackmailing me, then."

"That's an ugly word. I have two options open to me: bring you onboard or segregate you from society. Call it blackmail if you will; I call it being pragmatic."

"You said I could leave."

"You could have, yes. And we would have detained you twenty feet from the door."

"Not much choice then. Either I do as you say or I am incarcerated and lose my mind."

"We always have a choice. Sometimes one choice is abhorrent to us. For what it's worth, I'm sorry. I limit my team to people that have encountered The Other. I won't destroy a person's life by forcing them into an encounter. It's why you are under strict orders to limit other people's exposure."

"You started this off by saying that people with unique talents and skills make up your team. What if I offered nothing?"

Harjit sighed. "I don't present those people with two options. Only one. And the option is not presented so much as enacted."

Now it was Joe's turn to sigh. "And what happens to my wife?"

"Call her and tell her she doesn't have to move. She can stay in Cape Breton. Tell her you were offered a job high in the government, great pay and opportunity, but classified, and you can't tell her the details. It will take you away from home, but the work is important, and your government needs you. It's not like you can't go home, but your stays will be short, and only if you continue to pass our assessments proving to us you are not a threat to her safety. Or call her and tell her you want a divorce. Those are my two suggestions."

"You're obviously not married."

"I was. I chose option two. She and my daughter are better off away from me. She's remarried and has another kid now. My ex thinks I'm an asshole and a deadbeat dad; I'd rather that than the alternative." Harjit got up from the table. "I'd recommend starting with option one; you can always switch to option two if it comes to that. Given the time away from home, she might choose option two for you. I assume you're in?"

"I was in before you added the fact you'd have me arrested if I wasn't. Whatever was in Gallou Cove, it changed me. I recognize that I can't go back to my normal life. Let's figure out what the hell is going on with this shit."

"I expected this from you. Your first assignment is waiting. A suspected bear attack in Muskoka; a family is dead."

"And you don't think a bear was the culprit?"

"I'm sure it wasn't. Go investigate and give me your initial assessment. Here are the details," said Harjit, handing over an envelope. "I've booked you a room; nothing fancy, I'm afraid. Our department might not show up on the government books officially, but they still give me grief if I spend too extravagantly."

Thus Joe found himself in the shower of a motel that had seen better days.

Joe left his room and got into his rental car. He'd kill for a cup of Tim Hortons' coffee, but he'd have to go without one as the nearest one was ten kilometres away in the opposite direction. The case file Harjit gave him told him to meet Tim Keddy at the Thompson Marina at Eight Mile Lake. Tim worked for the Ministry of Natural Resources and would take him out to the site of the supposed bear attack. The police had removed the bodies three days ago. Joe hoped they had not contaminated the scene in the interim. There were clues the police would not recognize as relevant; he did not know what they were.

The gravel parking lot of the marina was almost empty. Cottage season was still a few weekends away, but the weather had been uncharacteristically warm. Some had gotten a jump on opening up their cottages, like the unfortunate family at the heart of this case. Joe never understood the appeal of a cottage; the added work of maintaining a second home, coupled with the hours stuck in weekend traffic to get to one, did not seem worth it. To each their own.

Tim Keddy was standing waiting for him. "Are you Joe Mills?" he asked as Joe stepped out of his car.

"I am. Inspector Joe Mills, RCMP."

"Tim Keddy, Ontario Ministry of Natural Resources. You want to peak at the site?"

"That's right."

"Uh, huh. Little out of your jurisdiction, aren't you?"

"Someone has deemed this case a matter of national interest, I guess. I'm a civil servant, like you. Someone higher up the food chain tells me to go somewhere, I go."

"Yeah, and they never tell us why. Maybe you can figure out what the hell happened."

"They told me a bear attacked the family."

"That was no bear. At least not one native to these parts. Maybe a grizzly or a polar bear could do damage like that, but not the black bears we have around here."

"Why was that?"

"A black bear might break into a cottage in search of food. Maybe you left a greasy pan out or something. They'll root in your garbage or knock over your barbecue. Whatever this was, it broke down the door and attacked the family."

"A man, a woman and their two kids, a boy and a girl the file said."

"Yeah, a real tragedy. Normally you surprise a bear inside your cottage, and the bear gets out as quick as it can. A bear is as scared of you as you are of them."

"And this one didn't?"

"The damage to the door and the cottage itself, well I've never seen a bear do that before. As for the people, whatever attacked ate part of them. A bear, he's more interested in greens or nuts and berries. I suppose it might eat a person if it was starving, but I've never heard of that happening. An adult male black bear is one-fifty, one-eighty pounds, and they lose a chunk of that during hibernation. So, a single bear, coming out of hibernation, upon encountering four people in a house when it has a clear escape route; this doesn't happen."

"What do you think it could be?"

"I've been thinking about this. Lots of rich people got cottages here. I'm wondering if one of them didn't have an exotic pet that got loose. Something they shouldn't have, so they didn't report it was missing."

"What kind of exotic pet?"

"A tiger or something."

"You think a tiger did this?"

"I never said that," said Tim haughtily. "You asked what I thought. There's nothing in these woods capable of creating the damage at that cottage. Whatever it was, it had to be big and aggressive and hungry. I'm not a tiger expert, and this may sound far-fetched, but I got nothing else to go on. All I know is something tore that poor family apart, and it's not anything we normally find around here."

"I thank you for your candour. Far-fetched is what I'm looking for. My boss suspected this wasn't a bear attack. You make an official report?"

"Not yet," said Tim. "The police do not suspect foul play because of the elements of an animal attack, but they are not closing the case until I sign off. When they said the feds were sending someone, I decided I'd wait before I filed my report. I'd rather give them my thoughts on what it could be, not say what I think it isn't. The police and the local mayor are pretty hopped up to close this case. Cottage season is about to start, and they don't want to scare anyone away. Visitors inject money into the local economy. If we can't solve this case, they will not be happy."

"Well, we won't solve the case standing in this parking lot. Let's have a look," said Joe.

"Follow me. The cottage is out on an island."

"An island? How big of an island?"

"About twelve acres. There are six cottages in total; cops told the owners they couldn't go out until we clear this up. More pressure on me, I guess, to solve this," Tim said wryly.

A boat with the MNR logo was at the dock. They climbed in, and Tim edged the boat out into the open water.

It was a quick jaunt across the still waters of the lake to the cottage's dock. The rough rocks of the Canadian Shield rose before them; they could see the cabin perched on a cliff through the trees fifty feet higher than the water. Someone built the dock along a rocky wall; Tim pulled the boat up alongside.

A path wound its way through the trees leading up to the cottage. Mortared steps into the rock with a cedar railing positioned in steeper spots. Wooden stairs led up to the deck of the cabin; the nearest other cottage was five hundred feet west of their location.

"Were the neighbours at home when this happened?" asked Joe, pointing at the other cottage.

"No. Only one guy was on the island; his cottage is on the far side. He didn't see or hear anything."

They followed the path and the stairs and came out on the large deck. The cottage was modest compared to some that dotted the lake.

"What did the owners do?"

"The family was from Toronto. The husband sold insurance, and the wife was a small-time actress. You might know her to see her, one of those that show up in commercials and doing bit parts in TV shows, but not a household name."

"The police don't have a motive?"

"Naw, they led a squeaky-clean life. Well-liked by those that knew them, no financial troubles."

"And the others on the island? Any red flags there?"

"What, maybe they were up to shady shit, and someone hit the wrong house? You'd have to ask the police about that, but I don't think so. Folks have owned these cottages a long time; they don't come up for sale often as people pass them down to their kids. Most of them are boring. The guy who was on the island the night of the attack is a university professor. But let me show you the scene. I have to warn you, it's gruesome, even with the bodies removed."

Tim led Joe around the corner of the house past the patio door. The cottage had big windows facing the lake; Joe glanced in as they walked by to see the interior in evident disarray.

The door lay in pieces on the floor. "Black bear will not do that," said Tim. He pointed to the barbecue outside. "Another

91

thing is the barbecue. It was untouched — still residue from the last time the family used it. If a bear came to the cottage because he was hungry, he'd have a go at that first. Too many red flags for me."

Joe glanced at the barbecue and peered through the door. Gore dripped from the walls, and furniture ripped and flipped over. Something had torn the place apart. Stepping inside, he pulled out his notepad and jotted down items of interest.

"Kitchen looks untouched," Joe said.

"It was. Hungry bear will go for the kitchen."

"Where were the bodies found?"

"They found the adults in the living room. Police said they had been sitting on the couch when whatever it was came in. Don't suppose they even had a chance to stand up, the attack was so fast."

"Something came in killed them before they could react?"

"Yep. That's aggression. No way would a bear do that. Smash through the door and cover twenty feet of ground to kill two adults before they could move? Not a chance. It's why I can't tell them it's a bear."

"And the kids?"

"They found the boy inside his bedroom by the door. The little girl must have hidden in the closet because that's where they found her."

Joe shook his head. "This is a real mess." In almost fifteen years on the job, he'd seen auto accidents and investigated a few murders, but nothing like this. "And you said the bodies were partially eaten?"

"Each one of them had a chunk taken out of them. Bear will eat carrion, sometimes kill a fawn or a newborn moose. If they do that, they eat their fill and move along. This thing grazed around the place."

"Ok, you've convinced me it's not a bear. Still, that revelation doesn't bring us any closer to figuring out what it was." Joe started to walk from room to room, observing the carnage throughout the place. He closed his eyes and took a deep breath, and a tingle — similar to the disorientation he had when he and Adele cracked open the creature in Gallou Cove, was at the edge of his consciousness. Keeping his eyes closed, he forced his breathing to stay even. Joe's mind began to make sense of the cottage, reaching out to touch on the energies found in the room, as if his previous experience had attuned his senses to what lingered in the room. He opened his eyes.

The room looked different now. It was still in disarray, but he got the sense of a pattern amidst the chaos. Taking out his phone, he started to focus on different elements around the room and began to take pictures.

"You think you got something?"

Joe nodded. "I do. I don't know what yet." The random splatters began to take on shape and substance for him. "There is a pattern here. Look." He handed Tim his phone. "Look at that photo. Do you see the blood?"

"Yes. So?"

"And here," said Joe, pointing at the wall. "And then back to the picture."

"It looks the same," said Tim. "I mean the basic shape of the splatter is similar. So what? Didn't you just take that?"

"No. The photo is from the other wall. And the pattern is repeating. Here," Joe pointed to a spot on the floor. "Here." A similar spot was on the far wall. Joe walked into the boy's bedroom. "And here on the floor. This isn't random. Something deliberately made these splatters. They are too uniform."

Tim looked at Joe's phone again and then at the spots that Joe had indicated. It was his turn to close his eyes and try to calm his breathing. Sighing, he opened up his eyes and hastily thrust the phone back into Joe's hands. "I've seen enough. It's obvious to me that a bear came in and killed these people. Unfortunate, yes, but that's my official report."

"You know a bear didn't do this. Something sinister is at work here, and we should figure out what before we put others at risk."

"No, you figure it out. I'm done here. A bear did this. Case closed."

Joe was going to retort and then stopped, remembering Harjit's direction to limit other people from encountering The Other. He didn't want to expose Tim to any more than he already had. "Fine, it's a bear. Tell the cops and the mayor, but don't file your official report for a few more days. I need to confer with my boss and see what he thinks. He might have other ideas."

Tim nodded. "I'll give you a few more days, but I'm not changing my mind. I'm not coming back out here."

They headed back to the dock. Upon arriving at the marina, Tim turned and left without another word to Joe.

Joe got into his rental car and texted the pictures he had taken to Harjit, providing him with a synopsis of what he had seen, including the repeated pattern in the blood splatters. He sat there, waiting for Harjit's reply. It came a few minutes later:

Someone will join you. Stay at the motel. Do not investigate further until you have backup.

#

Joe woke up and glanced over at the clock beside his bed. Three twelve am said the red numbers. This was the first night he had not dreamed of Gallou Cove since it happened. His sheets were dry; what had awakened him was the mundane need to urinate. Perhaps he had moved past the nightmares.

Light from the parking lot of the motel filtered into the room around the edges of the curtains. He made his way in the pale glow to the bathroom to relieve himself. Sitting down on the toilet to not piss on the floor if he missed in the near darkness, Joe yawned. His mouth was dry; he needed a drink. The light didn't filter enough into the bathroom for him to see one of the glasses provided to him; he needed to turn on the light. Having finished urinating, he gave himself a shake and stood up, reaching back to turn on the light to find the glass.

As the light flicked on, Joe began to scream. He saw the mirror covered with the same blood splatters he had noted at the cottage; the familiar pattern repeated itself over and over. His form in the mirror was grey and desiccated; he looked like a corpse.

Joe bolted upright in his bed, drenched in sweat. Disoriented, he looked around. The room was normal. He glanced over at the clock which read 5:27 am.

He rubbed his eyes and willed his breathing to settle down, his heart racing in his chest. After composing himself, he got up and cautiously went over to the bathroom, sliding his hand in to flick on the light, glancing in with narrowed eye slits, afraid of what he would see.

It reflected his cowering form to him in the mirror. He didn't look like a corpse, but he looked like shit, as he had yesterday when he had woken up from his nightmare. He let out the breath he had been unwittingly holding and turned on the shower.

#

Unable to return to sleep, he found a diner to get breakfast. As he sat there contemplating the case, his sense of urgency and unease continued to grow. He kept picking up his phone and looking at Harjit's last text. No word when this backup would arrive. As a cop, he knew you waited for backup before going into a dangerous situation. It was in movies that cops went running in alone. His anxiety was peaking; he couldn't sit around and do nothing. Maybe if he drank himself into a stupor, he could get past it; he wasn't about to start that self-destructive behaviour.

He couldn't sit there any longer so, he paid his bill and went out to his car. A few minutes later, he found himself back at the Thompson Marina, renting a boat to head out to the cottage again.

The cottage loomed as he approached, innocent looking but harbouring dark secrets. Pulling the boat into the dock, he turned off the engine and sat there listening. Birds were chirping, and insects were buzzing in the still morning air. Everything was placid and regular in appearance.

Shuffling up the path towards the home, feeling both compelled forward and resisting, he emerged onto the deck. Lingering to look out over the lake, his back to the carnage visible through the windows, he rechecked his phone. No update from Harjit. He shouldn't be here, he should wait as instructed, but a gnawing in his brain forced him to turn and enter the cottage.

His eyes alighted on the patterns in the blood. No mistaking it, the designs were deliberate. But why? The undertaking to recreate these elaborate splatters throughout the home, even in other rooms, would have been painstaking. Whatever made them lingered over the bodies. It revelled in what it had done and left a signature.

Joe closed his eyes and focused on his breathing. His senses calmed, and he noticed details unperceivable to regular observation. The curse of The Other was on him, leaving him attuned to these subtle differences.

"Joe Mills," came a whisper in his head. It was not audible; he hadn't heard it, he'd felt it. A low broken cackle followed. "Joe Mills."

Whatever it was, it knew him, knew he was there. It was calling to him.

Joe looked into the woods. There was a path, barely discernible to the eye, but Joe could see it. It looked like a highway cut through the rocky landscape to him. He drew his service pistol he had tucked into his jacket pocket that morning as he left the motel and made sure there was a bullet in the chamber. Holding it loosely in his hand, he began to follow the path.

This is crazy, he thought. *What am I doing? I should listen to Harjit's orders and wait for backup. Don't take this on alone.* But his feet didn't seem to be following his directions, and he continued to proceed into the woods.

It grew darker under the canopy of trees, with the light filtering down through the cracks in the tall evergreens. Joe's mouth was dry, so he licked his lips and cast his gaze around furtively. The path led towards the centre of the island.

"Joe Mills." The cackle. And even so, he went forward.

A sense of foreboding hung in the air. He closed his eyes again, and when he opened them, the landscape had changed to black and white. The sounds had dimmed, became muffled, and the chirping of the birds and the buzzing of the insects took on an industrial, almost metallic tone. It was as if he was seeing a hellscape overlaying the real world. Joe paused to look around him.

The trees were subtly different. The buds, promising the return of leaves, were distorted, pulpy. Sap ran slowly down the trunks and provided the only tinge of colour in this dreamscape;

the sap was reddish and looked like blood. And while there was no wind, the trees swayed as if there was, driven by an internal source.

Glancing skyward, he noted a small flock of birds. Their claws and beaks appeared distended and razor-sharp, and their eyes had a wild gleam in them. They alighted to branches surrounding him, gazing upon him with barely contained malevolence. They began to screech in unison, the mechanical quality evident.

Joe started to move further along the path, picking up his pace. The ground before him roiled with hundreds of beetles scuttling in every direction. On their carapaces, Joe noted the same pattern found in the blood. Looking up, he saw a figure draped in a black coat, a hood obscuring its features. The figure raised a hand and beckoned Joe forward.

Joe stopped and closed his eyes. He gave his head a shake and furiously rubbed his eyes. When he opened them, he was once again standing in the sun-kissed forest, and the sounds had returned to normal. Forcing down the wave of panic developing in him, he continued to walk further into the woods.

The trees broke, and in the clearing ahead, he could see what appeared to be a mound jutting from the rock. An opening appeared there, the dark mouth of a cave beckoning to him. What appeared to be scrub bushes, dense foliage that had choked off the hole, lay scattered on the ground in front. Something had recently exposed the cave.

Making sure the safety was off of his pistol, Joe entered. He wished he had brought a flashlight with him, as the sunlight did not filter inside to any considerable depth; darkness obscured the back of the cave. Taking out his phone, he flipped the display to a white screen to have a source of light. The pale dimness that emanated from it cast a ghostly haze in the darkness but did not penetrate more than a few feet.

The cackle echoed in his mind, but this time, he heard it too. He was not alone in the cave.

Sanity returned to him; he should not be here. Backing away, holding his phone in one hand, his pistol in the other, he headed for the entrance. Too late.

Something emerged out of the darkness. It was over eight feet tall, and its multi-jointed arms, with two sets of elbows, splayed outwards, giving it a span of at least ten feet. The arms ended in long, thin hands, each with three fingers, the middle finger ending in a six-inch gleaming claw. Its skin was as black as night, and it was gaunt and brittle in appearance. The thing had no face; its head was long and misshapen. The black surface split vertically, exposing a red mouth lined with four rows of three-inch teeth. Moving to mimic speaking, he heard his name again uttered. "Joe Mills." It cackled, filling the cave with its malice.

Dropping his phone and steadying his pistol in both hands, Joe pulled the trigger. It barked three times, sending its deadly projectiles at the creature. He was sure he hit it at this range, but it did not react. It cackled again and came towards him.

Turning to flee, Joe took three steps before he felt a sharp pain in his left side. That claw had connected with him, and he felt the other fingers closing on his jacket. The thing, despite its brittle countenance, was strong; it pulled Joe deeper into the cave and threw him. Joe hit the floor hard, dropping his pistol. The creature was now between Joe and the exit, and he had no weapon.

Staggering to his feet and backing up to get away from it, Joe ran into the back wall of the cave. Desperate to get away, he scrambled to his right, deeper into the darkness. He banged into what appeared to be a low shelf; there were objects arrayed on it. His hands frantically felt the edge of the table, and his fingers encountered something sharp, slicing open his skin. Reaching for it with his undamaged hand, he closed his grip around what felt like the hilt of a blade. Spinning back to face the creature descending upon him, he lashed out, feeling it connect.

A scream of pain and rage filled the cave, as the creature recoiled from Joe. Pressing his slight advantage, Joe lunged forward, stabbing at it. He felt several superficial hits strike, and it backed away from him, no longer the aggressor. Realizing his only hope to survive this encounter was to attack, he drove himself forward.

The knife struck a hard, meaty blow, connecting with the creature's torso. It grabbed Joe from behind and threw him violently backwards, the knife slipping from his grasp. He struck the wall; the wind knocked out of him as he slumped to the floor. Highlighted in the dim light from the entrance, he could see the creature staggering back, its hands clawing at itself as an acrid stench filled the small confines of the cave. The sounds that came from it were of fear as it struggled to stay on its feet. Falling to its knees and hunched forward, it released a bellow that Joe both heard in his ears and his mind. The roar seemed to cross boundaries of reality, and in the distance, Joe thought he could hear an agonized reply. And then the thing in front of him withered and exploded outwards, covering Joe in its viscera. His skin burned where it touched him, and Joe passed out.

#

"Joe? Joe? Wake up, Joe!"

The voice penetrated his brain fog; it was vaguely recognizable. Joe tried to push the fog aside as he opened his eyes.

"You're not dead, so that's something," said Harjit, looking down on him. "I told you to wait."

Joe rubbed his head and forced himself to sit up. "I'm not dead, although I feel like I should be," avoiding the admonishment for not having waited.

"I was trying to dispatch another asset to help you, but everyone I have was on assignment. I rushed back from Halifax because I knew you wouldn't wait."

"What time is it?"

"It's." Harjit checked his watch. "One thirty-two."

"What day?"

"Saturday."

It was the day Joe came to the island, but four hours later. He held his hand up for Harjit to take and help him stand.

"Tell me what happened?"

"I'm sorry, I couldn't wait. Something was calling to me."

"I knew you wouldn't wait long. But I expected you'd at least wait twenty-four hours, though. I'm pissed you disobeyed me but impressed you took action to figure things out, so they balance each other." Harjit gave him a sly smile.

"I came to the cottage, and something whispered to me. It drew me out into the woods, and I found this cave."

"What was it?"

Joe described the creature to Harjit. "I've seen vague references to something similar, but none of my people have encountered anything like this. We may have a first."

"It attacked me, and I stumbled backwards. I hit something and found a knife; I cut my hand." Joe held it up to show Harjit. "I hit it with the knife, and it recoiled. I pressed the attack and stabbed it. Then it exploded."

"Let's shed some light on this place, shall we and see what we are looking at." Harjit pulled out a pair of flashlights and gave one to Joe. They both engaged their lights. Harjit gave a low whistle.

Someone covered the walls of the cavern with symbols, different from each other. "Are those hieroglyphics?" asked Joe.

"Egyptian, yes."

"What would Egyptian hieroglyphics be doing in a cave in the Canadian Shield?"

"I don't know. But these symbols here, they are indigenous pictograms. Here is a proto-kanji form of writing. Like the Chinese use, but earlier than the ones in common use today."

"So we're standing in the middle of some sort of Rosetta Stone?"

"Is that a joke? Because it's kind of funny," said Harjit. "These symbols scratched into the rock have been out of the weather, so I don't notice any real differentiation in age. Could be ten years old, or a thousand." Harjit shined his light further in discovering the shelf. Ritualistic items and symbols were scattered where Joe had knocked them. "Where's the knife you mentioned?"

Joe scanned the ground. "It's here," he said, picking it up and handing it to Harjit.

"We must get this studied," he said, slipping it into his backpack. "I will send a team out to catalogue everything in here. See if anyone knows what it says. We should swab some of that goo off you too."

"There are letters over here," said Joe, ignoring the goo. "It's our alphabet, but they make little sense."

Harjit came over to look. The letters on the wall formed the phrase 'ph'nglui mglw'nafh Cthulhu R'lyeh wgah'nagl fhtagn'.

"Any idea what it says?"

"I'm not familiar with this phrase," said Harjit. "But this name here," he pointed to the word Cthulhu. "This I've seen. It keeps coming up associated with a variety of cults all over the world. I don't know for certain what it represents."

"I guess we know what killed those people. We can tell the police it's safe to let people back on the island."

"Premature. There are things in this world that found their way here long ago. Other things are brought here by others."

"What do you mean brought?"

"Summoned. Through a ritual." Harjit pointed his flashlight back at the table with its artifacts. "These things look similar to other ritualistic items we've seen in the past."

"Rituals? Summoning? That's mumbo-jumbo."

Harjit stared at Joe. "You encountered that thing in Gallou Cove, discovered the patterns in the blood and fought a demon monster in this cave, and you are having doubts about rituals?"

Joe blushed. "When you put it like that, sure it sounds dumb."

"It is dumb. I thought you could embrace this whole thing we are doing. Don't weird out on me now. I need you to accept these things are real."

"I've got a wound in my side to remind me it's real," Joe grimaced.

"Why didn't you say something?"

"It's superficial," said Joe, waving Harjit off. "Don't worry about it. The bleeding stopped on its own."

"You're going to the hospital to get checked." He glanced around. "Nothing more for us to do here. I'll know more when I get it translated."

"You got someone?"

"I have lots of someones, all ideal for particular tasks. They'll let me know. Let's go."

The two of them turned to leave the cave when they heard a noise outside. "Shh," said Harjit, extinguishing his flashlight and indicating to Joe to do the same. Joe complied.

Something was walking near the edge of the clearing. They listened; the sound stopped.

Harjit peered around the edge of the cave opening. A man was standing there, gazing nervously at the cave. He was an elderly gentleman, wearing a Tilley hat, a fleece top and a vest, with cargo shorts and socks under his Birkenstocks. Harjit was about to signal to Joe to follow him out of the cave when the man reached into his pocket and pulled out a snub-nosed revolver. Gripping it tightly in his hand, the man moved hesitantly closer to the cave opening.

"You have your gun?" Harjit hissed. "I assume you brought one."

Joe had forgotten his gun, which he had dropped in the dark. "I dropped it. I will need a light to find it," he whispered.

"We can't chance it; he'll know we are here."

As if on cue, the old man's shaky voice called out. "Come out. I know you are there. You are trespassing on this island. Show yourself, or I'll go call the police."

They looked at each other in the dim light of the entrance. "Maybe he doesn't know we are both here," said Joe. "You go out, and I'll see if I can find my gun."

"Go out? That guy has a gun. Listen, I come off all badass when I'm wearing a suit and sitting in a meeting, but I'm not keen on facing down an armed opponent. That's more your thing."

"You know how to use my pistol if you find it?"

"Not really, no."

"Then you need to go out there."

"You have until the count of three," said the old man, his voice becoming more confident. "I saw you lurking around through the trees, coming up this way. Nowhere else for you to be. One..."

"You got to go."

"Who works for who? Remember, I'm the boss."

"Well, boss, if you don't distract him and give me the time to find the gun, we're both in real trouble. Maybe he's the self-imposed neighbourhood watch and wonders what you're doing out here."

102

"Yeah, and maybe he's got an itchy trigger finger and doesn't like brown people."

"Two..."

"Alright," hissed Harjit. "I'm coming out," he shouted, lifting his arms over his head and walking to the entrance. "Hey there," he said, smiling as he emerged. "My name's Rupinder; my friends call me Rupi. I was looking at the island. I'm a real estate agent, and my client is looking to buy a cottage here."

"Nothing for sale," said the old man, his eyes narrowing. "What were you doing in that cave?"

"What? Oh, it's-it's-a cave. Caves are cool. I thought I'd take a peek inside. Who wouldn't want to look in a cave?"

"What did you see in there?"

"Inside the cave?"

Joe was on his hands and knees, looking for his dropped pistol while this exchange was occurring. He was frantically going over the dark ground where he thought he might have lost it; he could easily miss it by less than an inch.

"Yes, inside the cave."

"I couldn't see anything. It was way too dark. I wished I'd thought to bring a flashlight. I didn't expect I'd be going spelunking," said Harjit, laughing.

The old man looked at him, testing his sincerity. He scowled and looked past Harjit to the cave mouth. "Hessanin mudath," he said, staring into the depths of the cave.

Joe's fingers brushed against the cool metal of his pistol. He picked it up and turned back towards the entrance.

Flicking his eyes from the cave mouth back to Harjit, the old man raised the revolver and pulled the trigger. The first bullet grazed Harjit's left arm, and he spun away, crouching and heading back towards the cave mouth. The revolver spat again, the round catching Harjit in the back of his right thigh, just above the knee. He screamed in pain and crumbled to the ground. The old man levelled his gun at Harjit's sprawled form.

Joe came out of the cave mouth and pulled his trigger twice. Both bullets hit the man in the middle of his chest, placed there with expert precision. A look of surprise and then pain gripped his face as he fell backwards, dead.

"Son of a bitch, that hurts!" yelled Harjit on the ground. "That old bastard shot me."

Joe took off his belt and fashioned a tourniquet to wrap around Harjit's thigh. The wound didn't bleed too much, having missed the artery, and passing clean through without hitting the bone, but he wanted to be safe. The wound on Harjit's arm was of no consequence.

"Here, hold these over the wounds," said Joe, pulling out two handkerchiefs. "Apply pressure to help staunch any bleeding."

"I'm familiar with first aid," said Harjit. "But why did you have a handkerchief on you? Who under seventy carries handkerchiefs?"

"Second nature. You might have to pick up something you don't want to contaminate. You ok?"

"It hurts, but I think I'll live."

"Give me your phone. I'll call for help."

#

The police came to the island and took Harjit and Joe to the nearest hospital. Joe's wound was worse than he had thought. He had internal bleeding as the creature's claw had made it through his flesh into his abdominal cavity. An infection had set in. Joe was treated with a round of antibiotics and kept overnight for observation. They gave Harjit a series of medicines, dressed his wounds and discharged him. He arrived the next morning at the hospital in with a car and driver to fetch Joe.

"My team will get out there today to check things out, take pictures, and dissect the scene. So that's taken care of." Harjit sat in the back with Joe as the driver pulled the car out of the hospital parking lot and headed towards the highway. "The old bastard that shot me? He was Professor Robert Bilson, a professor of Medieval History at the University of Toronto. He's the guy on the island the night it murdered those people."

"Medieval History?"

"Yeah, he was an expert in the Church's position on cults and Satan worshippers."

"Weird. You figure he knew what was in that cave?"

104

"Without a doubt. When the cops went to check on his place, they found a false wall in the basement. There was freaky shit in there they tell me. That's next on my team's list to go through."

"You think he summoned whatever it was?"

"Someone had to. The professor was coming to check on it. Maybe he saw me going up there. He probably wondered why it didn't tear me apart. Those words he spoke? I think he was calling out to it. Anyway, I've sent the description of what you encountered along with that phrase we found, the one with Cthulhu in it, to a bunch of my colleagues around the world. I suspect I'll know something soon."

"Did they summon it, knowing that the family would be on the island?"

"I don't know for sure. Not like they'd want to draw attention to themselves that way. The cult didn't expect people to be here yet, but with the great weather..."

"So, the wrong place at the wrong time?"

"Sometimes it's as simple as that. It was for you."

"Poor bastards."

"These cults, they are rarely a cult of one. I'm worried that Prof. Bilson is not the only person who is part of this. It might involve anyone that lives on this island."

"Maybe even the family. You never know."

"Good point. I'll have my guys comb through their stuff a little deeper, see if there is anything to that theory. Can't be too careful."

"Can we check the other cottages before the police give the all-clear?"

"Even my authority has limits. I can't draw attention to us, and if I can't tell people who I am and what I do, I don't have a lot of leverage. It was a bitch getting that MNR guy to wait for you; the provincial governments don't like it when we feds stick our noses into their jurisdictions. We'll monitor, but unless I have something solid, we can't be breaking into people's houses."

"So, now what?"

"So now, you go home. I will drop you off at your motel. At the airport, one of my people will run you through our assessment protocols, and if it comes out ok, you can visit your wife for a few days, maybe even a week. You've earned it; that was nasty for your first time."

"What about you? Don't you need a break?"

"Tick-Tock, time's a-wasting. Eight years is around the corner, remember? I have lots to do."

"Hey, maybe you'll be lucky and set the new longevity record."

"Oh, I intend to, but this is what I know." Harjit got silent and gazed out the window. "I may not be in her life, but I have a little girl out there, and I love her. I have to make this world safe for her. Knowing it could come crashing down on me drives me harder. I've got too much going on; there's something big in Nunavut. Maybe I'll give you an update on it next time I see you. You have any nightmares last night?"

"No. I thought maybe it was the drugs they had me on."

"They didn't give you a sedative. That was all you, buddy."

"That's something then."

"Embrace the small miracles. Sometimes it's all we have." Harjit pulled into the parking lot at the motel; they had recovered his rental car from the marina. "There should be a ticket for you at the West Jet desk at Pearson, and I'll have a car waiting for you at Halifax to take you the rest of the way home."

"Thanks."

"Got to look out for my people. Take it easy, and I'll call you when I need you."

"Before you go-" Joe struggled with what he would say next. "I see things. I could see patterns in the blood, and when I was out in the woods, for a time there, things took on this weird aspect. They were the same woods, but everything was black and white, and altered in subtle ways. The birds took on monstrous qualities. Is this normal?"

"It's not abnormal." Harjit sighed. "Things are sitting heavy on you. I've heard of people that could see things others could not see. I've read accounts of people who said there was another world, a dimension, layered over our own. Usually, though, people only see this in their dreams. You were awake when this happened?"

"Yes. It didn't last long, and things returned to normal."

"Curious."

"Yeah. Do your people ever get burned out doing this job? Like, they wake up one day and decide that the prospect of becoming catatonic is better than continuing?"

"All the time. No gold watches for long-term employees, you know."

"Yeah. Goodbye, Harjit. I suspect I'll hear from you sooner than I want to."

Joe got out of the car and watched Harjit drive away. He hadn't told his wife he'd taken this job; she assumed he was in Victoria. He looked down at the car key in his hand and then put it in his pocket. Turning, he went into the motel office to see about extending his stay.

Troy Young

It Hides In The Village

The phone trilled on the nightstand beside the bed. Joe Mills turned over with a groan. The red numbers on the clock showed 5:37 am.

He wondered who was calling. It was too early to be his wife. She thought he was over four thousand kilometres west of where he was, in Victoria, British Columbia. It was two thirty-seven there. But Joe had been lying to her.

Picking the cell phone up off the nightstand, he glanced to see who it was; it was Harjit. He let the call go to voice mail. The ringing stopped, only to start again a few moments later. He'd have to shut it off if he wanted a respite from the ringing, but Harjit would no doubt call on the room's landline. Worse, he might have one of the staff knock on the door. Harjit wouldn't give up until he reached Joe. Reluctantly he pressed to answer. "Hello?"

"Joe." Harjit's voice was stern. "You never picked up the tickets at the West Jet counter. Why not?"

"I didn't feel like going home."

"You're still at that scummy motel in Muskoka." It wasn't a question.

"Yes."

"And you still haven't told your wife the truth. She thinks you're in Victoria."

"How do you know that? You have my home line bugged?"

"Your landline in Cape Breton, your wife's cell phone and yours. I have to watch my people, to see if they are exhibiting undesirable behaviours."

"Is hiding out at a motel and not telling my wife the truth an undesirable behaviour?"

Pause. "No. But it's not positive either."

"I need time. I'm not sure if I shouldn't take the second option and let my wife go. That I might pose a threat to her..."

"If you posed a threat to her, I would never have booked you a flight home. You're making excuses."

"Yeah." Joe rubbed his eyes. "It was over a week ago you left here. Why are you only calling me now?"

"I figured you needed time, as you just confirmed. Your calls to your wife have been infrequent, and you haven't told her any details. You told her your transfer might not be permanent, and you might come back to Nova Scotia, so she should stop packing up the house."

"Not exactly a lie. You told me to tell her I was seconded to another department which required me to travel, but I could use Cape Breton as a home base."

"That's between you and your wife. But I'm not calling to discuss your home life. I'm calling because I have a job for you. Something has come to my attention, in a small town east of you called Little Brook. I want you to investigate the village."

Joe's emotions struggled with this news. He had accepted this assignment willingly; incarceration was the alternative if he'd passed on it. Joe hadn't known that when he'd accepted Harjit's offer of employment. He was trying to keep it together, but he wasn't sure how successful he was being. To do it again caused him to pause.

"It's probably nothing, but I can't leave loose ends. Someone needs to confirm there's no problem. And after you disobeyed me last time and went in without backup, I'm

110

assigning you a partner. Pete's flying into the Toronto City Centre airport from Ottawa. Go meet him there."

"I have to go downtown? Why not the main airport?"

"We get a discount from the airline that flies out of the downtown airport. I need to find savings where possible. Bureaucracies, am I right?"

"Whatever. I'll go. What's the case?"

"Pete, your partner, will have the details. Pick him up, and he'll fill you in on everything. You've got three hours until his flight lands, so get a move on." The line clicked dead.

The drive was two-and-a-half hours to Toronto; this didn't leave him much time.

Joe showered and checked out of the hotel. He pulled into the temporary drop off circle with minutes to spare.

Harjit had told him nothing about his partner, apart from his first name. Joe didn't know what he looked like and couldn't leave the car; his lingering in the temporary spot was drawing dirty looks. People were exiting the terminal and heading for the long line of taxicabs ready to whisk them to their destination. Taking out a pen he found in the glove compartment of this rental car, he scrawled the name Pete in large letters on the back of the Tim Hortons bag that had held his breakfast.

Joe stood at the end of the car, his makeshift sign held high and scanned the crowd. A slight man of indigenous origin was heading towards him, a broad grin on his face. "Joe Mills?" the man asked. "I'm Pete Ivalu. Nice to meet you."

Joe popped the trunk for Pete's bag. They got into the car and left the crowded zone.

"I have a copy of your photo; it's in your file. I knew what you looked like," said Pete. "The sign was a nice touch, though. Made me seem important."

"Oh," said Joe sheepishly. "I know nothing about you. Harjit just said to pick you up, that you'd have the details."

"I do. I've got your file and the case file. There's a file on me for you to read, but I can fill you in on the details as we drive."

"Where are we headed? Harjit mentioned a town called Little Brook."

"We're going to another town first — a place called Orono. We are to meet Molly Saunders at a bakeshop in the village. She has information on Little Brook, a tiny village a few kilometres northeast of there."

"What details?"

"The file is vague on specifics. Harjit believes the village harbours a threat but doesn't say what."

"Sounds like Harjit. He loves being vague. Wants us to discover things on our own, without prior prejudice."

"You're more familiar than I am with how he works. This is my first assignment."

"It's my second. Apparently, there is a heck of a turnover rate. So, what was your first encounter?"

"Abandoned Inuit village at the top of the world. We tracked the people from the village to an ice flow that had trapped something big and nasty. They were trying to free the creature and didn't want us interfering with their task. We had to wipe the whole village out."

"What? That's horrific."

"It wasn't pretty. They came at us in a tunnel in the flow. Lucky for us, I had my rifle; I'm a Sergeant in the Canadian Rangers, the group of soldiers tasked with keeping up Canada's presence across the Arctic. In case the Russians get cute. Although the Americans worry us more these days as the ice is receding and opening up the Northwest Passage."

"What does that entail?"

"We spend our time on snowmobiles, going from place to place, keeping our claim to the territory. Although for fun, we pop over to Hans Island now and then. Hans Island is a disputed territory between Canada and Denmark. The Danes show up and leave a bottle of schnapps and a sign that says 'Welcome to Denmark.' We collect the schnapps and leave a bottle of Canadian Club and change the sign to 'Welcome to Canada.' Closest I'd come to combat until the ice tunnel."

"How did that go?"

"It was a slaughter. The tunnel prevented the villagers from surrounding us, and they couldn't match my firepower. One got by us and ambushed me later; my first taste of combat and I got stabbed with a whalebone spear. I'm just now recovering."

"You weren't alone, I assume."

"No, I was with two others. For the task, we should have brought more help. Adele was under strict orders to limit exposure to the three of us."

"Adele?"

"Yep. Dr. Adele Kramer. She told us about Cape Breton. I read in your file you were with her in Gallou Cove."

"I was. How is she? She's ok, I hope?"

"She had a rough time. The other guy we were with, he lost his mind. The thing in the ice hit us with a psychic attack. I was far from the monster when it happened; I sensed it, but Adele and Scott, that's the guy with us, took the brunt. He lost his mind and attacked her. Bit off the tips of two of her fingers and chunk out of her cheek. He forced her to kill him; that will leave more lasting damage to her than the physical damage will."

"Damn." Joe liked Adele. She was smart and driven and had trouble taking no for an answer. "Where is she now?"

"I'm not sure; I wasn't told. Harjit isn't forthcoming with information if he doesn't consider it necessary."

"He enjoys being vague. He thinks it adds an air of mystery to him, makes him more interesting."

"The military runs on a need-to-know basis. Makes the higher-ups feel important."

"Like having your name on a sign at the airport?" Joe smiled.

"Yeah, like that. Listen, can we stop at a McDonald's?"

"McDonald's?"

"We have few fast-food outlets in Iqaluit. A KFC, Pizza Hut and a Tim Hortons. I'd kill for a Sausage McMuffin with egg."

"I'm sure we can find one on our route to- where did you say we were going?"

"Orono. On the way to Peterborough."

"I have no idea where either of those places are. I'm not from here, remember?"

"Cape Breton by way of Fredericton. In the file. Good thing you have me then."

"Why?"

"Toronto is a second home to me. I attended the University of Toronto; lived here for seven years."

"What brings someone from the far reaches of the north to the big city?"

"Medieval history. I was into knights and dragons and wizards and stuff. So, I enrolled at U of T to study Medieval History. The problem with that is, dragons and wizards aren't real, so you don't study them. Instead, you study a serf's typical day. If I wanted monotony in life, I could have stayed home. And as interesting as learning of a monk who starts an affair with his young student and gets castrated by her uncle is, it wasn't what I'd expected."

"What we study at university often isn't as interesting as we hope it will be. Hey, did you know a Professor Robert Bilson?"

"Bilson? The name sounds familiar. Why?"

"He was a professor of Medieval History at the University of Toronto. He was older, so he should have been there when you were there. He specialized in the Church and Satanic Cults."

"Oh, that guy. Yeah, I took one of his classes, but he was too intense for me. Most academics have an unhealthy fixation with their specialty, but he took it to another level entirely."

"Harjit and I encountered him in Muskoka. I'm sure the file says I had to shoot a man; that's the guy."

"Professor Bilson?"

"Yeah. We think he summoned the creature that murdered the family. He also shot Harjit."

"Unbelievable."

"That's the biggest issue with this Other; it can be anywhere, even right before us. So why didn't you pursue your studies further? Not much need of a medieval scholar patrolling the far north."

"I wasn't a medieval scholar, just a dabbler. Living here was great; I worked at the Royal Ontario Museum as a docent and slung drinks in clubs around town, but I grew homesick. You can take the boy out of the tundra, but you can't take the tundra out of the boy. I still travel to the city at least once a year to meet up with old buddies and get drunk. As they are getting married and having kids, the numbers keep dwindling. Soon it will be two guys that will never get married and me."

"So, soldier, medieval historian and slinger of drinks; you're quite the renaissance man."

114

"That's me. As far as our mission today, Molly Saunders lived in Little Brook. The file alludes to the fact that she has information on strange occurrences in the village. Any guesses on what we might find there?"

"No idea. There are no details on what these occurrences might be?"

"There isn't much information in the file."

"So far I've encountered two things associated with The Other; a sea monster and a... I'll call it a demon for lack of a better word."

"Great. More monsters. I hope this isn't another one."

"I don't think it's always about monsters. Let's hope not. Sometimes it is about the people who reach out to them. The demon was in a cave with strange writing on the walls. Someone had to write it there."

"Let me guess, did you see the word Cthulhu there?"

"Yes. Was that in my file?"

"No, but we found the name Cthulhu on the walls in the village Adele and I investigated, in an underground shrine. It was part of a phrase, but the word stands out to me."

"The same for me. So this term, Cthulhu, links a cave in Muskoka and a village in the Arctic. My cave even had Egyptian hieroglyphics written on the walls. We couldn't figure how long ago they'd been written."

"Confirms Harjit's claim that it's a global phenomenon. Ours had no hieroglyphics though."

"I agree this is worldwide. The more I learn, the more I'm freaked out how these things connect. A malignant power is at work here, directing things across the globe and over millennia."

"And our job is to root it out and end it."

"Do you think we can? End this power, I mean?"

"Doubtful. But I will still do my part to try. On a related note, how are your nightmares?" asked Pete.

"You've got them too?"

"Yeah. I dream of the creature in the ice. I keep picturing it opening its eye and assaulting us, even though when the attack happened, I wasn't near it. As if I'm feeling guilty for not being with them."

"Mine are becoming less intense. Harjit said they would if we kept 'confronting' was the word he used. My mind has either become used to The Other, or something else is happening. The nightmares are images of things I don't recognize, more a prophetic dream of places I haven't seen yet."

"Such as?"

"I see myself entering a cave, different caves, but never the cave in Muskoka. Sometimes Adele is there, and sometimes not. The visions, if they are visions, are not consistent."

"Beats sitting around becoming catatonic, though."

"Does it? Some days I'm not sure. On those days, I want to sit back and let the bliss of ignorance subsume me."

"That assumes its bliss and not sheer terror that will take hold."

That brought the conversation to an awkward end.

Once they had left Toronto's city limits, Joe got off the highway so Pete could get his McDonald's. They were back on the road in a few minutes, with Pete enjoying his greasy treat.

"Harjit told me I needed a partner," said Joe.

"Mmm," mumbled Pete, his mouth full of Sausage and Egg McMuffin. "Your file said you didn't wait for backup. I hope I'm not babysitting a loose cannon. Loose cannons get their partners killed."

"No. I shouldn't have gone, but something was pulling at me. I found it hard to resist."

"This is not comforting me. Scott had trouble resisting. He went insane."

"I've learned my lesson. I didn't expect to meet an entity. After running into that demon, I won't be in any rush to run in half-cocked."

"Now you're disturbing me the other way. I need to know you've got my back. I don't want you stuck on the threshold, leaving me exposed. If we're a team, we need to depend on the other person."

Joe nodded. "It's the same in police work. I made a rookie mistake, going off by myself. I know better, but..."

"This is not normal stuff we're up against. I understand."

"What other secrets are in the file?"

"That you were a solid cop but lacked ambition."

"That's in the file?"

"Yes. Harjit included your RCMP files."

"And what does it say in your military file? What kind of soldier are you?"

"A solid soldier that lacks ambition," smiled Pete.

"We're a great pair."

"We'll see."

They drove the rest of the way in relative silence. Soon they were pulling off the highway into Orono. It was a quaint little village, a block long. An old town hall dominated the main street. The bakeshop where they were to meet Molly Saunders wasn't hard to find. Inside, the shop was bustling with activity. Molly was the only person sitting alone. In her mid-twenties, thirty pounds overweight, her hair dyed black, wearing thick make-up and a hoop ring in her nose, she stood out from the other residents in the shop. She sat at a table, obviously nervous, an untouched cup of coffee before her, glancing furtively towards the door.

"Grab us something. I'll introduce myself to her," said Joe. Pete nodded.

Joe walked over to her. "Molly Saunders? I'm Joe Mills. My partner, Pete Ivalu, will join us soon; he's grabbing us coffee."

She nodded at him and rubbed her hands nervously on the table in front of her. "Thanks. I don't want to linger. People, well, they talk. We're near Little Brook; someone might enter. We should have met further away. I didn't think when I suggested we come here, and now I'm wigging out."

"Why should it matter? Who cares if someone from Little Brook saw us?"

"You don't understand. That village is... weird. Something strange is happening in it. The people... they're not right."

"Ok, let's wait for my partner. He'll want to hear this too."

Pete took longer than expected to get to the table. He had two coffees and a plate of sausage rolls. "The shop's specialty," said Pete as he sat.

"Ok, Molly. You mentioned something was weird in the village. Care to elaborate on that?"

117

She shifted nervously. "It is a series of things. On their own, they seem like nothing. But after being there a few months, they start to add up and collectively they are not right."

"You're not from Little Brook originally?" asked Pete.

"No, I'm from near Kingston. A friend- she doesn't seem much like a friend now, convinced me to move to the village seven months ago. I had a rough upbringing, and my life was in turmoil. This was to be a new beginning for me. The village was nice at first; everyone was friendly, too friendly. I thought they were trying to make me feel welcome."

"I sense a 'but' coming," said Joe.

"There is. I noticed strange occurrences after three months. That's when I started to see... things. For one, I wasn't the only young woman that had recently moved to the village."

"Why is that strange?"

"Fifty people live in the village. Three young women move in from elsewhere, with no prior connection to the place and no means of support. We stood out."

"You didn't have a job?" asked Pete.

"No. I didn't need one. The villagers let me live with them; my friend... the woman who brought me to the village, Jessica, let me stay with her. They collectively took care of my needs."

"They made no demands of you?"

"No."

"Ok," said Joe, taking notes. "So, let me check if I have this right. Three new residents, young women, with no visible means of support or prior connect to the place, move into this village and they take care of your needs. Could their motivation be to save you from yourselves?"

"At first, that's what I thought. That they were a group of religious people, trying to save sinners and put them on the path of righteousness, or whatever. An old church is in town, but they don't use it as a church. They've converted the building into a community centre. They never held a mass, no one ever talked to me about God or made me read the bible. The things you'd associate with religious indoctrination."

"What happened next?"

"One of the other girls, named Stella, she disappeared. I never saw her again."

"She left town?"

"I don't think so. I didn't know her well. Even though the community welcomed us, they did a good job of keeping us away from one another. We were never alone with each other."

"That is weird," said Pete.

"Right? I didn't notice these things at first, but then they started fitting together. As for her leaving town, to run away as I've done now, I don't think she did that. Stella came to the village a few weeks before I did. She loved the place, and they loved her. I was getting leery, but she was not only oblivious to the things that were bugging me, but she embraced them. Not the person to run away."

"Maybe she relapsed into whatever was in her past?" said Joe.

"It's not the only weird thing in the village. It became more significant as things unfolded. Not something I dwelled on, but now... it's sinister."

"When did this happen?"

"Three months ago."

"What happened next?"

"Another young woman showed up in town. Followed the same pattern as I did. No means of support, but everyone took care of her. She was living with a family. I started to get agitated, stopped leaving the house."

"Did you ever get the sense you were a prisoner?" asked Pete.

"Eventually, yes. The village is distant from other villages. There is no reason for anyone driving by to stop. Isolated without being totally isolated. I realized one day that the house I was in didn't have a phone."

"So? Many people have given up their landlines for cell phones."

"Yeah, that's true. But I never saw Jessica with a cell phone. That's almost unheard of, someone my age to not have a cell phone."

"Did you?"

"I did when I first arrived. But I lost it."

"You lost it? How?"

"My phone disappeared one day."

119

"What did you do?"

"Nothing. During the first month, I was free from the bad things in my life. I didn't want to connect with anyone from my past and was glad to be off the grid. But I started to get bored with the isolation. I wanted access to a phone, to the Internet, but Jessica didn't have a computer. I started to realize I had no way to connect to anyone outside of the village. That's when I started to sense I was a prisoner."

"Did you ever leave town?"

"If I started to get stir crazy, they'd bring me here, to Orono, or Newcastle, south of here. Someone always chaperoned me. They never let me out of sight. The appearance of freedom, when there was none."

"What made you leave? What has brought us here today?"

"Two nights ago, I was having trouble sleeping. I heard Jessica getting up and exiting the house. It was two a.m. Strange time to be leaving the house. I got out of bed and looked out the window and saw her walking towards the church. I then noticed that most of the town was outside, heading for the church. In the middle of the night? It spooked me. I watched them enter. I noticed Stella was with them."

"Then what happened?"

"The village was quiet. No lights were on in the church. I had no idea what they could be doing in the dark. I sat staring at the church door, waiting to see what happened next. An hour passed, and they returned. Everyone started coming out of the church and heading back to their homes as if this were normal. Stella wasn't with them. She never came out of the church."

"What did you do?"

"I got back to bed and pretended to be asleep. Next day, I booked it out of the village. I don't know what happened to Stella, but I wasn't sticking around to let them do it to me. I took off cross-country through the woods."

"Ok," said Joe, looking at his notes. "You got out. How did you contact us?"

"When I was far enough away, I hitched a ride. Dude dropped me off here in Orono. I asked to use a phone, and I called the cops."

"What did they do?"

"Asked me similar questions to the ones you just asked. Was I a prisoner? Was I threatened in any way? They told me it didn't appear anyone committed a crime, so there wasn't anything they could do. I was pissed and frightened. No one believed me, and no one wanted to help me or find out what those crazy people were doing in the village. I was getting ready to hitch a ride out of here when a police cruiser appeared. The officer said he had orders to take me to a local motel, and that someone would be in touch with me. He dropped me off, and I checked into the room set aside for me. The phone rang, and a guy named Harjit asked me questions and said he'd send people to question me. And then you showed up here."

"Why didn't we question you at the motel?"

"I'm freaked out by this. The motel was isolated. I couldn't sleep last night, kept waiting for someone to kick in the door and drag me away. I felt safer in public. The bakeshop seemed safe. Harjit, whoever he is, said that someone would pick me up and take me wherever I want to go. I want far away from here. He said he'd make it happen, but I had to talk to you first. Not sure I can trust him or you, but I can't get away on my own. I have no money, no means and nowhere to go. So here we are. Are we done? Can I leave?"

Pete and Joe looked at each other. "I don't think you can add more for us. Do you, Pete?" Pete shook his head. "We believe you. Whatever is going on in the village is not normal. We'll go check things out, see what's happening. If we confirm anything untoward, you have our word we'll put a stop to it."

Molly sighed, relief flooding her face. The tension in her body released. The three of them got up from their table and left the shop.

Outside on the street, a man in a black suit was stepping out of a black Lincoln. "Harjit sent me. I'm here to escort Molly Saunders. Ms. Saunders, if you are ready?"

Molly nodded. "Let's go." Turning back to face Pete and Joe, she said: "Thank you. I needed to unburden myself of this. I think I escaped something terrible. For someone to believe me, that means a lot. I hope you find out what's going on and help the new girl get out before she disappears like the rest." She got into the car.

Pete and Joe watched the car drive away. "What do you make of her story?" asked Pete.

"I'm not sure. The circumstances in the village are not normal, but why involve us?"

"Appears to be a David Koresh-Branch Davidian thing. We've got our very own Waco, Texas."

"Except for the lack of religious ceremonies. Cults need a vibrant leader to keep them focused. Molly didn't mention a leader in the village. This village has the hallmarks of a cult, but is missing key components."

"We need to go see for ourselves."

"Yes, but how? We can't stroll into town and start demanding answers to difficult questions. We have no legal authority here. I'm on leave, so I can't use my authority as a cop."

"And we'll stand out in a small, insular community. No reason for us to be there. We need a story."

"Any ideas?"

"We could be scouting locations for a movie?"

"What? That's obscure."

"Obscure enough. We're seeking the perfect small town to shoot in, and Little Brook's name was mentioned. Might enable us to walk around, ask questions and take pictures of the place."

"You know what a location scout does?"

"No, but I'm counting on them not knowing either. You got a better idea?"

"Off the top of my head, no. How far is Little Brook from here?"

"Fifteen minutes, according to Harjit's notes."

"I wonder how he found Molly? What did she tell him to get us to investigate?"

"I don't want to hazard a guess how he operates. It doesn't matter. He told us to investigate the village, so we investigate. On the surface, it's something mundane. Perhaps something illegal, but mundane. Harjit has a nose for this stuff. If he thinks it's connected to The Other, it probably is."

Joe nodded. "I suspect the same thing. Let's go find what we can."

#

Nestled in a valley just past a ski hill, Little Brook was a simple rural village. Two arterial roads passed by, creating a t-intersection at the northeast corner. It was close enough to larger centres that no one would come to it for services, but far enough removed to be isolated. The houses clustered around the old white wooden church, whose steeple rose above the other buildings, marking the location.

They pulled into the village. Apart from the church, the only other public building was an old gas station. No gas pumps remained, and the bays now held an antique shop, with the rest of the station housing a small convenience store. They parked their car in front of one of the bay doors.

Their immediate impression was of a boring place to live. Nothing to show anything might be amiss.

"Hello. Can I help you?" came a friendly voice. An older woman was getting up off her knees from where she had been tending her lush flower garden. A wide smile beamed on her face. "Roy only opens the antique shop on appointment during the week. If he knew you were coming, he'd have opened up for you. I can see if he's around?"

"No, thank you, ma'am. We're not here for the antique shop. My name is Joe, and he's Pete."

"We're location scouts."

"Location scouts? For what," she asked.

"For a movie. I can't say which. The producers keep these things secret, you understand," said Pete.

"A movie? In our little village? How exciting. I'm Laura," she said, pulling off her glove and extending a hand. "Nice to meet the two of you. Not sure what you're looking for, for your movie. But head over to the church. Dale would be the best to help you out; he runs our little coffee shop. I'll take you over and introduce you."

"That's very kind of you."

"The church brought us here. We heard Little Brook had the style of church we needed for a few of the shots," said Pete. "That and a few shots of period homes; exteriors only. We'd only be in town for a few days."

123

"Any big stars?"

"A few are attached to the picture. We'd shoot a pivotal scene here, so the stars will be on set. Can't tell you who."

"I understand. Wow, I hope we're everything you want. Everyone will be so excited." Laura led them up to the stairs of the church and held open the door for them. "Dale," she called. "These movie scouts want to film a movie here in town!"

Laura led them into the community centre. The interior no longer resembled a church. The pews were long removed, with a few remaining along the side walls to offer seating. Where the altar had been a counter now stood, complete with a large silver espresso machine. A few small tables and chairs clustered near the bar. In the central open area, a woman was leading a group of older men and women in a yoga class, and off to one side, two women sat at easels, painting a still-life of a bouquet.

"A movie? Here in Little Brook? Exciting stuff!" said the man behind the coffee counter. He had a long ponytail pulled back from his balding pate, shot with grey. He was wearing big, square glasses and had a small moustache perched over his lip. "I'm Dale. Welcome to the Starry Wisdom Cafe. Can I get you fellas anything? On the house."

"Thanks, I'd like a coffee," said Pete.

"Thank you, but nothing for me."

"Espresso or Americano? I'm sorry, but I don't have drip coffee."

"Americano, thanks."

"Coming right up. So, you fellas were looking for a place to film your movie? Is it a big-budget one?"

"Yep, but I can't tell you its name or any stars attached. Not until we pick the location."

"Makes sense to me," said Dale, working on making the coffee. "What brings you to Little Brook? Just driving by?"

"We heard about this lovely little church you had. They want a church interior and the exterior. When did it stop being one?"

"Oh, we converted this church into a community centre ten years ago. The building sat empty for years after the congregation shrank. Most people around here don't follow organized religion anymore. We didn't want to see it deteriorate,

124

so as a community, we pooled our resources and bought the place. The best thing we ever did." He passed the disposable cup of coffee to Pete.

"Thanks. We might still use the outside of the church for exterior shots. We can always recreate the interior on a set. Do you mind if we walk around the village? Might be other locations we can use. Are you okay if we take pictures?"

"By all means. Go ahead. We've got nothing to hide. Little Brook's a pleasant spot; everyone will welcome you. If you see a house that might suit your needs, knock on the door. People will invite you in to look. If you need anything, come see me."

"Much obliged," said Pete, lifting his coffee. "And thanks. We'll be back." Pete and Joe left the church.

"You slipped into that lie easily," said Joe. "Almost like you were enjoying deceiving them."

"I did improv when I was living in Toronto. I enjoy playing a role. What do you think of the place?"

"On the surface, it's a quaint little community. Too quaint. It seems too perfect. Something is in that church, though."

"What do you mean?" asked Pete, taking a sip of his coffee.

"You didn't sense it? I could. The Other was present in the church."

"I sensed nothing."

"I've become sensitive to The Other. In Muskoka, I could make out patterns in the crime scene, sensed the path I had to take. I can sense it now. Faint, as if it's not in the church itself, but somehow connected." Joe pointed to the east of the doors. "Something is pulling me this way. Let's check it out."

They ambled east. "The Other is getting stronger," said Joe. "Something is here." He stopped. "Beneath us, right where we are standing now."

"So, what are we going to do?"

"We need to check the church when it's empty."

"Molly said she saw villagers going into it at two a.m. You think it's ever empty?"

"I don't know. Probably not. But it bears further investigation."

"You want to come back tonight? See if we can't force our way inside?"

"Yeah. Whatever is at the heart of this, we'll find it in that building. Let's contact Harjit, bring him up to speed, and tell him we want to come back, to check out the church and see what he says."

"Fine," said Pete. "But we need to keep up appearances. Let's wander around, let people see us taking pictures and report back to Dale. People will talk, and we want our story to sound legit."

Joe and Pete wandered around the village, Pete taking photos on his phone, and Joe appearing to be taking notes in his notebook. They checked back in at the church with Dale.

"So, what do you think? See anything you like?" asked Dale.

"This place is awesome. Very picturesque. The village would look great on film," said Pete. "The church's exterior is exactly what we wanted. But the interior of the church; it would be easy to replace pews, but it would be too much work to dismantle your shop."

"There is a limit to our hospitality," said Dale smiling. "I'm not letting you tear down my shop!"

"Of course not; we'd never ask that of you. Is the basement still in the original condition? Can we look at it?"

"Nothing to see. It's small, and we use it as storage. Card tables, things for the shop, stuff like that. The rest is crawlspace and not accessible. Won't be any use to you."

"I figured. Still, I had to ask because the producers will ask me. I'm as thorough as possible. Do you mind if I take pictures of the interior to show them why it's not usable for a church scene?"

"Sure, go ahead."

"Thanks," said Pete, pulling out his phone and taking photos of the interior. "I like this town. You have a great thing here. I'm worried though that this interior might be a deal-breaker. They could always build a set, but if we find another church that is still a church, they'll go with it."

"That's too bad. It would be exciting to have a movie shot here. They'd need extras, I don't doubt. Wherever you film, the locals have a chance to be in it, am I right?"

"Usually, that is the case, yes."

"It would have been fun. I hope you find no village better than Little Brook."

"There are a few more locations for us to visit. We should go; we might have enough time left to check out one more location today. Do you have a card with a number we can contact you at to call you once we know more?"

"Sure do!" said Dale, picking one up from the holder near the cash and handing it to Pete. "Your visit will be the talk of the village for the next few days."

"Thanks, I promise I'll let you know as soon as we decide. You guys have been most hospitable; thanks for everything. That Americano was great; one of the best I've had."

"Thanks," beamed Dale. "I roast the beans myself. I take pride in my product."

"And it shows. Good luck and talk to you soon."

They returned to their car and got underway. "You loved that, didn't you?" said Joe "You were in your element."

"All the world's a stage," said Pete. "This is fucked up shit we're involved with. We should have fun where we can."

"Let's call Harjit." Joe pulled out his cell phone and hit the number for Harjit. The phone connected to the car's Bluetooth and the ringing came over the car speakers. On the third ring, it picked up.

"Wondered when you'd call. Give me the rundown."

They gave Harjit the details of what they'd seen. "I sensed The Other in the church," said Joe.

"I figured. You must check it out."

"We were thinking of going back tonight."

"The sooner, the better. You're good to go. Send me any photos you took in case my team sees anything you missed."

"How's Molly?" asked Pete, pulling out his phone to text the photos.

"She's fine. I've transferred her to a facility for a medical and psychological exam. I want to make sure her time in Little Brook didn't leave a lasting mark on her. If she's clean, she can go wherever she wants."

"If nothing else, we've helped her."

"I expect more than that. Discover the truth of what's in the village. Tonight." Harjit ended the call.

"So, the boss man has green-lighted the mission. We go into the church tonight. How do we prep for it?" asked Pete.

"We can't go back to scope it out without drawing attention to ourselves — no idea what we'll expect in there. We should go to a hardware store, pick up a bolt cutter, at least. I hate for a simple combination lock to impede us."

"Good idea. Anything else you can think of?"

"Yeah, I'd love a shotgun. We might run into opposition, and they might outnumber us."

"Well, we can't get shotguns on short notice. You have your sidearm?"

"Yeah. Do you have one?"

"I do."

"It will have to do then. Hopefully, we won't need to use our weapons."

They drove to Newcastle to the hardware store and had dinner at a local pub. After midnight, they drove back to Little Brook. Not wanting to draw attention to themselves, they parked their car on a rural side road and travelled cross-country through a farmer's pasture to get to the village.

They slinked into the village under cover of darkness. Everything was quiet. Joe checked his watch; it was 2:37 am.

"How are we getting in?" asked Pete. "I didn't notice a back door."

"Nor I. I noted that there were no windows in the foundation. The front door may be our only entry point."

"Leaves us exposed. What if someone is keeping their eye on the front door?"

"Based on Molly's statement and my sense of the church, the key to whatever is going on is in there. Harjit told us to do it tonight. We have to risk it. I don't think putting it off will help us, nor does coming back during the day. We've learned all we are going to learn. This situation stinks, I know. But what choice do we have?"

"You're right. About the timing and the shotguns. We should have shotguns."

They listened to the night air; silence hung over the village. The single pale bulb hung over the door of the church, casting its yellow light on the entry. The church interior was dark. They made their way to the church stealthily and reassessed. They noted no movement or sound near them.

"Can you pick a lock?" asked Pete.

Joe nodded. "I glanced at it today. It's a simple lock. It should be easy to bypass. I'll work the lock while you give the bulb a turn or two. I don't want us on display while I try to get past this door."

"Got it. Go on three?" Joe nodded again. Pete counted under his breath. "One, two, three."

They sprinted to the door. Pete leaped on the metal pipe railing and leaned towards the light. He pulled his hand into his jacket and used the material to protect it from the hot bulb. The light above the door winked out.

"Shine your flashlight on the lock, but use your body to block it while I work. I need to see what I'm doing."

"Try the door first. Molly said the villagers entered the church at night. Maybe they keep it unlocked?"

"That would be convenient." Joe pulled on the handle; the door opened. "Now, does this mean that people are coming later, or that someone is already here?" he asked as he slipped inside the doorway.

"Might not mean either. Small towns. Not everyone locks their doors."

They waited until their eyes became accustomed to the dark. The moonlight filtered in through the windows, allowing them to navigate through the church. They entered the sacristy, assuming they'd find the stairs to the basement there. Locating the stairs, they began to descend, closing the door behind them.

They were in complete darkness and had to use their flashlights. Twin beams chased back the dark, illuminating their path.

As Dale had said earlier, they used the small basement for storage. There was little to see. The room was half the size of the church above them.

"You sense anything?" asked Pete. "This can't be it."

"It feels the same as the rest of the church," said Joe. "Let's look along the eastern edge of the room; that is where I got the sense underground earlier today."

They walked along the edge, shining their lights at the wall. They saw nothing.

"This makes no sense," said Joe. "I can feel it. There is something here. Where is it?"

"Turn off your flashlight," said Pete as he turned off his own. Joe did as instructed. There in the instant darkness came the faint glimmer of light along a seam in the wall that was not visible prior.

"A hidden door," said Joe. He pushed against the wall, and it pressed inward, allowing him to slide it back. They could now hear voices.

"They're here," said Pete.

"It appears so."

"This is hitting too close to home for me," said Pete. "Villagers leaving their homes to go underground, chanting; I'm experiencing déjà vu." He blanched.

"We can't go back. I can't go back. I need to follow through with this. Earlier, you said that you needed to know you could depend on your partner, know that they were behind you, not afraid to cross the threshold. Now I'm the one that needs assurances. Don't wig out on me."

"Lead on; I won't desert you."

The two of them crept along the brick-lined tunnel, and the chanting sounds grew louder, the light ahead brighter. They pulled out their pistols. Pausing at a doorway, they took in the scene below them.

The tunnel opened up into a natural cavern, forty feet across. The villagers were here, on their knees, chanting and bowing. They wore formless masks covering their faces. A man dressed in the garb of an Egyptian Pharaoh, with a gold headpiece framing his face and a purple vestment draped over his naked chest, was leading the chant. A black mask obscured his face, a horrific visage carved upon its surface. At the back, resting on three lush divans in an honoured berth, were three young women, two of them in advanced stages of pregnancy.

The language of the chant was unrecognizable. No one had noticed their approach.

"What the hell is this? Who's the Pharaoh?" hissed Pete.

"A ritual? The cave I found in Muskoka had Egyptian hieroglyphics in it, remember? I guess this helps explain why that is." Joe's eyes widened. "Pete! This cavern! It's a cave from my dreams! I've seen this before!"

"What? Was the ritual occurring in your dreams?"

"No, it was empty, except for a black misty manlike shape. It was always indistinct. This is the cave in my dreams."

"Well, what do we do? We've found them. Do we bug out and call Harjit? Let him send in someone to round up everyone?"

"Sounds like a plan. Too many cult members for us to engage by ourselves. They don't appear armed, but I don't want to risk it."

Pete nodded, and they started to crawl back towards the tunnel to the church. At this moment, the woman on the divans who did not appear to be pregnant cast her lazy gaze towards them. She noticed them retreating from the cavern.

"Brother Dale! Intruders!"

The chanting stopped, and all eyes turned towards them. The man in the Pharaoh garb spun on them, chanting something. Dark purple energy enveloped his hands, and deadly rays shot from them towards Pete and Joe.

"Down!" said Joe, pushing Pete aside as he flattened himself on the floor. The purple ray passed between them, narrowly missing both. Pete rolled to his knees, his pistol levelling as he crouched. Joe aimed his gun. Both firearms barked twice, and four red wounds appeared on the Pharaoh's chest. He staggered and pitched forwards.

"Protect the vessels!" shouted one villager, and they surged forward en masse.

Pete assessed the scene and fired off a single round. It impacted on the back wall near the pregnant women. "Joe, quick! Aim your gun at the pregnant women! They are the vessels!"

"What?"

"Do it! Now!" Pete rose to his feet and yelled at the villagers: "Take another step, and we'll kill the vessels!" Joe catching on, stood beside Pete, his gun now pointing at the women behind the villagers, who stopped in their tracks.

"Stop!" yelled a woman in the crowd. They recognized the voice as Laura, the woman who had greeted them. "As much as

I think they are bluffing, the risk is too great. We cannot allow the intruders to harm the vessels. They carry his seed!" She turned towards Joe and Pete, ripping her mask from her face. "You. I should have known not to trust you. But Dale urged us to embrace any who came through the village, to give no one a reason to suspect. You will not win. The Haunter of the Dark favours us! He honours us as we honour him. He entrusts us with his future progeny. We will forfeit our lives to protect them!"

"Pete!" said Joe beside him. "What do we do here, buddy?"

"You've shot two rounds; I've shot three. We don't have enough to shoot everyone here; they'd be on us before we can reload. The pregnant ladies are our only play here. If it comes to that, shoot them!"

"This is madness, Pete! I will not murder pregnant women!"

"It won't come to that if everyone keeps their cool. I'll do it if they make me. What happens next depends on what they do."

The villagers tensed, as if ready to spring forward. The woman in the most advanced stage of pregnancy rose from her divan. "Do as they say. These intruders will not harm us - the Black Pharaoh will not allow it. This is happening as he foretold! These men are part of his plan; the God of a Thousand Forms wishes us to go with them. It is time they brought us forth from our shrine. Do as I say, for He Who We Follow speaks through me. His child grows in my womb, and I hear his whispers. Stand down."

Pete and Joe shuffled in their place. Tension hung over the cavern.

"Do as the sacred vessel tells us to," said Laura. "Submit to the intruders." The villager's stances softened, and they removed their masks. The tension in the cave abated.

"Everyone, backs to me, get on the floor! I want you to lie on your stomachs and place your hands on the backs of your head! Do it now!"

The villagers complied; the fight had gone out of them, and they followed Joe's orders.

"Keep your gun on them. I'm calling Harjit." Joe looked at his phone. "Damn it, I can't get a signal here."

"Where are you going, Joe?" Pete said as Joe headed towards the tunnel.

"We need to contact Harjit. I told you, there is no signal. I'm going upstairs to see if I can make a connection to a network."

"You're going to leave me here alone with them?"

"What else can I do? You want us to stand here indefinitely? If any of them moves, shoot one of the vessels. You were willing to minutes ago."

"Hurry back."

Joe nodded. He glanced back before he entered the tunnel. The triumphant smile of the pregnant woman who spoke was unnerving.

He held his phone up as he moved back into the basement. He was halfway up the stairs to the sacristy when he got a bar on his phone. His thumb stabbed the dial symbol, and Joe waited for Harjit to answer his call.

"Joe?" came Harjit's voice. "What's the situation?"

"We encountered a cult. They were in the basement conducting a ritual. We shot the leader, and the rest have surrendered to us. There are three women here they keep referring to as the vessels. Two of them are pregnant; I assume the other one is too."

"Pregnant women? Did you get details on the cult? What they follow?"

"They mentioned the Black Pharaoh and the Haunter of the Dark."

"Did they?" Harjit paused. "Good job. You and Pete secure the cult. Let nothing happen to the pregnant women. A team will arrive in three hours to lock down the village. Can you last three hours?"

"What choice do we have? They are docile now, listening to what we tell them to do. One of the pregnant women told them to listen to us, and they've complied."

"Ok, just keep your heads, and everything will be fine. Help is on the way." The line went dead.

\#

A week after their visit to Little Brook, Pete and Joe were sitting in their car, listening to Harjit speak to them over the car speakers. Joe had rejoined Pete in the cavern, and they waited until Harjit's team found them under the church. The villagers had lain on their stomachs docilely while the three women had lounged on their divans. The triumphant look of the pregnant woman shook Joe. She'd kept it even as the government team showed up to secure the village.

"Gentlemen, good job. You unearthed a dangerous cult. They'd have unleashed devastation on the world. We recovered tomes and other sources of knowledge that will shed light on The Other."

"What will happen to the villagers?" asked Pete.

"They are being held at a remote facility while we debrief them to find out what they know. In most instances we have encountered, the personal charisma of a high priest or priestess holds the cult together. Remove the leader from the equation, as you have, and they return to normal. Most will regret their involvement in the cult if they even remember it. Those we can rehabilitate may return to society. The others we will keep safe and take care of as long as necessary. We have facilities that are housing uncovered cult members and have a long history of rehabbing and releasing recovered cultists into society again."

"Was it necessary to tell the press an underground methane gas pocket killed everyone in the village?" asked Joe.

"Unfortunately, yes. How else do we have an entire town disappear? Charge them with a crime? No, it's better to create a believable disaster and say that's what happened. Inform the public a homeowner was drilling a new well and cracked into the methane deposit. Unbeknownst to the village, throughout the night, the methane seeped out and asphyxiated everyone. The explanation will scare the public but satisfy them at the same time."

"The concentration of methane to cause an entire village to asphyxiate would have to be enormous."

"True, and we're lucky that nothing caused it to explode, which would have been an even bigger disaster. The unintended negative consequence of the story is now petroleum companies will want to come and search the area for more natural gas deposits."

"Geologists and others will doubt the veracity of the story. They will try to disprove it," said Pete.

"Yes, and we have enough of our own experts that depend on government grants who will counter with their research that says it's unlikely but plausible. The story will fade over time. There might be the odd person who keeps it up, but they'll have as much credibility as the people pushing the conspiracy jet fuel isn't hot enough to melt steel beams. We'll label them as conspiracy theorists and kooks and move on to the next story."

"What about the families of the villagers? They think their loved ones died. Won't the rehabilitated ones, once you release them, go back to their families and prove your story wrong?"

"No, most are estranged from their families or didn't have any family. This makes them attractive and susceptible to the cult. If they have strong family networks, they are tougher to indoctrinate, or they invite their families to join them. No one will miss the villagers from Little Brook, at least not long term."

"This still makes little sense. Estranged or not, you'd think part of their recovery would include wanting to make amends with their family and friends," said Pete.

"I appreciate what you are saying, but have you executed an undertaking like this before? Because I have. Trust me; this is the best approach. Drop it."

"Sounds like you have it tied up," said Joe. "Just like Gallou Cove."

"We've done this for a long time, and in more circumstances than you'd think. Sometimes actual disasters are staged to cover up the activities: a train derailment, a plane crash or release of toxins from a chemical plant. The media reports the disaster, the public feels sympathy or outrage, and in time it settles into the back of society's consciousness as a vaguely remembered event. Have you seen much in the news about Gallou Cove? It was a global news event for a week, and now everyone has moved on to other things. This incident will be the same."

"Still wrong to me," said Pete.

"Do you think the public could handle the news of cosmic horrors waiting to plunge the world into a miasma of chaos and insanity?"

"No."

"Nor do I, so this is our solution. I don't like it either, but I understand the need for it. To preserve stability and promote the greater good. But enough about Little Brook. I will send the two of you to Arkham, in Massachusetts to visit a colleague at Miskatonic University. I want you to take the knife you found in the cave, and a few of the tomes we recovered. He's the expert on The Other, and you can learn much from him. I will have Adele Kramer join you. He'll want to hear your experiences first hand."

"Whatever you say, boss," said Pete.

"Gentlemen, until you hear from me, enjoy yourselves. Do something fun. You've earned a rest." Harjit hung up the phone and took a sip from his cooling coffee. There was a knock at his door. "Come in."

The door opened, and a man entered. "Sir, we've confirmed the connection to Nyarlathotep."

"The pictures from the church, the Starry Wisdom, tied this to Nyarlathotep."

"I thought they eradicated the Church of Starry Wisdom?"

"In the US, yes, but the cults linger in Canada. What's the status of the Little Brook villagers?" Harjit asked.

"Typical responses. Ranting and raving about the Black Pharaoh. Nyarlathotep is nearing completion of his great work, only a matter of time, the Unbelievers will perish, blah, blah, blah. We couldn't learn anything new from them, nothing more than we've heard many times before."

"I figured as much. Still, we had a significant breakthrough in Little Brook. We recovered lost knowledge. Have you enacted the final solution?"

"We have terminated the villagers as per protocol."

"Good. Thank you. That is all."

The man paused at the door. "Sir, do you think it wise what you are doing?"

"We've never had an opportunity like this. This could tip the scales in our favour. Nyarlathotep is preparing the way for something. We need to know what that is."

"By keeping them, aren't we aiding Nyarlathotep?"

"Who knows? He's an enigma, and he's come by the name the Crawling Chaos honestly. I'm not sure he has a plan, but he sows discord wherever he can. I may be giving him too much credit. I'm assuming there is a strategy he's following, even if we figure it out, he might dodge in a different direction."

"All the more reason to dispose of the women and their potential offspring now. We could be adding to the chaos."

"If we destroy them, he'll create more progeny. Do you think Little Brook is the only place on the planet he's made contact with a cult and fathered children? He might have hundreds, thousands of offspring out there. Knowledge is power. I want to know everything we can. We learn nothing if we destroy them. We need to see this through to its conclusion."

The man nodded. "I can't disagree with your logic. It is worrisome though that we are contributing to his endgame. But as you say, destroying them now doesn't prevent the creation of more."

"Tell those whispering and questioning this course of action I've harboured the same doubts. This decision was a tough one, but ultimately the right one. I won't be changing my mind."

"Yes, sir." The man exited the office.

Harjit looked at his now cold cup of coffee and walked over to the coffeemaker to refresh it. He took his warmed cup and went to the window in his office.

His office was underground. The window didn't look out onto a pleasant vista, but to a medical facility behind the thick glass. Three women, in various stages of pregnancy, were tethered to beds, a myriad of tubes and monitoring devices attached to them. They kept the women sedated, for their safety and the safety of the people working near them. Harjit sipped his coffee as he leaned against the window, looking at each woman. When his eyes alighted on the most pregnant of the women, she turned her head towards him. With her level of sedation, she should be unconscious. Her eyes fluttered open briefly, locking with Harjit's, her lips curling into a smile before she drifted off into a drug-induced sleep.

Harjit pressed a button, and the windows turned opaque, blocking his view. The window was made of one-way glass; how could the woman know he was standing there? Disturbed by this, Harjit sat at his computer and opened his file on Nyarlathotep. While the name had its roots in antiquity, it had been showing up more and more in the past decade. Reports from across the globe showed that the followers of Nyarlathotep were becoming increasingly active. The entity had a plan and was moving on it. But what was it?

Pondering the file, Harjit sighed and rubbed his eyes. The strain of the position got to him and this was one of those times. He wasn't sure if he was doing the right thing regarding the women. Ultrasounds confirmed the fetuses of the first two were developing as expected; a test confirmed the third woman's pregnancy. The three women were otherwise healthy, with nothing to show there was anything different about their pregnancies. A thought made Harjit chuckle. What if the cult leader, Dale, had convinced the women that Nyarlathotep worked through him, and he had been the one to impregnate them? He made a note to have a non-invasive fetal DNA test completed on the two fetuses and an additional one when the third woman's pregnancy had progressed far enough. The results would confirm if the fetuses shared the same father; they could compare it to the DNA of Dale and the other villagers to see if it matched.

The most likely scenario was the village housed a secret sex cult with no tie to Nyarlathotep, not directly anyway. If the DNA matched with Dale or any of the other villagers, Harjit would order the final solution enacted on the women. They were too dangerous to keep alive and potentially expose the lie around Little Brook. It pained him that the blood of innocents would be on his hands; perhaps he'd keep the women alive to term regardless of the DNA findings. They could adopt out the infants and execute the mothers after they delivered. Yes, this is what they would do. It would assuage his guilt.

It's not possible to confront the monsters around us without becoming a monster ourselves, he thought. *At least this is what I keep telling myself. It's easier if I can justify my actions.*

Convinced what he was doing was for the good of humanity, Harjit turned back to his computer and opened up an email. Yet another potential encounter with the Other, this time in Edmonton. Realizing he'd let his coffee grow cold again, he rose and poured it out while brewing a fresh pot. Turning, he glanced at the darkened glass of the windows again. He thought about turning off the electric privacy glass so he could watch the women, but pushed the idea from his mind. Instead, he returned to his chair and got back to work. The Other never stopped, so neither could he.

Troy Young

It Lurks In The Basement

Adele was back in Halifax. The black eyes from her broken nose were fading. She was getting used to the missing tips of her left pinky and ring fingers. The scar on her cheek was more devastating. She had lost a significant chunk of flesh when Scott had bitten her face. Harjit assured her that the government would cover the costs associated with reconstructive surgery, which she had so far not pursued. For now, when in public, she hid the damage under a large bandage.

It wasn't her physical scars from the incident that troubled her the most, but the mental ones. Images came to her in her nightmares. The creature in the ice, its baleful eye opening to leer at her malevolently, was the strongest of them. Images of sunken cities populated by creatures resembling it, the architecture of the cities alien to her. Black, bubbling shapes, enslaved by the creatures, filled with teeth, gnashing and silently screaming, tortured and full of hate. And lingering above lay a great shadow, with wings and a bulbous head set on thick shoulders waiting to arise. She could not shake the abject fear incited by these images.

Harjit told her to rest, to recharge and to be ready for the next time he called her. She knew she had no choice. With what she had learned, it was impossible to return to her old life. So, she waited for his call.

The advantage of not having tasks to handle at her sham job meant that she didn't need to go to her office. No one would notice she wasn't there as her office was in an unused part of the building, ostensibly under renovation. Harjit had confirmed there was no expectation for her to set foot in her office, so she was free to use this time for herself. She wished she had something mundane to occupy her mind and time but made the best of it.

Adele had been a runner at university. Not competitive, but still active. As the years passed, she found less and less time to pursue it until her runs were so infrequent as to be non-existent. She remedied this. Finding her old running shoes, she realized that the foam cushioning had hardened over the years. Heading to the mall, she bought herself new running shoes and an outfit to match. The normalcy of the outing had made her smile until her mind drifted back to darker thoughts.

The running was doing the trick. It had always been liberating, kept her mind devoid of distractions and helped her focus when she was feeling overwhelmed. After a long run, she felt energized, and the fears pushed away. She even started to do yoga in her apartment, and her tea consumption ballooned.

This period of self-healing was doing what Harjit intended. It was, however, short-lived.

It had been two weeks since she returned to Halifax. Getting up early one morning, she had a coffee and a slice of toast and warmed up with twenty minutes of stretching. When she was ready, she grabbed her phone, picked a new playlist from her streaming service, put in her earbuds and headed out for her run.

She had lived in the same apartment since her graduate school days at Dalhousie, so she knew the neighbourhood. She had wandered these streets for years. Today, she ran a different route. Her run took her on a path she had walked hundreds of times before, but not since she returned from the Arctic.

Something was amiss. She sensed something up ahead, coming from a house, an unassuming old building made of grey brick with an orange door. She'd remembered walking by this house before, but today something was different. Slowing, she looked at the home as she passed by — nothing extraordinary on the surface. But something emanated from within its walls.

She felt a sense of foreboding as she passed. Every fibre in her being urged her to run, but she didn't. But she didn't stop until she reached the end of the block. Once she did, she stood on the corner, gasping from breath, both from her run and from a deep and primordial fear.

Adele didn't know what to do. There was something wrong with the house. Something was there. She got the same impression she had in the forgotten village in the far north, in the shrine filled with human bones, with pictograms and words written on the walls. Reading the phrases had made her lightheaded; she'd had the same feeling when she had viewed the insides of the creature at Gallou Cove. Now she had the same unnerving sensation on this street. The sense was stronger than she had encountered in either locale but less than the full force of the creature trapped in the ice. In the village and Gallou Cove, there was an obvious source of the discomfort. There was no obvious source this time.

The discomforting impressions passed as she resumed her run and left the house behind her. An uneasiness that The Other was in her neighbourhood replaced them. She cut her run short and headed home.

Her mind was a jumbled mess of thoughts and emotions as she opened the door to her apartment. Throwing her keys in their usual bowl, she went to the kitchen and opened a bottle of wine. She gulped half of her first glass and topped it back up, pacing around her apartment. Her heart was racing, and she was having trouble keeping calm. She needed guidance.

Pulling out her cell phone, she dialled Harjit's number. "Come on, pick up," she said to herself impatiently. It rang five times before Harjit's voice cut in.

"Hello? Sorry, I'm on the other line, something urgent. Can I call you back?"

"There is something urgent on my end, Harjit. I need to talk to you."

143

"Ok, you've just moved to the top of the list. Right after I finish my call." He hung up on her.

Adele couldn't believe he had done that. She sat at her kitchen table and refreshed her glass a second time. Starting a yoga routine, she used deep breathing techniques to cause her heart and breathing to calm. She was focusing on centring herself when her phone rang.

"Sorry about that. I was on a call from a police detachment in Ontario. Something concerning a woman in a village. I will call her as soon as we're done. What is so urgent?"

Adele told Harjit about the house, and the signals originating from within. "Do you have an address?" She gave it to him. "I'll have my people here do some detective work into the house: who built it, who owns it, etc. In the meantime, I want you to do some detective work yourself. Keep going by at different times of the day. See if you ever see anyone coming or going and document any changes to your sense of the house. I want to know if it's the house itself."

"Okay. It was a powerful emanation. Almost as strong as when whatever trapped in the ice attacked me. I hope whatever is the source isn't out in the world."

"I'll call you when I find the history of this house. If you discover any details, call me at once." The line went dead.

Adele picked up her wineglass and sipped thoughtfully. Harjit's request to keep her eye on the house was an easy one to fulfil; even though the house scared her, it would continue to draw her to it. The mark of The Other prevented her from staying away. The more she resisted, the more agitated she got. It was calling to her, even now.

Nothing she tried to do the rest of the morning eased her mind. It kept going back to the house. In the early afternoon, she took a walk along the same route she had taken that morning.

The house silently loomed, innocuous in the sunshine. She stood across the street, suppressing the terror that gripped at her, willing herself to observe her surroundings, to see if she could comprehend something, to discover any clues to what might hide inside its walls.

Suddenly it was obvious. The day was warm and sunny, and birds chirped in the trees. It was a riot of sound now that she was

144

focusing on them. Birds avoided the trees nearest to the house. She stood, observing them. When a bird took flight, it swerved, giving the house a wide berth. They were attuned to the strange emanations coming from the house and avoided it. She watched a man walking his dog. As they approached the house, the dog's tail curled between his legs, and he moved to the other side of his owner, closest to the street, putting as much space between him and the house as the leash allowed. The dog gave the house a nervous glance.

"So, animals can sense this presence," she murmured to herself. How often had a pet's nervous reaction to something unseen been The Other? Owners often dismiss an animal's response to something that isn't apparent. Adele began to wonder how The Other imprinted itself on individuals. Had people who believed they could sense ghosts been unknowingly exposed? Were psychics charlatans or sensitive to the impressions left on the world by this cosmic horror? What was real, and what was imagined? Did the human mind fill in the blanks and hide the incomprehensible reality of existence? If so, the more she and others tried to pierce this veil, to learn the truth, were they hastening their descent into madness?

Suddenly she looked around her. The sun was lower in the sky. Glancing at her watch, she noticed three hours had passed since she had approached the house. But that couldn't be the case. She had only been here a few minutes, hadn't she? Where had the time gone? Had she stood in a daze for three hours in the middle of the street?

Adele looked up at the house again. There was a dark form in one of the upper windows watching her, obscured by a gauzy curtain. She stared, and the figure withdrew. Fear gripped her, and she fled.

Slamming the door to her apartment behind her, Adele tried to get a grip on her racing heart and wild emotions. She needed to call Harjit.

"So soon?" he asked her as he picked up the call. "You've got something for me?"

"Yes." She related her observation of the dog and the birds and their ability to sense the presence.

"We've known this for decades. Investigators often take dogs with them to give advanced notice when they were getting near a target. You can only take an animal so close to a source before they become terrified and run away."

"So why didn't the dog in Gallou Cove run away from the creature on the beach?"

"The specimen was dead. Their impressions and power are diminished after they perish."

"The remains had a profound effect on me. I'd hate to see the effect if it was still alive."

"You're lucky you didn't meet the thing that smashed the pier. But you didn't call to rehash Gallou Cove. This revelation on the animal was not what I meant when I said to call me if you discovered something. I hope you have something more interesting to tell me?"

"This is news to me, ok? Maybe if you briefed us better..."

"I know. Circumstances prevented that from happening. If I can't do it right, I'd rather not do it and make things worse. I tell you what I think you can handle as the circumstances dictate. Letting too much slip without the proper context is not advisable."

"Why? Does exposure turn people into assholes?"

"I'm lax with my team, but there is a limit to insubordination. Now, do you have anything else to tell me?"

She related the loss of time and the figure in the window.

"You stood catatonic on the street?"

"I don't know. I suppose so. Is this common?"

"It's not uncommon. I'm more concerned with the current state of our society that people let you stand there incoherent for three hours without intervening. If society has become so cynical, why am I trying to save it?"

Adele wasn't sure if he was serious or not. "What do you want me to do?"

"Enter the house."

"How do you propose I do that?"

"That's up to you. I tell you what, not how. Your judgment and skills are what I rely on in the field. Just don't get caught. Once you involve local officials and police in your investigation, I have less influence. It's easy for me to send a cease and desist order along the chain of command for federal agencies, but get a local do-gooder on the case, they get their backs up when the feds try to muscle in on their jurisdiction. If I tell them to look the other way, it's likely to have the opposite effect. I may have to abandon you, release your medical records that show you've been getting delusional and making outrageous claims; it's why you're on administrative leave."

"I'm not delusional, and you know that. And I'm not on administrative leave. You said I didn't need to go to the office."

"Yes, but the Department of Fisheries and Oceans will point to your empty office and people will testify that they haven't seen you there."

"My office is located in an empty wing. No one is there to see me."

"You're assuming you only have one office."

"I've only ever been to one office. Are you saying that I have another one somewhere?" It dawned on her what that meant. "You son of a bitch. You've created a separate profile for me, haven't you?"

"The most important thing we do is uncover The Other's secrets. The second most important thing we do is keep our secrets hidden. You have the full support of the Canadian government as long as you keep to the shadows. Get yourself or The Other exposed to outside scrutiny, and you're a loose cannon suffering from a mental illness."

"What if I quit? Walk away?"

"You can't. The Other will keep calling to you, forcing you to search for more truth. And I won't let you either. You know too much. I'll have you picked up within minutes."

"So that day in the car, when we were heading to the airport, you kept encouraging me to leave. You said I could walk away. Were you lying to me?"

"You were getting on the plane to Alert, or I would have had you detained. People like you and Joe Mills or Pete Ivalu, you are too dangerous to have walking around in public without my involvement. You know too much, and loose lips to the wrong person could have detrimental effects on society."

"And those whom you consider dangerous and don't agree to your terms? What happens to them?"

"You don't want to find out. Check out the house." A click on the line signalled the end of the conversation.

"Asshole," said Adele as she put away her phone.

Harjit was right. He may be an asshole, but he was right. She couldn't walk away, not with what she knew. She needed to find what was in the house as much as he did, and she'd do what was necessary to discover it, whether or not she worked for Harjit. Harjit's point of view that she was a danger if left on her own irritated her, but the idea of him observing others comforted her. The wrong person could snap under the strain of this knowledge. As much as she hated him at that moment, she respected him for what he was trying to manage. She'd discover the house's secrets-

"Or die trying," she said out loud. This was her reality she could not escape.

What was her plan? She'd rather not try to break-in. She'd never broken into anything in her life and was sure someone would discover her clumsy attempt. Harjit had recommended that she scope the house out, at different times in the day, to determine any routine. Adele needed more surveillance before she formulated her plan. She worried she might have another episode and blank out for a few hours, drawing more attention to herself, but had no other choice.

She'd go out after dark, limiting her chance to be seen. The figure in the window had seen her earlier; if they noticed her observing the house again, they might not react well.

The next few hours were hard for Adele. The house kept calling to her, and she struggled to resist. She found it impossible to focus on anything for long as her thoughts kept drifting back to the house. She had to stop herself on three occasions from rushing back. She couldn't survive this way; she had to discover the secret of the house.

Just after ten p.m., she headed back out into the chilly spring night. Apprehensive, she turned down the street. The house had no exterior light. From within, pale light filtered out of a few windows — not the white light of an electric bulb, but a dull orange light that rippled. The occupant of the house used candles or another form of flame to light the rooms.

148

Someone moved through the house, as the orange light travelled through rooms on the main floor. One by one, the lights in the windows winked out. An orange glow appeared on the upper level, and then moments later disappeared, plunging the house into darkness.

She observed the house for a few minutes, growing more confident and less afraid. Undercover of darkness, she moved closer to the home. The familiar uneasiness and discomfort grew as she drew nearer. Was it the house itself or something living inside it? The figure who stared at her from the window had not produced a sensation, so she concluded the occupant wasn't the cause of the emanations. Was it imbued in the structure itself? She dared to approach, walking hesitantly up the stairs to the door. Her flight instinct told her to run, but she ignored it. Reaching out, she placed her hand on the door.

Nothing. She reached out to touch the painted brick and also felt nothing. It wasn't the house then, but something it contained.

With great effort, Adele pulled herself away from the house and crossed the street. She lingered a while longer, gazing intently, the building only a black silhouette against a star-filled sky. A cosmic evil pulsed within its depths. Then she turned and headed back to her apartment.

A fitful night followed. She tossed and turned, her mind racing, dreaming incomprehensible dreams. Her first dream was of large cyclopean cities that rose out of nothing, being constructed by shapeless beings. The beings ebbed and flowed, becoming whatever shape they required to complete their tasks, made of iridescent slime, as black as night. Shining green eyes floated on their surface, making them appear as the cosmos itself, with a myriad of mouths gibbering silently. She woke drenched in sweat, compelled to jump out of bed and race to the house, but she resisted this summons.

As the night continued, the dreams began to change. A battle raged around her, with men on horses, wearing armour and wielding swords, the red cross on the while mantel marking them as members of the Templar Order. A city burned around them; Jerusalem or another city in the Holy Land. A scene of them meeting with Muslim clerics and shown a scroll bearing a picture of a winged being with tentacles protruding from its lower face.

149

Adele awoke at this image. The creature trapped in the northern ice sprang to mind; the two were similar. Could they be connected? But how? What part did the Crusades play in this house in Halifax? She realized these were not random dreams, but visions of reality too horrifying to consider.

As she drifted off to sleep, another vision leapt into her mind. A prison started to rise, the stone foundation built around the prisoner, a prisoner hidden from her. A man oversaw the development, the grim determination evident on his bearded face. The prison began to take shape, forming into the house that haunted her. Adele realized she had not yet fallen asleep when this vision materialized. This was no random dream. Something was trying to communicate with her.

The sun was rising as Adele left the house dressed in her running gear. She went for a run, planning her route to approach the house near the end. It took great willpower to stick to her path and not immediately detour to the foreboding building.

At last, Adele arrived at the street, slowing to a walk to examine the house as she passed. What she saw caused her to freeze; a man stood on the porch.

Old, stooped and bald, he wore a pair of tweed pants, too big for the slight frame underneath, held up by a pair of suspenders. He had on a dress shirt which may have at one time been white, but was now a faded cream colour, with the sleeves rolled up on his forearms. He had on a pair of worn slippers. A newspaper had landed on the front steps. Adele held her breath, trying to blend into the background, intent on any clues the old man might give.

He, with an effort, bent over to pick up the paper and stole a glance up and down the street. Adele tried to duck, but the movement caught his eye. The old man stared at her. Shooting a grimace in her direction, he moved with as much haste as he could muster and slammed the door behind him.

He was likely the figure from the window and who carried the light through the darkened rooms. His presence didn't match the menace associated with the building. Adele hurried by, catching a glance of one curtain pulled to the side, gnarled fingers clutching the faded fabric; he was watching her.

Back at her apartment, she paced around, determining her next course of action. She felt compelled to call Harjit but resisted. Perhaps she wanted his reassurances, but he had dismissed her report the previous day, and she had less to say now. That wasn't entirely true, she realized. She could add that the old man had seen her again, in broad daylight. The occupant of the house was aware the house was under surveillance, and she was unsure how this person would react. Harjit was unlikely to respond well to that information.

Adele was brewing a pot of coffee when her phone rang. Harjit was calling. "Hello?" she said excitedly.

"My people have found interesting things concerning the house," said Harjit. "A simple search of the land registry records revealed much. The house has been in the same family for four generations. The current owner is the great-grandson of the original owner. Built in 1842 by William Eddoes, an adventurer and collector of rare artifacts who became a recluse after he completed the house. Newspapers of the day carried several stories on his adventures. But the stories stop after he finished the house and there's next to nothing concerning his descendants. No stories on them, no mention of anything. A name at the land registry office transferring the deed of the house and other records to show they were alive, but not much else."

"This is weird. You don't think it's..."

"The same person? That the current Mr. Eddoes is the same Mr. Eddoes that built the house?"

"It's far-fetched, but nothing would surprise me now."

"My first thought was similar. Each of the Eddoes descendants have birth records and marriage certificates along with death certificates. Enough to prove the person existed, but nothing to show they lived. I think if the person were the same, they would have assumed the identity of a dead child or someone to pass on the ownership of the house. While we have more digging to do, a cursory investigation shows a legitimate transfer of ownership within the same family. I've encountered nothing that granted immortality in my experiences with The Other; I believe these are real people, but people who kept a low profile."

"Is having the same family own a house for generations strange?"

"On its own, no. But the owners never hooked the house up to the City's electrical grid. The city tried to force them to hook up to the water and sewer supply, but the family sued to stop them. It's the only house in the neighbourhood still on well and septic. There are no records of gas or anything being attached to the house. None of the owners has ever appeared to have held a job, yet they've never fallen into debt. We found no medical records, no driver's licenses, not even a library card registered to any of them. The current occupant is Walter Eddoes, 81. He married in the early sixties, but his only child was stillborn. His wife divorced him soon after and moved to Montreal."

"Does he have a will?"

"A will?"

"The house has to go to someone. They have been cautious in establishing the transfer of this house from one generation to the next. I'm curious who gets the house now in the absence of an heir."

"That's a good point. I'll check if we can find a will for Mr. Walter Eddoes. Have you learned anything?"

"I can confirm they don't use electricity in the house. I observed someone walking in the house last night using a candle or another type of open flame to light their way. And I believe I saw Mr. Eddoes this morning; an elderly man retrieved a newspaper off the front step."

"Interesting. Did he notice you?"

"Unfortunately, yes. I believe he is the figure in the window from earlier."

"You're drawing too much attention to yourself. I'd tell you to be subtle, but the time for subtlety might have passed. Anything else?"

"I don't think he causes my sensations on The Other. And it's not the house itself. Something inside the house is the source; I'm almost sure of it."

"Almost sure?"

"I won't know until I get into the house."

"Do you have a plan?"

"No."

"Well, come up with one. I'll try to discover more information about the house." He hung up the phone.

Adele finished making her pot of coffee and poured herself a cup. The house was getting stranger. What secrets did it hold? And how would she find out?

She sat at home for a few hours, wracking her brains for a logical way she could get into the house. If not actual entry, at least a glance into the interior. Perhaps she could pinpoint the source of The Other? But nothing came to her. Frustrated, she began to pace; in the back of her consciousness, the source tickled her mind, pulling on her. The temptation was too strong. Almost against her will, she left to revisit the house.

The stress of this investigation was getting to her. She had returned to Halifax to relax, to recharge after her harrowing adventure in the Arctic. Instead, she felt herself losing her grip on her sanity. The fixation on this house, her inability to disassociate, to focus on anything else; she had to overcome it lest it destroys her. She couldn't move past this; she had to confront what lurked within the home.

Her sight blurred as she got closer to the house. She had a vision, the source communicating with her, imploring her forward. The entity in the home identified her, sensing the blight from The Other. One of the enslaved beings, the ones constructing those ancient alien cities, flashed in her mind. It was in pain, trapped, and it desired freedom. She shook her head, and the vision momentarily faded, soon replaced by another. An image of a creature, similar to the one trapped in the ice, tormenting the slave came into her mind. Adele reached out and steadied herself on a tree lining the street. The tormentor loomed, its malevolence palpable and conjuring memories from her time in the ice. It terrified her. She had empathy for the misery the trapped entity suffered at its hands. Her heart raced, and she panted as sweat appeared at her brow. Forcing the image from her mind, the street came back into view, replacing the terrifying visions.

Collecting herself, she looked towards the house. Harjit believed the time for subtlety might have passed. So, she wouldn't be subtle. She crossed the street, walked up the steps and knocked on the door.

The door opened hesitantly, and Walter Eddoes looked out the crack. His eyes narrowed in hatred. "You. What do you want? Why are you spying on me?"

"Hi," said Adele, forcing a smile and friendly demeanour. "Listen, I've been looking for a house to buy in this neighbourhood, and I have to tell you, I have fallen in love with your home. I'm sorry to be so forward, but do you think you'd ever want to sell?"

"It's not for sale," growled Walter as he started to slam the door. Adele stuck her foot in the doorway in time to prevent him from closing the door.

"Please hear me out, sir. I want a chance to buy this house. It speaks to me."

"You have the mark upon you," said Walter. "I can smell it. You're tainted. That's why it speaks to you. Get out of here."

Adele tried to look past Walter deeper into the house. A musty smell emanated from within, the furnishings and decor old and in rough shape, untouched through the years. A door at the far end of the hall, marked with a symbol, undefined at this distance; The Other lingered behind that door. She pushed, causing the old man to stumble.

"No! Go! You're not welcome here. Be gone, foul woman!" Walter began to pull himself back to his feet.

"I'm sorry, let me help you," said Adele, reaching out to him.

"I said, be gone!" Something flashed in Walter's hand, a sharp pain cut across Adele's forearm, warm wetness following the sting. She sucked in her breath and grabbed her forearm. A pitiful wail sounded in her mind, and she staggered.

This gave Walter the opportunity he needed. He made it to his feet and leaned his full weight against the door. The door slammed into Adele, pushing her backwards. She lost her footing on the top of the stairs and tumbled unceremoniously onto the sidewalk. The locks clicked into place.

Adele lay on the sidewalk, stunned. The primordial black form writhed in her mind; she perceived its anger lashing out, its freedom denied by an old man and a lock. The fury at its jailer made her wince. She looked at her arm, a deep gash bled profusely.

She pressed her hand hard on her wound and staggered towards her apartment, drawing looks from the few passersby she encountered. Reaching her building, Adele forced herself up the two flights of stairs to her apartment.

Once inside, she turned on the water in her kitchen sink, flushing out the wound. The ugly gash showed no signs of stopping; she needed medical attention. In her first aid kit, she found a sterile pad and gauze and did her best to staunch the flow of blood. Changing her shirt, she left to go to the emergency ward.

The wound required stitches to close. Her phone rang while the nurse stitched her injury, but she let it go to voicemail. Harjit, but she didn't know what to tell him.

The sun was setting when she returned to her apartment. She couldn't put off calling Harjit any longer.

"Where the hell were you?" he demanded. "What happened?"

"Nothing," she lied. "I'd fallen asleep. I haven't been sleeping much, and I guess it caught up with me. When I woke, I checked my phone and noticed you had called."

"Uh, huh." He sounded skeptical. "Well, we learned more on the property. You'd never guess who gets the house."

"I hate when someone asks that. Too many variables and possibilities exist for me to get the correct answer. Stop playing games and tell me."

"The Freemasons."

"The Freemasons?"

"Yep. The local chapter in Halifax becomes the proud owner of the house. William Eddoes had been a Mason but gave up his membership soon after construction ended. None of his descendants have ever belonged to the Masonic Lodge."

"That is weird."

"It gets weirder. The wills of the descendants of William Eddoes each had a clause that if their heir could not discharge their duties, or in the absence of an heir, the house passed to the ownership of the Freemasons."

"Could not discharge their duties? What does that mean?"

"I don't know. The documents don't clarify what those duties are supposed to be."

155

"Why the Masons?"

"Your guess is as good as mine. If William Eddoes believed in the tenets of Freemasonry, why did he stop going to the Lodge? If his descendants included this clause in their wills, why did they not join? Other than being an old and secretive organization who counted among its members many influential men throughout history, I cannot think of any reason to link this family and this house to the Order."

"The plot thickens."

"It does. Do you have a plan to get inside?"

"Not yet."

"We're running out of time. This discovery could be significant. Do I have to send someone to help? Someone more experienced?"

"No, I'm fine. I can do it."

"Tonight?"

"Yes," she sighed. "Tonight."

"Good. Call me at once. I don't care how late. And when I say at once, I mean as soon as you are outside of the house. If you haven't contacted me by five a.m. local time, I'm sending in the cavalry. If you haven't entered the house by then, you're off this case."

"I understand."

"Good." The line went dead.

Tonight. It had to end tonight.

Adele waited until midnight to head out. She did not know how she would get in and had no skill at breaking and entering. Not only did she have to worry about Walter, but any neighbours that might notice her skulking near the house and call the police. The darkness and the late hour helped her. Normally a meticulous planner, she'd been improvising ever since Gallou Cove.

The front door would be locked, as would the windows facing the street. The house likely had a back door, but presumably locked. Maybe she'd get lucky and find a window unlocked on the main floor or a way up to second-floor windows. She was sick of this building consuming her every thought. The house mocked her. Arriving at the home, and with a glance to determine if anyone was there to notice her, she slipped into the backyard.

Tall trees cloaked the yard in darkness, cutting off the light pollution from the city. It was difficult to see, but gave the benefit of shrouding her from unwanted attention. The main floor extended further than the second did. Where it sat on the street, the two storeys were flush, but in the rear, the first floor continued. The roof over this extension offered access to the second-floor windows.

The back door was indeed locked. A quick inspection of the windows on the main floor proved fruitless, as they too were sealed. A tree growing near the house in the back yard allowed her access to the roof. She'd climb and swing out onto it.

Adele had not climbed a tree since she was a kid. Awkwardly she pulled herself up into the lower branches of the tree and caught her breath, listening to hear if her efforts had attracted any attention. Then she climbed higher. Once she was in the tree, the climb was easy. The tricky part was shimming out onto a branch to get the roof under her.

"What the hell am I doing?" she whispered to herself. "This is crazy. I should tell Harjit to go to hell and let him send someone to lock me up. Being incarcerated would be preferable to this. And now I'm talking to myself too. Get it together, Adele."

Choosing the thickest branch, she crawled out. The limb started to droop under her weight sooner than she anticipated. She wasn't over the roof, so she had to keep going. The branch continued to bend under her; she held her breath and hoped it supported her weight long enough for her to get to her destination.

The roof was now beneath her. She worried if she crawled any further, the branch might crack under her weight. Lowering herself, she positioned the limb under her armpits; she had to release her hold on the branch as she did not have the strength pull herself back up. Tentatively she reached out with her foot, but the roof was still two feet below her. She had no choice but to drop.

Grabbing the branch in her hands, she attempted to lower herself, but she slipped. The limb flew from her hands, and she fell the two feet to the roof, landing hard and twisting her ankle. The branch whipped upwards, and she made a horrible sound when she landed. Falling onto her back, she began to slide to the edge of the roof but caught herself before she fell to the ground.

Adele lay panting, the pain in her ankle stabbing up her leg. Someone must have heard her trying to gain access to the house. Lying still, she listened for a few minutes, hearing no sound that indicated anyone noticed her. From below, she sensed the thing in the house pulling at her; it was aware of her presence.

Rolling on to her front, she crawled upwards to where the roof met the wall of the second storey, aiming for the closest window. She poked her head over the edge of the sill to peer inside the room. It appeared to be an unused bedroom filled with old boxes and furniture. She tried to lift the window, but it was locked.

Crawling over to the next window, it resisted her attempt to enter. This left only one window; if locked, she needed to break the glass. While the occupant of the house would hear it and awaken, she had run out of options. Harjit had said get in tonight, or he'd find someone else. Gritting her teeth, both in determination and against the pain in her ankle, she made her way to the last window.

This window led to a small bathroom, with dirty fixtures and mildewing walls as if the old room was rarely cleaned. The window was unlocked; the old man opened it to air the room out and hadn't locked it again.

Sliding the window upwards to make minimal sound, Adele hissed in frustration when it stopped halfway. Something prevented it from moving any further. Thankfully, she was petite; with an effort, she could worm her way in, but her injured ankle worried her. She stuck her good leg through the opening, looking for purchase on something. Her foot alighted on the toilet, a minimalist porcelain affair at least one hundred years old. She got her foot onto the rim of the seat and lowered her other foot. Pain shot upwards as she attempted to put weight on her injured ankle. Her sudden shift in reaction to the pain caused her uninjured foot to slip off the seat and land in the water with a soft splash. This caused her to fall off the rim, and her injured foot hit the floor and buckled under her weight. She caught herself on the window frame before she fell into the room.

Cursing her clumsiness under her breath, Adele composed herself. Her breathing rapid, and her heart racing with the fear she had revealed her presence, she used the wall to steady herself and keep her weight off of her injured foot, and inched towards the door.

An orange glow appeared at the crack under the door. Someone was in the hall.

Escape by the window was impossible before Walter Eddoes grabbed her. Caught from behind and off-balance, she'd be vulnerable to attack. Her only choice was to face her adversary; he would not react well to her being in his house and was likely armed.

Tensing, wishing she had a weapon to defend herself with, Adele slipped behind the door. The knob began to turn.

The orange glow filled the room as the door opened. Adele hid behind the door. It creaked open more and stopped. She saw a blade clutched in a fist withered with age. Reacting, she threw her weight against the door, pushing off from the wall behind her. The move caught Walter by surprise. The door slammed hard, trapping his arm between it and the frame. He uttered a curse, and the knife clattered onto the tile floor.

Kicking the knife into the bathroom, Adele wrenched open the door and threw herself against the man. The candle he held in the other hand dropped to the floor, fluttering out as it hit, plunging the hall into darkness.

"You bitch! You don't know what you are doing! Get out of my house!" Walter cursed.

Adele pressed her advantage. She tried to find stable footing, but her injured ankle collapsed under her, pitching her forward into Walter. He stumbled backwards; she heard him stagger into something, and then he screamed. His scream faded and was replaced by the sound of him falling down the stairs.

"Walter!" she yelled, reaching out as she crawled forward, trying to find the top step. When she did, she shimmed down the stairs on her backside, not willing to trust her footing.

Reaching the bottom, her outstretched foot encountered something soft, which she assumed was Walter. He did not react to her pushing him with her foot.

She needed light as the blackness was too deep. The forgotten candle lay somewhere at the top of the stairs; she had no means to light it even if she found it. Another option was to stumble blindly in the dark, hoping to find a window and throw open the curtains and let in the ambient light from the street. Or, she thought, open the front door and let light into the hall. The door was to her right and easier to locate than a window. She could walk along the wall until she reached it. The front door posed the problem that someone might notice her. Determining the risk to be minimal, she made her way to the door.

Turning the two deadbolts and lifting the chain, she opened the door halfway. The glow from the street shone in palely, illuminating Walter's crumpled form at the bottom of the stairs. The light showed her something useful: a kerosene lamp and a box of wooden matches sat on a shelf just inside the hall.

Adele limped over to the lamp and lifted the glass chimney. Striking a match, the flame flared as she touched it to the wick. Warm light filled the hall as the fire took; she blew out the match, lowered the wick, and replaced the chimney. Then she returned to the front door to close it.

A cursory look at Walter confirmed what she already knew: he was dead. His neck bent at an impossible angle, and his lifeless eyes peered at her accusingly. She had now killed two people. Scott had been in self-defence; this was not self-defence. It had been an accident, but she had broken in, hadn't she?

What could she do with the body? Leave it here? Even in a house this large, the smell might reach the street. Walter didn't seem to be one to fraternize with his neighbours, but his newspapers would pile up, and someone would grow suspicious. It was only a matter of time before someone found Walter's corpse.

The scene appeared to be an accident. The old man had tumbled down the stairs and met his untimely demise — death by misadventure. Unless someone had noticed the incident between them on the front porch earlier or witnessed a strange form prowling around the property, then questions might be asked. Still, would they lead back to her?

The guilt of having caused Walter's death fought her fear of being caught. Harjit had said if she got caught, he'd abandon her to the graces of the local police. He even had a back story prepared to implicate her. She had to overcome this guilt and concentrate on what she needed to do. Her first task was to uncover the source of her visions.

At the end of the hall was the door she had seen earlier from the street. She sensed the glee from beyond the portal. Her vision faded, replaced by images of a great battle, the black amorphous creatures from her earlier visions fighting against oval beings with tentacles and wings. The oval beings defeated the black monsters, but a few managed to flee to freedom. That emotion washed over her: freedom.

She traversed the hall, noting the paintings on the wall. In one, Masonic imagery surrounded a barrel-chested man with a great beard and wearing an apron emblazoned with the Masonic symbol. She realized with a start it was the man from her vision, the one overseeing the construction of the prison. A corroded metal nameplate at the bottom of the frame identified him as William Eddoes.

Other old paintings showed knights heading off to battle; the one constant being at least one knight in every picture wore the distinctive red cross on a white tabard of the Templar Order. What did an ancient European knightly order, long gone, have to do with her in twenty-first-century Canada?

On the door, she got a better look at the painted crude sign she had noticed earlier. The sign resembled a warped, five-pointed star with what appeared to be an eye in the centre. She pressed her hand against the door; the source of The Other lay beyond. Reaching out, she expected a sensation when her fingers gripped the doorknob and was almost disappointed when nothing extra happened. Cautiously she opened the door.

The light from her lamp showed a short set of stairs leading to a landing. On each stair and on the walls of the narrow stairwell, she noted the same five-pointed star carved into the wood. She listened at the top of the stair; a pitiful moan and gibbering sound proceeded upwards from the depth of the house.

161

Favouring her leg, she held on to the railing in one hand, while the other gripped the kerosene lamp. She inched her way to the landing and gazed towards the bottom of the second flight of stairs that led into the basement.

At the bottom, held at bay by a mysterious force, appeared the creature from her visions. It stretched into the basement beyond her sight, it's dimensions massive. The surface of its slime-like body undulated, forming and un-forming eyes that floated and glowed with an eerie green luminescence. Misshapen mouths gibbered and formed unknown words. Her presence excited the creature. A series of voices, some shrill, some deep, began to speak in unison: "Telkeli-li! Telkeli-li!"

Revulsion and horror filled Adele. Any allusions to sympathy for its imprisonment and plight washed away. What monster had the Eddoes been keeping in the basement of their house for the past four generations? Whatever plan they had, she had stopped it. She could not allow this creature to escape its confines. The tangible malice exuded by the entity assaulted her, a being of unadulterated evil, that she needed to destroy.

The sinister being sensed this shift in her emotions. Its anger rose, and the timbre and tone of the voices changed. It surged forward, smashing itself against the invisible barrier keeping it at bay.

The thing lashed out with its mind, crushing Adele and forcing her to her knees. The kerosene lamp almost fell from her · grasp. Frantic, she forced herself to crawl as fast as she could back up the stairs and out of the basement.

Closing the door blunted the anger coming from the entity. It reached out to her, trying to force her to return, but Adele resisted its call. How would she destroy the beast?

Her eyes rested on Walter's body and then on the lamp in her hand. She'd burn it and the whole place to the ground. It would appear as if Walter had fallen, a kerosene lamp in hand, to smash at the bottom of the stairs and ignite the old dry timber in the house. Kerosene lamps sat in every room, with extra kerosene stored somewhere in the house. As the fire spread, the dry wood, coupled with the flammable material, would feed the inferno.

Limping along the hallway, she passed Walter's body. Raising the glass lamp over her head, she threw it to the ground near where Walter lay. The thick glass shattered, spraying kerosene over the corpse and the old rug in the hall. The flame from the wick spread, starting a conflagration that threatened to get out of control fast.

Adele rushed out the front door. She had no choice but to risk someone seeing her as she had to get out of the burning house. Crossing to the other side of the street as fast as her injured ankle allowed, she melted into the shadows and watched as the flames began to spread.

Palpable fear emanated from the monster in the basement. She sensed its agitation, heard it screaming. The screams changed from fear to anger, as it accepted its fate. The orange flames began to glow at the windows of the first floor, before moving on to the second floor. Minutes later, flames licked from the roof as the fire spread to the rafters. By now, someone had noticed the fire, and a small crowd began to gather on the street. In the distance came the peel of a fire engine.

Reaching out with her mind, she tried to sense the creature lurking in the basement, but the screams had grown silent. With a loud crash, the roof caved in, and the crowd gaped and gasped. Adele took advantage of this to retreat from the house and head to her apartment.

She called Harjit as soon as she slipped in her door. "Well? What happened?" he asked.

"I made it inside the house. And then it went to shit."

"Give me the details."

"A ninja, I am not. I woke up Walter, and he confronted me. In the struggle, he fell and broke his neck."

"Problematic, but something we can control. Did you find the source of your impressions?"

"Yes, a creature held captive in the basement. Huge and black with a multitude of eyes and mouths. The wickedness of the being was overwhelming."

"Wait, a second. I'll be right back." Harjit put her on hold, and a few moments later was back on the line. "Does this description match? 'It was a terrible, indescribable thing vaster than any subway train—a shapeless congeries of protoplasmic bubbles, faintly self-luminous, and with myriads of temporary eyes forming and un-forming as pustules of greenish light'[1]."

"Sounds like what was in the basement, yeah. Where did you get that description?"

"I told you of the report from William Dyer, the Antarctic expedition? They encountered a creature in Antarctica. In my opinion, what you described matches the description. The big question now is, what is it doing in the house?"

"The house was built around the creature, made to contain it, like a prison. Symbols carved and painted on the stairs and entrance kept it in place."

"Symbols? Describe them."

"A misshapen five-pointed star with an eye in the middle."

"The Elder Sign."

"What?"

"Nothing. How the hell did they trap one? And build the house around it? To keep it trapped, the risk, it's unfathomable. Wait, you referred to both the creature and the house in the past tense. Where is it now?"

"Gone."

"Gone? What? How?" The anger in Harjit's voice clear to her.

"I set the house on fire. That entity was dangerous, a being of vast power and indescribable evil. I had to destroy it so it couldn't get out."

"Why did you do that? Having a chance to study the creature could have given us insights into its masters. This was an amazing discovery. I've never heard of anyone having one in captivity. The opportunity for research was limitless."

"I don't understand."

"No, you don't. And that's my fault. Circumstances beyond my control necessitated rushing you into the field before you were properly trained. Your knowledge has huge gaps, and I'm not the best one to teach you what you need."

"You're not making sense."

---

[1] Excerpt from "At The Mountains of Madness" by H.P. Lovecraft, 1936

"I thought sending you out would not cause problems. But your lack of knowledge has cost us an opportunity to study one of those up close."

"Study what? What was it?"

"Not that the name will mean much to you, but it's called a Shoggoth. My knowledge is limited, but there are scholars dedicated to their study."

"I'm sorry. I didn't know."

"How could you? It's my fault, really. I should have expected this. But then again, we didn't think you'd meet something on your rest and rehab. I wonder what else the Eddoes had in their home? They might have owned tomes, artifacts, other lost knowledge, now lost. I should have told you to cease your investigations and sent in a proper team."

"What's next? Are you going to fire me?"

"No. Everyone makes mistakes, and I share this one. You need to be educated on The Other since you can't make this mistake again. You're going to Miskatonic University in Arkham. Professor Sean Stoker is the Dean of the Occult Studies department there, and the world's leading expert on The Other. You can ask him any questions you want. I'll send Joe and Pete along too as soon as they finish with what I have them working on for me. They also lack the knowledge they need. You can spend time together, learn what you can, enjoy the clam chowder and rest up for your next assignment. Sit tight until I call you."

"Thanks. I won't let you down. Again."

"For what it's worth, I should apologize to you. I sent you out ill-prepared for the danger you are facing. It's time we remedied that. Rest up, relax and get ready. Next stop, Arkham."

Troy Young

It Ends Where It Began

Dr. Adele Kramer stood up as the plane taxied to the gate at Boston's Logan Airport. *Why do I always do this?* she mused to herself. *I can't go anywhere until they open the door and everyone else ahead of me gets off first.*

The anticipation of getting to her destination usually motivated her, but in this case, she was hesitant. Harjit had sent her to Arkham to visit Dr. Sean Stoker at Miskatonic University. Dr. Stoker was the Dean of Occult Studies at Miskatonic, and one of the world's leading authorities on the phenomena she was chasing.

These last few weeks were a far cry from her career in marine biology. Sea monsters, alive and dead, plus strange alien beings trapped in basements, were eroding her sanity. She wasn't sure she wanted to learn more than she knew.

Harjit said Joe and Pete were heading to Miskatonic University too. That was the one bright spot on this excursion.

167

She had become close to both of them as one does when forced into stressful circumstances.

The line of people started to move. Adele got her bag from the overhead compartment and filed out of the plane. Fishing out her passport, she got in line at customs.

After a grilling by an official who took his role as the first line in defence a little too seriously, she wandered through the doors and out into the concourse, wondering how she was getting to Arkham. It was too much to hope that Harjit had arranged a car for her.

"Adele! Hey, over here!" shouted Pete, waving his hand in the air. The Inuk man was not tall, and he had to bounce for her to see him over the crowd. A smile creased his face as she came over to him. He wrapped her in a firm hug. "Good to see you, Doctor."

"It's good to see you too. I didn't expect you to be waiting for me at the airport."

"Joe and I just arrived from Toronto. He's in the can."

"How do you know Joe? Harjit said he was out West?"

"No, Joe's been working near Toronto. Harjit paired the two of us to investigate a cult operating outside of the city. It was... weird. And you?"

"I went home to Halifax. I found a literal monster living in a basement. Can we get a break from this shit?"

"Apparently not. What do you know about Dr. Stoker?"

"Nothing apart from what Harjit told me. I know that Miskatonic University has an extensive library on the Occult, and I had a colleague working there that was studying aberrations in sea creatures. The university has a reputation for its studies into weird things."

"Going to study us then, I guess," winked Pete. "Be careful if he offers you a drink; we might wake up in a lab."

"Funny. No, not funny. Your joke might have been funny a few weeks ago, but now... I'm not sure. There's a ring of truth now."

"There she is," said Joe, striding up to them. He had a smile on his face, but it did not reach his eyes. They had a haunted look to them. He leaned in and gave her a hug and a clumsy kiss on

Adele's undamaged cheek. She blushed and felt flustered. The two of them pulled away awkwardly.

"Good to see you, Joe. Pete says you've been in Toronto, that you've been working together?"

"We had one mission, yeah," he said, nodding. "A cult. Before that, I was in Muskoka, investigating multiple homicides. It was a demon or whatnot. I'm not sure what the proper term is."

"That's why we're here, to learn about the things that go bump in the night," said Pete.

"I wish I were still blissfully ignorant," said Adele.

"I rented a car," said Pete. "We can drive to Arkham. I checked the GPS; it's forty-five minutes northeast of here."

"Do we have an appointed time to meet with Dr. Stoker?" asked Joe.

"I don't recall seeing one. I guess we just arrive at his door," said Adele.

"Let's hope he knows we're coming; it would be just like Harjit to have us show up unannounced."

It was a lovely spring day, and the drive through the Massachusetts' countryside was soothing to their collective angst. "I never realized it was so rugged and beautiful here," said Pete. "I figured it would be end to end sprawl."

"Never been here before?" asked Joe.

"No, you?"

"Came with a few guys from the detachment to catch a Red Sox game, but we never left the city."

"I've been," said Adele. "Even visited the university. There are two campuses; the old campus and a modern one on the outskirts."

"Which one are we visiting?"

"I'd suspect the old one. Let me check." Adele pulled out her phone and looked at the details Harjit had forwarded. "Yes, Dr. Stoker's office is in the Randolph Carter Memorial Hall on the corner of West St and College."

Arkham was a small town, dominated by the university. Much of the streets on the south side of the Miskatonic river were old, tree-lined streets filled with houses built in the Georgian or

Federalist style. Parking was at a premium; they were forced to park a few blocks away from the university.

"How old is this school?" remarked Joe as they walked up to the old cast iron and stone gates.

"One of the oldest in North America," said Adele. "It was founded in 1690 if my memory is correct."

Entering the Hall, they located the number of Dr. Stoker's office on the directory. They headed up to the fourth floor and found the open door to his outer office. A young man with curly black hair and a black goatee and wearing a black turtleneck was typing at the computer on his desk. "Hi, can I help you?"

"Yes, we're here to see Dr. Stoker. We're not sure if he is expecting us. We didn't receive an appointed time to meet him."

"Are you the people that Mr. Singh has sent?"

"Yes, that's us."

"Excellent. He has been expecting you. Please, take a seat, and I will let Dr. Stoker know you are here." The man exited the anteroom via a different door. Pete, Adele and Joe found seats and waited.

They did not wait long. The man in black returned, leading an older gentleman. He had a shock of white hair, slicked to the side and was wearing a pair of thick-rimmed tortoiseshell glasses. His tweed coat and waistcoat were worn; the thread holding on one of his elbow patches was coming undone. "I'm Dr. Sean Stoker, Dean of the School of Occult Studies. You must be Pete Ivalu, Joe Mills and Dr. Adele Kramer. I was reviewing the notes that Mr. Singh forwarded me. Please, come in. William," he said, addressing the other man. "See if our guests want anything. I'll have a tea myself."

"I'm good, thank you," said Adele. Joe and Pete both nodded in the negative.

Dr. Stoker walked into his office and swept his hand towards the three chairs set in front of his desk. He eased himself into the well-worn leather office chair and let out a sigh. "So, Harjit claims that you've had encounters with something of an unusual nature?"

"Yes. Joe and I first encountered a dead sea monster in Cape Breton, and Pete and I later found something trapped under the ice in the high Arctic."

"I came across something that attacked me in a cave. Later Pete and I uncovered a secret cult."

"And I discovered something in a basement in Halifax."

"Harjit claims the thing in the basement was a Shoggoth. Most interesting. To think not only did someone trap one but to keep it imprisoned that long."

"What's a Shoggoth? Harjit didn't give me any specifics. He just read a description out of an old journal."

Dr. Stoker adjusted his glasses. "A terrible creature. The journal you mentioned is Professor Dyer's tale of an expedition that this university sent to Antarctica in 1930. He claims to have encountered a creature that has since been labelled a Shoggoth."

"It was terrible," agreed Adele. "It attempted to implant images in my mind. The creature hoped I'd free it."

"You were susceptible to its call because of your prior exposure to the Mythos."

"The Mythos?" asked Joe.

"Ah yes, I forget, Mr. Singh likes to buck convention. He calls it something else, doesn't he? The Irregular?"

"The Other," said Pete.

"Right," smiled Dr. Stoker. "The Other. Most scholars refer to this as the Cthulhu Mythos."

"Cthulhu? We've encountered that name before," said Adele.

"I'm not surprised. The Cult of Cthulhu is the most widespread, hence why the study of these phenomena was named after it."

"There are other cults?"

"Oh, yes, many. Cthulhu is one of the Great Old Ones, a pantheon of alien gods come to this planet from amongst the cosmos. Others include Yog-Sothoth, Shub-Niggurath, Father Dagon and Mother Hydra." He rose and headed for a bookshelf. He picked up something and came back to his desk, placing the item in front of them. "This is Cthulhu."

A bas relief made of clay lay there. One inch thick and six inches square, with strange hieroglyphics carved into it, along with the image of a winged being, with a tentacled head: part dragon, part octopus and part human. "Pete," began Adele, rising from her chair. "Look at that."

Pete licked his lips. "That's what was in the ice."

"Cthulhu? No. Cthulhu is immense, hundreds of metres tall. No doubt what you encountered was one of his minions," said Dr. Stoker. Seeing the distress on their faces, he scooped up the square of clay and put it into his top drawer, out of sight. "This came to us from a young man named Wilcox, who dreamed of this creature. He crafted it upon waking. It has been in the school's possession since 1925."

"I heard the name Cthulhu. It was written on a cave wall in Muskoka, along with other languages, including Egyptian hieroglyphics."

"We saw it in the Arctic, written in a lost Inuit village."

"There is a connection, most definitely. Cthulhu is an ancient entity that has existed on earth since before the dawn of recorded history. You most likely saw the phrase 'Cthulhu fhtagen'?"

Adele swallowed hard. "We did."

"The whole phrase is 'Ph'nglui mglw'nafh Cthulhu R'lyeh wgah'nagl fhtagn'; it means 'In his house at R'lyeh dead Cthulhu waits dreaming'. Quite a fanciful bit of prose."

"Where is this R'lyeh?" asked Joe.

Dr. Stoker shrugged. "No one knows for certain, but there is a record of an encounter in the South Pacific by a Norwegian named Johansen. He rammed a yacht into a thing hundreds of metres tall that resembled Cthulhu."

"And these things are related?"

"The information is disparate. There are similarities, a cosmic tie, but we cannot confirm the phenomena are linked. You three have seen a reference to Cthulhu, you said. An abandoned Inuit village, and a cave? Was there anything else in these locations?"

"The village had been abandoned, but we tracked the villagers to an ice flow, where we encountered a creature that bore a resemblance to Cthulhu," said Pete.

"Interesting. And in the cave?"

Joe rubbed his hands on his thighs. "I found something. It was..." He collected himself. "It was unlike anything I've seen. Eight feet tall, and its arms had two sets of elbows. The creature was black and faceless, and it knew my name, repeated it to me. I shot it, but I didn't wound it."

"This is a creature I've not encountered. Recount your experience if you will to my assistant, William. William Akeley has been a great addition to my staff; his family has been in Arkham since its founding and has witnessed many strange things firsthand. Notes on this undocumented Mythos being would expand our knowledge. But tell me, if you could not harm it, how did you escape?"

"I didn't say I couldn't harm it; I said that I shot it, but my bullets did no damage. There was a knife; I brought it with me." Joe reached into the breast pocket of his jacket and pulled out a knife, putting it on the desk in front of Dr. Stoker. "Harjit asked me to bring it to see if it meant something to you."

Dr. Stoker picked up the knife reverently. "The craftsmanship is exquisite. I recognize these markings but want to compare it to other things in the university's collection if I may. If I were to guess, I'd say this dagger is made of star metal."

"Star metal?"

"Iron from a meteorite. Metal from the stars, not originating on our planet. Before the Bronze Age and the introduction of smelting, the only usable metal was meteoric iron. Early humans used this iron to craft items of exceptional value to them. A bracelet, headrest and dagger made of meteoric iron were found in the tomb of Tutankhamun, King Tut, by Carter in 1927. The Inuit used star metal. It is not an uncommon material but was always given great significance. I can keep this to study?"

"You can. It's why Harjit had me bring it. Why was this dagger able to hurt whatever was in the cave?"

"The creature was not of this world. You needed something not from this world to harm it." Dr. Stoker put the dagger in his desk drawer.

"Wait a second," interjected Pete. "Are you saying these things are immune to harm by terrestrial items? Because we blew the shit out of the thing in the ice."

"No," said Dr. Stoker, smiling and looking at Pete over the rim of his glasses. "Johansen tells us they ran a ship into Cthulhu, though Cthulhu appeared to be regenerating from the damage. It is possible that whatever you found in the ice could survive, but unlikely. These alien beings are tough to kill, but not impossible. Significant damage can harm them. Mr. Mills' bullets could not harm the being in the cave, but if he had hit it with an artillery shell or something equally large, he might have harmed the creature."

"The Shoggoth?" said Adele aghast. "It was trapped in the basement of a house; I burned down the house. Did I destroy it, or let it loose?"

"We don't know enough about these creatures," said Dr. Stoker. "Fire may not have harmed it. It may have convinced you to set the fire. You said the Shoggoth was implanting images into your mind, asking you to free it?"

"Oh, God," said Adele, putting her hand to her mouth.

"If you freed the creature, we can't change that now. Let us focus on what we know and can do going forward, shall we? What is it you intend to do? What does Mr. Singh expect of you?"

"We're not sure," admitted Pete. "He's not always forthcoming. Only that the Other exists, and we must stop it."

"But you can't. This force is intergalactic and ancient. It is unlimited in its power. How did Harjit convince you to join him in this?"

"The nightmares," said Adele. "Once we were exposed to the Other, he said that they would continue to get worse, that our minds would collapse in on themselves and we'd enter a vegetative state. The way to stave it off was to confront it; by continuing to search out the Other, we could delay the inevitable."

"I see," said Dr. Stoker. He tugged on the end of his nose nervously and shifted in his chair. "That's not, um, not entirely…um, I shouldn't say any more."

"What? Dr. Stoker, tell us what you know," said Joe.

"Please, sir. We came here to learn from you. If you know something, you need to tell us," added Pete.

"Your boss, I don't know him well. We've talked on the phone, ran into each other at international symposiums on the topic. I don't know where he could have gotten this idea, but in my experience, it doesn't happen this way."

"What do you mean, Doctor?" said Adele icily.

"Exposure to the Mythos can impact the mind of the subject, leading to insanity. This has been well documented. But madness is a by-product of the initial exposure. Its effects are immediate and permanent, but I have never read of an account that they grew worse in isolation. The conditions worsen through repeated exposure. The madness can grow more pronounced, but only when the subject encounters the Mythos on a subsequent occasion."

"Sonofabitch!" said Joe, getting up out of his chair.

"He lied to us," said Adele. "He used our fears against us, convinced us to join him on his cause."

"It doesn't matter," said Pete. He was the only one not visibly affected by this news. "I'd still be here, even if Harjit hadn't lied. There are things out there that need to be stopped, or at least challenged," he said, cutting off Dr. Stoker before he could repeat his line on how stopping them was impossible. "The same is true for you. You're scared, and tired, and angry and are looking to blame your condition on someone. If Harjit had said your nightmares could improve on their own, and that you'd forget, would you? He's a bastard, yes, but we knew that before discovering his lie. Now that we've come this far, are either of you thinking of backing out? I'm not."

"Doctor," said Adele, still seething with this revelation about Harjit. "In the basement, I noticed a curious mark. Someone carved it throughout the place, on the walls, the stairs; it seemed to keep the Shoggoth at bay."

"Let me guess," said Stoker. "It was a misshapen star, with an eye in the centre, bisected by a pillar of flame?" He got up again and returned to his bookshelf, taking down a tome. He flipped through the pages as he returned. "Here," he said, sliding the book towards her. "Is this what you saw?"

The basement sign was on the page. "Yes. It repelled the creature."

"That's the Elder Sign. It is often associated with Mythos entities and is rumoured to have the power to keep evil at bay. I remember a curious case of it being used in a town called Innsmouth-"

The door opened, and William walked in with the tea. "Dr. Stoker, I hate to interrupt your chat," he said, placing the tea on the desk. "You have a meeting with the President of the University this afternoon. I can schedule a time for you and your guests to resume your conversation at a later date."

"Oh, dammit, I almost forgot that blasted meeting. William is right; we must set aside time to continue our discussions." Dr. Stoker took a sip of his tea, and his expression changed. His eyes became distant. "Although I don't think it will be a good use of your time. Its myths and unsubstantiated legends."

"What is?" asked Adele.

"All of it. Cthulhu, Shoggoths, Elder Signs; it's a lie, just fanciful stories told throughout the years to gullible fools.

The three visitors sat forward in their chairs. "Dr. Stoker," began Joe. "Harjit sent us here to learn from you about the Other."

"Harjit and his 'Other'; just another bureaucrat wasting public money, convincing the politicians he's working on something important. There is nothing to this."

"What?" shrieked Adele. "And the Shoggoth?"

"A hallucination on your part. Maybe a gas leak in that home, and it caused you to imagine things."

"What about the monster we came across in Gallou Cove? The one that destroyed the pier?"

"It was reportedly caused by a tsunami. You are suffering from survivor's guilt."

"And the cult we stopped?" said Pete.

"Misguided fools, like those that believe the earth is flat. It doesn't take much for a dynamic personality to convince the weak-minded to believe something."

"I see," said Pete calmly. Joe and Adele were staring at Dr. Stoker with barely contained anger.

"Cthulhu in the South Pacific? The ramblings of a drunken Norwegian. Dr. Dyer's account of the Antarctic expedition? Covering up for a mistake he made that led to the deaths of the rest of them. He develops a fanciful tale to cover off his incompetence. Most of these tales are just that, tales. There is no truth to them. The world is filled with such superstitious foolishness, and it is easy to find people willing to believe them. Your Mr. Singh has taken advantage of you and spun you a fairy tale. William, after further consideration, do not set a future meeting; we have nothing of importance to discuss." He rose from his desk. "I'm sorry that he sent you on what amounts to a grand waste of your time. I suggest that you forget this 'Other' nonsense and tender your resignations to Mr. Singh. You'll find yourself much happier, not chasing after ghosts and boogeymen. Now if you will excuse me, I have a meeting to prepare." Dr. Stoker walked out of the room; William held open the door for them, nonverbally indicating to them it was time for them to leave.

They didn't speak until they reached the sidewalk outside the building. "What the hell happened?" said Adele.

"Notice how everything changed when William came back? Dr. Stoker goes from telling us details on the Mythos to saying it's a lie," said Joe.

"Harjit expected Dr. Stoker to help us," said Pete. "We didn't get a return ticket, and we're booked at the hotel for at least a week. He expected Dr. Stoker to have much to say, even let us into their library; they have many books on the occult that may have shed light on things."

"Not going to happen now," said Joe. "The meeting had a sense of finality. He won't meet with us again."

"We should tell Harjit."

"We should," admitted Adele. "But not today. I'm fucking furious with him and don't want to talk to him at the moment. He can wait. Let's go check into our hotel and find a bar; I need a drink."

#

"This was a waste of time," huffed Adele. A half-empty pint glass sat in front of her, and she was absent-mindedly playing with a coaster bearing the name 'McElhenney's' on it.

"Not a total waste," said Pete.

"How do you figure?"

"Dr. Stoker gave us solid information before he went squirrelly on us. We have an idea what Cthulhu is, that these things are from outer space, and they can be harmed by something from out of this world-"

"Ah, shit. The dagger. He still has it," said Joe.

177

"Damn, it'd be useful to have on us if we run into another cosmic entity." Pete shrugged. "We can't help that now, I guess."

"We go back and get it," said Adele.

"I don't think it's wise," began Pete.

"That's bullshit. It's our dagger, and it might be one of the few things we can use to kill these things. Joe killed something with it. The thing in the basement, the fire may not have killed it. I'll bet that dagger could. We need to get it back."

"Dr. Stoker will not give us the knife. Maybe Harjit could request he return it?"

"Screw Harjit. I say we get it ourselves."

"What are you saying? How will we convince Stoker to give it back?" asked Joe.

"Screw Stoker too. I say we take it. Break-in if we need to. You're a cop; you should know how."

"Yeah, I'm a cop, not a criminal. We're not breaking into his office."

Adele slumped in her chair and fumed. "This whole thing is bullshit. Harjit, the Other, Stoker, all of it. Bullshit."

"Hey." Joe leaned forward and patted her arm. "We've been dealing with heavy stuff, but it isn't as bad as it could be."

"Really? It could be worse than this? What are we doing? We stumble along into things we can't comprehend. I had to kill someone driven insane by this shit. I'm a killer."

"I killed someone over this, too," said Joe.

"Yeah, but you're a cop. You might not have killed someone before, but you know it's a possibility. Pete's a soldier, so he knows it could happen too. I'm a goddamn marine biologist! A researcher! I shouldn't be killing people with an ice axe and burning houses!" She slumped forward, her head in her hands, stifling a sob.

"Are you out then?" asked Pete.

Adele contemplated this. Then with a sigh, she said: "No. How can I be? After what I've seen, with the imprint this has left on my psyche, I can't stop. Even if I told Harjit to go to hell, I will walk around and get impressions of unseen cosmic entities and relapse. If I had gotten out of his car at the airport and-"

"He'd have you detained. He said so."

"Can we trust anything he says? He's been lying to us since the beginning."

"Do you think he has much choice? Imagine what he has seen. He knows more than he is letting on to us. The threat the Other imposes is real, and he understands how real. He needs people to help, people with skills he can use. They are hard to find, especially if he limits his search to those who encountered the Other. Is he a bastard? Yes. Has he lied to us? You bet. He is desperate, and he'll do whatever it takes to limit the damage the Other can do to humanity."

"You sound like you respect him," said Joe.

"I do. Not saying I like him, but I respect what he's trying to do. If I was in his position, I might act the same way. What other choices are there?"

"Pete, stop making sense and let me hate Harjit the way I want," said Adele, a slight smile cracking her face. "He didn't need to lie to us. We might have gone along with his plan if he had told us the truth."

"You might have. But you don't know how many people he's approached in the past that said no. If he has a limited pool to draw from, every potential asset is an opportunity he can't risk losing. Harjit may have been a normal, truthful guy at one point, and this job has changed him into the shifty bugger he now is. We don't know what he's dealing with, or how many assets he's managing. We've survived this long; let's give him the benefit of the doubt."

"This anger isn't helping our plight," admitted Joe. "My life's been in greater turmoil than yours. You guys only have you to worry about; I've got my wife too."

"How is she handling things? What does she know?" asked Adele.

"Nothing. We were set to move to Victoria. She thinks I'm there now. I told her they had seconded me to another government department, and I'll be on the road, but we could stay in Cape Breton. I haven't been home since. We'd be moved and settled into our new life by now. Instead, I've been hiding out in cheap motels and lying to her."

"That has to be putting a strain on your marriage."

"Yes. Harjit… he suggested I divorce her. Said it would be easier for her. Told me that's what he did."

"Joe, man, sorry. It must be tough. What are you going to do?" asked Pete.

"I may take his advice. It's unfair to her. I can't go back and put her at risk. And we can't lead our lives apart with me lying to her."

"Sounds to me, if anyone had a reason to walk away from this job, it's you. Why don't you?"

"I can't. The nightmares, what if they get worse? I'm not myself anymore, and I can't be just her husband again. What if I wake up one day and take my service pistol and end it and take her with me? She deserves better than the man I've become."

"You've decided then," said Adele. "You just haven't done it yet."

"I guess," said Joe with a pained smile. "I'm a coward, but yeah, I know what I've got to do."

"Don't be hard on yourself. It's difficult dealing with this. You've got it harder than Pete and me; we only have ourselves to worry, as you said. You've got a whole other layer to sort out."

"Thanks. When we are done here in Arkham, I should go back to Cape Breton and talk with her. Tell her the truth. Well, maybe not the whole truth; no sense telling her we are surrounded by powerful cosmic beings intent on harming us."

"You'll feel better for it, I'm sure. If we're finished here, what do we do next? We should start developing our own plans, instead of being Harjit's errand people."

"Where could we go? What is there for us to find? Either we hope to stumble onto something, or we wait until he tells us what he's found," said Pete.

"I agree with Pete on this. Going around blind is no plan. We need intel; we need Harjit as much as he needs us."

"You're right," sighed Adele. "I don't enjoy depending on him. My life was structured, and now it's a mess."

"Get used to it. We're at war now," said Pete, finishing his beer. "Anyone want another? I'm getting another. I want to get bleary if it's ok with you."

Joe and Adele both nodded, and Pete headed to the bar to order three more beers.

"We've come a long way from Gallou Cove, haven't we?" asked Adele.

"Yeah," nodded Joe. "It seems a lifetime ago, but it has only been a few weeks."

"Wish you'd never taken the call?"

"Yes. But..." his voice trailed off. "No. Not going to Gallou Cove doesn't change the fact the Other exists. I'd be ignorant, but it would still have happened. The thing in the ice would be free, the thing in the cave may have murdered another family, the-"

"The thing in the basement might still be trapped where it was for one hundred and seventy years."

"It may be dead. Assume it is. These incidents would still happen even if we didn't go to Gallou Cove. We'd be trusting these tasks to someone else, someone who may not be as capable as we are."

"We're capable?" Adele shook her head and laughed. "I don't know what I'm doing. This has been a joke. I might have on mismatched socks."

Joe snickered. Adele looked at him and started to laugh harder. It was infectious, and now they were both laughing until tears ran down their faces.

"I miss something?" said Pete returning with the beers.

"No, just laughing at the absurdity of our circumstances," said Joe.

"This has been fun, fellas. Sure, the visit to Stoker was not what we'd hoped, and we still don't know what will happen, but this is the first real human interaction I've had in weeks. It's good to relax. Let's make the best of it while we're here, maybe see the sights. Salem has a statue of Bewitched I'd like to take a photo with, or we can head to Kingsport; I hear they have an amazing lighthouse, or-" She stopped mid-sentence as her phone buzzed. Each of their phones sounded. They took them out to look. There was a text from Harjit.

They found something in Gallou Cove. Sending the three of you tomorrow. 9:37 am flight to Halifax.

"Gallou Cove?" said Adele apprehensively. "What's there? They levelled the town. The army has that place shut down."

"It's serious if Harjit wants us to go back."

181

"I don't think I can."

"We need to," said Pete. "I wasn't there, I didn't see what you saw, but it's where it began for you. Maybe you'll get answers to what the hell happened. It might help you make sense of everything."

"He's right. We need to do this. You going to be ok, Adele?"

"I don't like it. But, maybe Pete's right. Maybe we'll find information that makes sense of things."

"Drink up. It doesn't appear we'll be getting drunk tonight, but no sense letting these beers go to waste," said Pete.

They finished their beers in silence, brooding on tomorrow's travel. No one was excited about the prospect, and the tension that had broken returned. They hailed a cab and headed to their hotel.

Pete pushed the number three. "What floors are you on?"

"Seven," said Joe.

"Twelve," said Adele. Pete pressed both.

"Well, see you bright and early. We need to arrive at the airport three hours before departure, so we need to leave by 5:30 A.M. No rest when fighting the wicked, eh?" Pete winked at both as he exited on three. "Sleep tight."

The door closed, leaving Adele and Joe alone in the elevator. Joe smiled at Adele, and she averted her eyes. When she glanced back, he was still staring at her. "Joe..."

He reached out to her, taking her hand in his own. She felt him tugging her towards him. She hesitated, but only for a moment, then went forward and placed her lips on his, wrapping him into a firm embrace. Joe returned the kiss. The doors on seven opened, but they were so intent on each other they missed them. Closing, the elevator started to rise once more. They broke the embrace, embarrassed, as the car stopped on twelve.

The doors opened, and Adele stepped out into the hall, pausing in the doorway. "Goodnight," croaked Joe.

Adele lingered, her body in the entrance, preventing the doors from closing again. Then she reached out and took his hand, guiding Joe forward and off the elevator. She led him towards her room. They didn't say another word to each other as she took out her key card and waited for the light to flash green.

Opening the door, Adele again took Joe's hand as she walked into the room. They closed the door behind them.

#

They were in the car driving the four-hour trip from Halifax to Gallou Cove. Joe and Adele were exhausted; they did not get much sleep, and 5:30 A.M. came early. If Pete suspected anything had happened between the two of them, he was wise enough to keep it to himself.

Adele and Joe had not talked that morning. At one point, on the plane, Joe had tried to reach over and hold her hand. Adele gave his hand a brief squeeze and then pulled away. She was a whirlwind of emotions. She had slept with a married man. True, his marriage was not on solid ground, and if it ended, it wouldn't be because of her. Being with Joe was the most normal thing she had done in the past few weeks. While she was in turmoil today, it was an ordinary turmoil, and not something related to the incomprehensible cosmic entities they were battling. It gave her something to dwell on that didn't involve things trapped in the ice or basements, and that made it worth it.

They had been driving in silence the two hours it took them to get to the Canso Causeway to Cape Breton. As the car touched the ground on the island, Joe said: "I should go see my wife before we leave." Adele sunk lower into her seat and closed her eyes, pretending to sleep.

The road to Gallou Cove had redirected around the town. It was surprising how fast they had completed the work on a rudimentary detour. Ahead, a barrier blocked the old road, an RCMP car parked behind, lights flashing. Pete drove their vehicle up and rolled down the window to speak to the officer that approached.

"Afternoon, officer. I'm Sergeant Pete Ivalu, Canadian Rangers," he said, holding out his ID. "We've been called into Gallou Cove on official government business."

The officer glanced at the ID and looked into the car at Adele and Joe. His eyes widened in recognition. "Hey, Millsy, is that you?"

Joe gave a brief smile. "That's Inspector Mills now, Mike. How you keeping?"

"Good, Mills... uh, Inspector-"

"Mike, I'm joking. Relax."

"Ok. I heard you were out in B.C.?"

"Um, yeah, that's where I'm stationed. But the bosses called me back; told me the investigation needed me here."

"There's nothing left of the town, but the soldiers are still on site. We keep traffic away; lots of nosey people want to check out where they found the sea monster. If they get past us, the army comes down hard on them. Don't worry, though, they are expecting you. I was told to let VIPs through this morning, but they didn't tell me you were one of them. I'll radio ahead and tell the army guys you're here; they are getting itchy trigger fingers."

"Why? I thought you said nothing was happening?"

"Nothing specific, but the soldiers are freaked out. They find the place unsettling. Army's taking to rotating them out every few days, so they don't stay on-site too long. These guys are due to muster out."

"Thanks, Mike," said Joe. "Say hi to Karen for me."

"Will do, Inspector." Mike gave him a smile and a nod. "Give Shelley my love."

Pete pulled away from the roadblock. "Shelley?" said Adele.

"My wife's name," said Joe.

"I figured," said Adele. *Great,* she thought. *Now I have a name. It was easier to confront the adultery when she was nameless. Now she's Shelley.*

Ahead of them was a chain-link fence with a gate and security shed. Two soldiers carrying assault rifles, one pointed at their vehicle, stood in front. They came over to the car.

"Sgt. Ivalu, Canadian Rangers. What's the word, soldier?"

"Your ID?"

"I showed the officer at the roadblock."

"And now show me."

Pete handed over his wallet to the soldier while the other one circled their car. He looked at the ID and back at Pete. "I need IDs for the others in your vehicle too."

184

Joe and Adele passed their passports to Pete, who gave them to the soldier. He took them and went to the security shed while his companion continued to eye them suspiciously.

"I'd hate to see how they'd be acting if they weren't expecting us," said Pete, trying to break the tension. The door to the shed opened, and the soldier returned and gave them back their IDs.

"Drive straight to the old centre of town, towards the trailers. Don't stop. Colonel Jeffers will be waiting to meet you." He signalled back to the shed, and an electric motor hummed to life as the gate started to open.

Pete drove through the gates. "They are taking security seriously."

"What the hell did they find? What did they learn?" said Joe.

Ahead, one trailer opened, and two figures emerged. One was a soldier, likely Colonel Jeffers, and the other was a woman. They stood in what was once the street in front of the Shoreline Café, which along with the rest of the buildings, had been demolished.

Pete brought the car to a stop, and they got out. He snapped to attention and saluted the Colonel who returned it. "Sgt. Ivalu. And you are Inspector Joe Mills and Dr. Adele Kramer. Welcome to Gallou Cove. I'm Colonel Jeffers, ranking officer here at the site. This is Molly Xiao; I believe she works for your boss."

"Hi," said Molly. She shook each of their hands. "I work for Harjit Singh, same as you. I'm to update you with what we've discovered here. Colonel Jeffers," she said. "I need to speak with my colleagues alone."

"Understood. I handle the security, and you handle the other stuff." He gave them a nod and left to check on his troops.

"A full Colonel on-site managing security; they aren't messing around," said Pete.

"You know what we are confronting. We aren't messing around here."

"Does the Colonel know the truth?" asked Joe.

"No, and he doesn't want to. The rumour that has stuck with the locals is there was a secret facility with toxic waste the government stored under the town in the 1950s. The tsunami disturbed it, and the government is trying to cover it up. It's like a bad Sci-Fi movie; expect giant ants to descend on the countryside."

"More likely giant lobsters," said Adele.

"We're not setting the record straight. The soldiers stick to the perimeter and don't have a clue what's real." Molly looked at her watch. "Let's go in the trailer. It's more comfortable."

She led them into the trailer. It contained a desk with a laptop and a table with four chairs spaced around it. "Anyone want a coffee? I brewed a fresh pot."

They all said yes and took seats at the table. Molly brought them their coffees and sat. "We found little here. The incident seemed to be an isolated one. At least until we found the journal."

"Journal?" asked Adele.

"Sorry, I'm getting ahead of myself. Let me back up to the day you and Inspector Mills left Gallou Cove. We started to evacuate the residents, but one family refused to go."

"Just one? Holding out for more money, were they?" smirked Joe.

"No, their daughter, Daisy, was missing. They didn't want to leave without her. She was fifteen; we figured she ran away. The family said she had been acting strange the past few months, but didn't think it was like her to run away. They were worried that she was near the pier when it was destroyed."

"No way," said Joe. "It was only me, Adele, Mary-Margaret and Cecil at the pier. My officers did a great job of keeping everyone else away."

"That's what we told them, but they were beside themselves. We had to extract them from the town and place them in a secure facility."

"You locked them up?" said Adele.

"We did what we needed to do. Two days ago, we discovered Daisy's body; she had committed suicide. Amongst her things was a journal. The information in the journal has raised our concerns." Molly got up and went to her desk and returned with a spiral-bound notebook, covered with scribbles and stickers. She slid the diary to Adele.

"What does it say?" said Adele picking it up and leafing through the book.

"Daisy found something. Something is hidden here in Gallou Cove. She discovered it a few months ago. Most of her entries are the ramblings of a typical teenage girl, the type you read five years later and get embarrassed. But start on January 14."

Adele flipped through the journal and found January 14 and started to read aloud. "*I found this wicked cool cave today, under the town. I don't know if anyone knows it's here. I only went in a little because it was dark, but I could hear waves splashing. I will come back and explore.*

"Next date is January 16. It says: '*Brought a flashlight with me and surprised to find stairs in the cave. I thought this was a natural cave. But someone had been here. It was much bigger than I thought it would be and cold. Then I found a switch. I feared what it would do but flicked it. There was a weird hum and lights came on everywhere. I followed the path.*' What the hell was she thinking, going into a cave by herself?"

"It gets weirder. Keep reading," said Molly.

"*Whoever built this had attempted to fix it up. It was an underground home. The floors were smooth, and there was furniture. It was a large grotto open to the ocean; it was low tide when I went in, and stairs were cut into the rock leading to the water. On a balcony built near the water, I found an altar. Weird freaky shit went on in this cave, I can feel it. I got spooked and ran away from that weird place. I think I'll tell Johnny and bring him here; he'll think it was cool.*"

"Adele could keep reading out loud to us, or you could sum up and tell us where this is going," said Joe irritably.

"Ok," said Molly. "She doesn't bring Johnny. I think she chickened out; she had a crush on him but was afraid to talk to him."

"Let's skip the teen angst and get to the point."

"Oh, sorry. Daisy goes back on her own. She finds several things she doesn't know what they are, along with a small library. Most of the books are written in a strange language she didn't recognize, but she reads the ones she can understand.

Daisy ends up spending a lot of time on her own in the grotto. Jump ahead to March 17."

Adele nodded and flipped ahead. *"It's weird, but the books that I couldn't read before are making sense to me. I still don't know what the language is, but I find I can read it. One of them talks about Dagon, how he lives under the sea."*

"We heard that name. Dr. Stoker mentioned Dagon," said Pete.

"Dagon is the Mesopotamian god of fish and the sea," said Adele. "Marine stuff, you know." She blushed as the others looked at her.

"The name has come up many times in our research," said Molly. "Always in coastal communities."

Adele turned back to the journal. "She goes on for pages of nonsense, but wait, here's something. *'The ritual says that the Servants of Dagon will do the bidding of the one that completes it, working to grant whatever your heart's desire. I can't wait to try it out.'* She completed a ritual hoping to attract these servants of Dagon? What was she, crazy?"

"She was a teenage girl that wanted to be popular. She'd been spending more and more time in the grotto, reading books related to the Other for weeks. I can't fault her; I've seen reports of people doing far worse with less reason than Daisy where the Other is involved."

"So, did she do it?"

"Read April 6th's entry."

"April 6th?" said Joe. "But that's the day they found the monster on the shore."

"I'm very aware of that. Read."

"Omigod, what have I done?" read Adele. *"That thing, I know it's here because of me, because of the ritual. They did it. They brought it to me to show their devotion."*

"Who are they?" asked Pete.

"It doesn't say. Daisy's handwriting gets messy here, and her entries ramble and repeat. She keeps saying it's her fault repeatedly."

"So, this teenage girl finds a hidden cave complete with Other-related items here in Gallou Cove and completes a ritual.

The ritual summons something, and next, we've got a strange sea creature washed up on the shore?" asked Joe.

"That's the thrust, yeah," said Molly.

"Have you found the grotto yet?"

"No. I haven't looked for it. We don't want the army involved in the search; that's why you are here."

"You haven't been curious? You didn't try to find it?" asked Adele.

"No," said Molly. "I'm not a field agent; I'm a researcher. I interpret what the field agents discover."

"Harjit uses researchers?" said Adele, flabbergasted.

"Yes. The data needs to be analyzed and catalogued."

"Sonofabitch!"

"What else was there?" interjected Joe.

"Not much. Daisy's journal continues to ramble on, saying Cecil Walker is dead because of her and everyone has to move because of what she had done, and that she was sorry, and she wished she'd never summoned the Deep Ones."

"Deep Ones?" asked Pete.

"I don't know what those are. Whatever she thinks she summoned."

"So, you say that the monster washing ashore was not a random incident, but something because of these 'Deep Ones' Daisy summoned?" asked Joe.

"Who knows for sure? It could be a coincidence. We're trusting the ramblings of a disturbed teenage girl. The journal might not even be real."

"Why?"

"A cry for attention? Maybe Daisy wrote it after the creature washed ashore. She wanted to be part of the most significant event to ever happen in her town. So, she wrote this journal."

"And then killed herself?"

"Just a theory. Until we have evidence to the contrary, we need to account for all possibilities, no matter how far fetched."

"It's not a fake. The grotto is real, and what Daisy wrote is true." Adele got up and began to pace. "There is something here, and we need to find it."

"How?" asked Pete.

"It can't be that hard. Daisy found the way. She said it was under the town, so it can't be far away. I'm sure the entrance is within the perimeter fence."

"Why hadn't someone else found it before her if it was this near town and easy to find?"

"If we find it, we might know the answer to that question. It doesn't matter. It may have been under a house, in a crawl space." Turning to Molly, Adele asked: "Do you know what house Daisy's family lived in?"

"I can get you that information, yes," said Molly.

"We start there and fan out. It can't be hard to find; the town isn't that big. The entrance wasn't in a conspicuous spot before, but with the buildings gone, it should be visible."

"You make it sound simple-" began Pete.

"You got any better ideas?" said Adele angrily. "We have to find this fucking place, see this goddamn altar, and recover the books Daisy mentioned in her journal. That's why we're here, isn't it? It's our job. We're field agents!" She stormed out of the trailer, slamming the door.

"What's gotten into her?" said Pete, puzzled.

"Let me go talk to her," said Joe getting up.

Joe left the trailer. Adele was standing near the car, her face in her hands, her body wracked with sobs. Joe came up behind her, stopping a few feet away. "Hey. You ok?"

"No," she said, wiping tears away from her eyes. "I am not ok. And neither are you, or Pete, or even fucking Molly, sitting in her goddamn office waiting for others to do the hard work. None of us are ok. This is fucked up. This town's cursed and we have to figure out why. I don't want to know why. I don't want to go digging for a stupid underwater cave for evidence of the Other."

Joe nodded and looked at the ground. He didn't disagree with her and needed to choose his words with care in her agitated state. "Beyond that. Snapping at Pete; he's on your side, you know?"

"I know," she said, hugging her arms around her. "It's not Pete I'm mad at; it's Harjit. Pete and Molly were convenient targets for my anger. Harjit has been lying to the three of us since the beginning."

190

"Yes, but I thought we discussed that. We're too valuable of assets to him to risk losing us."

"Joe, Molly's a researcher."

Joe shrugged. "Yeah, so what?"

"That means Harjit employs researchers. I'm a researcher, a marine biologist. You're a cop, Pete's a soldier. It makes sense why he has you in the field. Why am I in the field? Why the hell does he have me running around in ice caves in the Arctic and breaking into houses instead of sitting behind a desk and cataloguing what you and Pete are finding? Look at my cheek, Joe. At my goddamn fingers. Not to mention the mental scars I'm now carrying. I've killed two people in the last few weeks. Yes, they were in self-defence, but why am I being put into positions where I have to defend myself when he has smug little Molly sitting and waiting for us to get our hands dirty?"

"I don't know. You must have impressed Harjit with how you handled the sea creature. You are smart and tenacious. You categorized the specimen we found as something otherworldly and didn't balk at that hypothesis. This sets you apart from most people. Most would not keep pushing, wanting to discover figure it out. Even after we were overcome, your instinct was to go back in and find more. That's a rare quality, and one he values."

"So, my tenacity got me here?"

"Curiosity kills the cat."

"Not the best analogy to use here, Joe."

"Sorry. Is that the main issue bothering you?"

"Yes. I'm over his lying on how the Other would consume us. I get why he did that, his need to convince us. It is admirable he is trying to limit others from being exposed to this. Knowing what I know, I'd want to help, to continue to make sense of this — but knowing there are other ways I can contribute? I can help without having to crawl into caves and break into houses. He should have given me a choice."

"Now that you know, when this is over, tell him. Tell him you aren't going back into the field and he should find another spot in his organization for you. If the alternative is he loses you as an asset, I'm sure he'll accommodate your request."

"Yeah, maybe." She took a deep breath and let out a sigh. "Being back here is weird. I look around at the piles of destroyed buildings, and I'm seeing their ghostly forms overlaying the space. This town is burned forever into my mind. Everything started here. I sacrificed a part of my soul by coming here the first time, and I'm back. I'm afraid I'll never escape Gallou Cove."

"Yeah, it sticks with you. But we're tougher than that. We'll get past it in time."

"I don't think so. I'm not dealing with things as well as you and Pete."

"I'm not handling things well. Pete is, I think. He's tough, tougher than I am mentally. But he's seen far less than you or I."

"What do you mean?"

"He didn't get his mind messed up here in Gallou Cove with that creature. When the thing in the ice attacked you, he admitted that he was far away from it, and that spared him from the brunt of the attack. He never saw the demon I met in the cave. Compared to us, he's had limited exposure to the 'Other'. You shouldn't compare how you are doing to others since they haven't seen what you have. You've handled this better than I have."

"Thanks. It's hard, though."

"I know."

"Joe, about what happened, about your wife-"

Joe's face went red. "I'm sorry, we shouldn't have-"

"That's not what I was going to say. What we did was the most human thing I've done since that night in Gallou Cove. Yes, your wife, Shelley, is an unfortunate casualty in this, but she was before we got together. She deserves to know the truth from you. But I don't regret what happened between us."

"I will tell her. She needs to be free of me and start over again. I can't bring her into this, and I can't be the man she needs. I know what I said yesterday at the pub, but now after... after us, it's clear what I have to do."

"What are you going to say?"

"Now I can say I cheated on our marriage vows. I didn't know what to tell her before because it's so abstract. She'd never believe it, tell me to get counselling and want to stay with me. This is something she can understand. It will hurt her, but she'll get over me easier this way. It's tangible, something she can comprehend."

"Did you do this on purpose? Was last night a ploy to give you an easy out?" asked Adele, anger rising in her.

"No. There was no calculation on my part. I needed someone, some human contact, to allow me to put everything behind me and not dwell on this madness even if it was only for a brief time. It was a matter of convenience because of our shared history. Why did you do it?"

"It just happened for the same reasons you stated. I needed something to break me from what was living in my head."

"It's like Harjit, not wanting to expose new people to this. I didn't want to expose anyone else to what I have going on inside of me."

"Did you just use Harjit as an example of why you had sex with me? Gross."

Joe started to chuckle. This caused Adele to laugh. Joe's laughter became stronger too. "Sorry, that's not what I meant."

"I get it. I know what you meant. The absurdity of the statement set me off."

"While this was not a plan on my part though, it gives me a reason to end it with Shelley that doesn't involve cosmic monsters."

"Glad I could be of help then."

"You helped me in many ways last night. Thank you."

"You helped me too."

"Well, this is getting awkward. We should go back inside. I'm sure Pete and Molly are growing impatient. We need to plan our next steps."

#

"Molly said this was Daisy King's house," said Joe pointing at the tangled remains of the home.

"Do you want to start here and move out in circles?" asked Pete.

"We have no idea where to start, so this is as good a place as any. If we don't find anything near here, we can do the same near where they discovered her body. The best way to search is with a team of people in a line, a few feet apart from one another. But with only three of us, that doesn't work. If we keep this to our right at all times and spiral at an interval, we should come across something."

"What are we looking for?" asked Adele. "What if the entrance to this grotto was in a home?"

"I doubt it. The people living in the house would know it was there."

"Those living in it could have been part of the cult that built the altar."

"I think whoever built it is long gone. If they were here, I'd expect there to be more activity. Daisy's journal implied the place had been abandoned for a time."

"Not that long," said Pete. "Remember the switch and lights? Someone had modernized it."

"Electricity is not modern. That could have been added fifty years ago, hard-wired into the town's electrical grid. Besides, if it was in a home, how could Daisy find it? I think it is outside but not obvious. We can skip looking at the remains of the houses and concentrate on the gaps in between them."

"Are you guys armed?" asked Adele.

"No," said Joe. "The paperwork for us to take our sidearms to Boston was tedious, and we didn't expect to meet anything. We didn't have time to recover them."

"Couldn't you ask the army? See if Molly can ask Colonel Jeffers for you?"

"I don't think we need them. Having a gun didn't help me against the demon."

"Daisy made it in and out for months. If a teenage girl was safe, I'm sure we will be too," added Pete.

"I'd feel safer if you did," said Adele. "Not everything bad is one of those cosmic thingys."

"With the soldiers crisscrossing the town, any cultists would have to keep a low profile. I doubt any are here. Daisy encountered none, and the locals were all accounted for. Someone would have to sneak in after the army locked it down. I wish we had the knife, though."

They spread out, ten feet between each of them, and started to walk around the remains of the King home. When they had completed a rotation, Joe, who had been the closest to the centre, moved to stand ten feet past Pete, the furthest. Adele and Pete mimicked the movement, so they were now spaced again ten feet apart. They resumed their steady pace.

They repeated this manoeuvre two more times, placing Pete now one hundred and twenty feet from the King home. "What do you think the entrance will be?" asked Adele.

"I don't know. With the houses gone, the land is unobstructed. It needs to be in plain sight, but not something that attracts attention to it," said Joe.

"I may have found something," said Pete. He pointed at the ground. "There is a small spring here; it flows this way. I want to follow it."

"Why?"

"Look around you. I see no pond or visible groundwater. There is a good chance it returns underground. That might be an entrance."

"Ok, follow it. We'll stay here in case it's nothing, and we need to start our search pattern again."

Pete followed the small spring, walking in a random pattern as the water's flow altered. Fifty feet away, he stopped and knelt on the ground, taking out a flashlight and pulling at vegetation. "There is something here," he said. "The stream disappears into an opening here. The opening is small, but it widens out."

Adele and Joe joined him. The opening was in hard rock, three feet across, and hidden by moss and grass. "What would possess a teenager girl to crawl into this?" said Adele.

"Assuming this is it," said Joe, skeptical.

"Good thing I'm small," smiled Pete. "I should be able to worm my way in with no problem."

Adele glanced at Joe with his athletic frame. Sensing her gaze, Joe looked back at her. "If Pete finds something, I'll try it. I'd rather not do a Winnie the Pooh impersonation for no reason."

Pete chuckled and squeezed his feet into the hole. "I'll fit, but I'm getting wet; that spring water is frigid. Daisy was motivated if she crawled into this. Although in January, it might be frozen solid."

"I'm wondering if she was sensing something," said Adele. "She may have encountered the Other before she found this hole. It could have drawn her."

"I'm not feeling anything. Are you?" asked Joe.

"No," she said, shaking her head.

Pete had slipped out of sight into the hole. After a few moments, his face reappeared. "It's big in here, and I can hear the ocean. If it was a rough day on the water, she might have heard the noise. Maybe she was just curious. Living in small towns, kids get bored. Finding this breaks up the monotony."

"I'm coming in," said Adele. Pete pulled back and allowed her to slip into the hole. The cave inside was high enough that Adele and Pete could stand up straight, although Joe would have to duck.

"You going to try?" Pete asked Joe.

"Can't leave you with all the fun," said Joe, resigned. He slid his long legs into the hole, but his shoulders got hung up in the narrow opening. It took several attempts, a reconfiguring of the placement of his arms and the removal of his jacket, but he made it in, with only slight scrapes.

Joe's flashlight joined Pete and Adele's in casting its illumination around the cave. It was rough and uneven, and large. The spring flowed through the hole where it collected in a small pool before draining into an unseen vent. The distinct sound of waves came from further in.

"There are stairs carved into the rock," said Pete, pointing the beam of his flashlight at it. The others joined him at the top to see where they led. The stairs disappeared beyond the range of the light.

"Just as Daisy's journal said. Constructing this, especially if by hand, was no easy thing. The craftsmanship is remarkable; volcanic rock is difficult to work with."

"I thought you were a marine biologist, not a geologist," smirked Joe.

"I'm a researcher, and you come across things. This part of the island is in the Avalon Terrane, and it differs from the-"

"Anyhoo, not sure how a geology lesson is helping here," interjected Pete. "Suffice to say this shouldn't be here, and someone went through an effort to make it so."

"Just trying to educate you," sniffed Adele. "A little knowledge is never a bad thing."

Pete led the way. The walls and ceiling of the path were smooth and cut like the stairs. They descended deep into the rock, going a significant distance downwards, with the ever-present sound of waves growing louder with each step.

The stairs stopped at a hall, equally smooth. Fastened to the wall was a sizeable electrical panel, a switch in the middle of it.

"I guess we flick the switch," said Joe.

"Do you think it's safe?" asked Pete.

"Daisy did it. Electricity is not our problem here," said Adele. "Our problem is what electricity might show us."

"Right," said Joe, who reached out and flicked it. A hum reverberated throughout the cave, and a pale blue light flooded the hall from recessed lights running along its length. The lights had blended into the rock when their flashlight beams had played across them, but now they were apparent.

"So how long ago was this installed?" asked Adele.

"Hard to say. These panels have changed very little. This could be fifty years old, or it could have been installed last year."

"Any markings on it?" asked Pete.

"No. No 'Fred's Electric' stickers with a service number."

They didn't need their flashlights anymore, so they put them away. The hall was wide enough for them to walk abreast. They continued to follow the path. It curved in a ninety-degree angle and went forward fifty feet before turning again. As they rounded that corner, they saw the way opening into a room ahead.

"I think this is it," said Pete, stopping.

"Agreed."

"So why are we standing here?" asked Joe.

"I don't see you leading."

"Well, Pete's been doing a decent job of it until now."

"Yeah, I'm going. I just needed a moment." Pete took a deep breath. "We've gone through a lot, and most was in worse conditions than this. But something about this feels... I wasn't scared in the ice, nor at the village. I am now, and I don't know why."

A sense of foreboding hung heavy in the air. They stood in silence, the only sound in the hall the crashing of the waves from ahead and the sound of their breathing.

"It feels as if it's the beginning of the end," said Adele. "Once we enter the room, things will take a dramatic and irreversible turn."

"But you still can't sense the Other ahead, can you?"

"No, and I should. The Other has been so pervasive and strong elsewhere, but here where you'd expect it to be, and I'm getting nothing. It's the nothing that is freaking me out."

"It's too late for us. There is no going back. The only way is forward," said Joe, steeling himself. Pete rubbed his hands on the front of his legs and nodded.

"Let's do this before I embarrass myself," said Pete, who pushed forward.

The room was a cavern, half-finished and half in its natural state. The unfinished part dropped twenty feet to the roiling sea. Stairs cut into the rock, leading into the water. It was at low tide; they could see that the stairs were slick with slimy algae. Spartan furnishings dotted the room. A wooden table with four wooden chairs around it was in the centre, and an old couch pressed against the wall.

Further on was a bed; it had bed coverings on it, but they had been pushed back as if someone had slept in it. A bookshelf dominated the back wall, filled with a variety of tomes. The air was cold, and the waves were loud, requiring them to raise their voices to talk.

"This is weird," said Pete. "Why would you live in this grotto?"

A rope bridge was suspended over the open water, leading across a narrow gorge to a balcony built over the sea. From where they were standing, they could see a stone altar and an image carved into the rock on the back wall.

"There's the altar the girl mentioned. Let's check it out," said Joe. He went out on the bridge and made his way over to it, followed by the others.

"What is that?" said Pete, pointing to the image in the wall. "It doesn't look like anything we've encountered so far."

"It looks like a fish head," said Joe.

"No," said Adele, pushing past them to get a closer look. "It has characteristics of a fish, with its large bulging eyes and that wide mouth with sharp teeth." She reached a hand out to touch it. "But look, it has small shrunken human-like ears. Fish don't have ears. They don't have necks either, and this here is a neck." She pointed at the area beneath the mouth. "If I'm not mistaken, these ridges in the neck appear to be gills."

"So, what, a sort of fish-man?"

"I don't know what the hell it is, but that's as close a description as we will get."

"Molly said Daisy had summoned something called a Deep One. Could this be how they look?" asked Pete.

"Maybe. But I'd guess this is Father Dagon. Daisy's journal mentioned him and that she summoned the Servants of Dagon. This is most likely who the Deep Ones worship."

"These Deep Ones built this as a temple? Did they install the electricity?" said Joe.

"Again, maybe. More likely, a cult was working with the Deep Ones. A human cult that worshipped Dagon and found kindred spirits in them. Whatever they were, they needed a place to meet unseen. This was it."

"The stairs, leading into the water, do you think they are for the Deep Ones? Their name implies they come from under the sea," said Pete.

"There is an undercurrent of nautical imagery in the things we've encountered. The sea creature that washed ashore, the monster in the ice; everything points back to the sea. Your guess is as sound as any."

Joe placed his hands on the altar, but withdrew then with an exclaim, as if it was hot.

"Joe, what is it?" asked Adele.

"When I touched it, there was a strong, overwhelming feeling of the Other."

"I don't sense it."

"Touch the altar."

Adele went to it and reached her hands out, stopping an inch above the surface. She hesitated for a moment and then pulled them back. "No, I trust you. I don't need to feel it myself. But why if it is localized that strong here, why can't we sense it?"

"I don't know. None of this makes sense."

"Does what we've been doing for the past few weeks made sense to you?" asked Pete with a grim smile.

"No, but when things fall into a pattern, and the pattern is disrupted, it makes you wonder."

"So, now what? We've found the grotto and confirmed that Daisy's journal is real. What's the next step?" asked Adele.

"We could look at the books. There's information in there that could prove valuable," said Pete.

"Yeah, Harjit will want access to them too. Let's pack a few and take them to Molly. Stick to the ones in English; we can come back for the rest later," said Joe.

"That's a plan. Finally, we have something concrete to do," said Adele.

"This place is weird, but mundane, except this altar over here," said Pete. "Why were we gripped with the fear of finality before we entered?"

"I don't know," said Joe. "Of the places we've been, it feels the least out of sorts, apart from the altar." He turned to cross the bridge and froze. His voice was a dry rasp. "Run!"

"What? Where? Joe?" Adele's eyes flashed to where Joe was looking. She noticed a greyish green head emerging from the water up the stairs. Wide, unblinking eyes sat on the front of its broad face. As it rose out of the water, she saw a ridged back, with a crest running to the top of its head. Its long-muscled arms, longer than a human of equal height, ended in large hands with webbed fingers, complete with a deadly looking claw. The creature made a lumbering, hopping motion as it climbed the stairs. It fixed its eyes on them and let out an unearthly croak. Behind it, a second and then a third head broke the water's surface.

Joe clenched his hands and bellowed at the creatures. Before she could stop him, he ran across the bridge toward the stairs. He came down the first few steps and aimed a powerful kick at the gaping maw of the first one, connecting below its chin. The creature staggered and slipped, falling back beneath the waves. Joe moved towards the second.

Standing knee-deep in the surging waters, Joe punched the next one in the face. The sharp scales of the crest slashed his knuckles, and his punch had minimal effect on the creature. It reached towards Joe, its sharpened claws cutting through his jacket as it clutched him. The monster outweighed Joe, and shifted backwards, pulling Joe towards it. The being behind it reached forward and caught hold of Joe's flailing arm. Both creatures slid beneath the waves, taking Joe with them.

"Joe!" yelled Adele, crossing the bridge and standing at the top of the stair. She searched for any sign of him in the surging waters. A grey-green crested head broke the surface, and another monster started up the stairs.

"C'mon!" yelled Pete, grabbing Adele by the arm and starting to tug her back towards the path they took to get here. "You can't help him. There are too many of them!" Three more heads emerged from the surf. The first creature was ten feet from her. Turning, she allowed Pete to steer her.

They ran along the twisting path towards the cave entrance. Behind them, they heard the flapping of webbed feet hopping on the smooth stone floor. The flapping was fading as the creatures could not match their speed.

Pausing at the bottom of the stairs, they listened for sounds of pursuit. Wild croaking echoed through the complex; they were not out of danger. "Go," gasped Adele, desperate for breath. She gave Pete a push.

Running up the stairs, they came to the cave. With the vegetation pulled from the mouth, it allowed pale moonlight to filter into the cavern. They had been underground longer than they expected. Pete helped Adele squirm through the hole and followed behind her.

They both lay on the cold ground outside of the hole, gasping for air. "I'm not as recovered as I thought," said Pete, a hint of pain in his voice.

"What the hell were those things?" said Adele.

"I presume those were the Deep Ones. You're the marine biologist, and they came from the sea. I'm looking to you here."

"I study normal sea creatures, not monsters. This is outside of my knowledge." She sat up and leaned towards the hole, listening. The sounds had not come closer; they were growing faint. "I'm sick to death of goddamn monsters. And Joe…" Her voice faded, and a tear started to run down her scarred cheek and was absorbed by the bandage she still wore. "We left him, Pete."

"We had to. If we had stayed, they would have got us too. There was nothing we could do to help him."

"Isn't there a 'leave no man behind' mantra in the military?"

"Unofficially, yes, but not doctrine. No sense getting half your unit killed to get one person. This isn't a movie in Mogadishu. We lost Joe the moment he hit the water."

Adele sighed and stood up. "We abandoned him when he needed us the most."

"Joe would understand."

"Why did he attack them?"

"He just snapped. We all have a breaking point, and it has affected him the most by everything we've seen. He focused his fears and frustrations on the Deep Ones."

"You guys should have gotten guns from the army."

"In hindsight, I think you're right. A bullet could have harmed those things."

"We all could have escaped. Joe didn't have to throw his life away."

"He may have wanted it this way. He was struggling with everything. You heard him talking about his wife and the strain on them. This gives him an out without having to confront her. He dies a hero, and she never needs to know any different."

He had his out, thought Adele. *I gave it to him.* She didn't believe that Joe sacrificed himself to avoid the issue, but when you added the other stresses they were under, it wasn't implausible. "So, what do we do now?"

"Let's go back to Molly. We need to report to Harjit, tell him about Joe and what we found under the town. He'll know the next steps for us."

"He can't expect us to go back without help."

"If he tries, I got your back. No way I'm tackling that without backup."

The moon was full, and the clouds sparse. The expanse of the demolished town spread out in front of them. In the distance, the pale light from the bulb over the door of Molly's trailer called to them. They started to pick their way across the rocky landscape back to it.

As they got closer, they noticed a black figure walking towards them. It was too big to be Molly. If it was a soldier, they were not carrying a visible weapon. "Who do you think that is?" asked Adele, suddenly nervous.

"Harjit? He likes to show up at weird times in strange places."

"It's not Harjit," she said, growing fearful. "We don't want to talk to this person." She stopped.

Pete stopped and turned to her. "There's nowhere for us to go. We can't avoid whoever it is. They've seen us and are coming here."

"I know. This is inevitable," she said serenely.

Pete and Adele turned towards the approaching person. It was a man wearing a long black overcoat, moving with purposeful strides towards them.

"Sgt. Ivalu. Dr. Kramer. I note that Inspector Mills is not with you," came a rich, sonorous voice. It was familiar but different. They struggled to place it.

"No. He's had an accident," said Pete.

"The Deep Ones. They can be a handful." The figure stopped twenty feet from them. In the moon's light, they could make out his appearance: William Akeley, Dr. Stoker's assistant from Miskatonic University.

"William?" stammered Adele. "What are you doing here? How did you get past the soldiers?"

"I came for you. The soldiers are of no consequence to me."

"What is this about?" asked Pete warily.

"Your visit with Dr. Stoker was cut short. There are things you should know. And I have a task for you. Well, for one of you. I only need one. Inspector Mills being removed from the equation simplifies things, but still, a decision has to be made. Eeny, meeny, minny, mo." The finger he was using to point at them stopped on Adele. "I'm sorry, Sergeant Ivalu, it appears your services are no longer required. Your part in this tale is over."

Pete froze. Adele glanced at him. His eyes rolled back in his head, and his body collapsed into a heap. "No!" shrieked Adele, rushing to his side. A quick check confirmed what she already knew; Pete was dead.

"What the hell did you do to him?" she screamed as she rounded on William. He stood there, his hands in his pockets, a bemused look on his face.

"You need to calm down, Dr. Kramer," he said. "I have much to show you, and I have other tasks that need attending to. Worrying on the fate of Sergeant Ivalu will not alter your own. You may as well make this easier on yourself." He took a hand out of his pocket and reached it towards her. "Take my hand, and the next phase of your existence will begin."

"I'm not touching you, you murderer."

He smiled at her. "I appreciate your spunk, but it will not change a thing. You are coming with me. It will be easier for both of us if you submit to the inevitable. Now, please take my hand."

His words were honey in her mind. She wanted to resist but reached for him. The instant her hand touched his, she felt a rippling sensation flood her body, as if she was being ripped from herself. Her senses mutated, and she began to see a spectrum of colours unseeable with human eyes. The full glory of the cosmos spread out in front of her. She realized that she was floating and looked at the ground as it faded. She saw her body lying on the ground next to Pete's.

Frantic, she glanced at William. He was solid. Her form was indistinct, a hologram of herself, lacking in substance. They continued to float higher.

"This rock is an inconsequential satellite floating in the great cosmos," he said to her. "It is only significant because The Great Dreamer Cthulhu chose it as his own. You and your kind are parasitic forms clinging vainly to life, waiting until Cthulhu wakes from his slumber. Once that happens, you will be without purpose and either be destroyed or ignored. You should be honoured that Great Cthulhu chose your kind."

"What are you talking about?"

"Your place in existence. Humanity believes it's special. It is not. You are but one of a myriad of life-forms that infest the dark corners of the universe. You're the cockroaches of the cosmos."

"Where are we going?"

"To the centre of ultimate Chaos. My father slumbers there."

They drifted in silence. Bright pinpoints of distant stars surrounded them, billowing clouds of dust and gases reflecting infinite colours. Giant beings floated in the ether, and planets loomed and retreated from their path. The speed at which they were travelling was immeasurable.

"My father is the blind idiot god. We are but figments of his dreams in the universe of his creation. We exist because he thinks we exist. He rules time and space from his black throne. If he awakes, all will be undone."

"Why are you telling me this?"

"You have many questions. You will learn the answers to them in due time. I am bringing you to my father's side so you may witness and learn. Perhaps you will be called upon to relate what you have learned to the rest of your insignificant peoples. Or not. I know not, and I care not, for I am madness incarnate."

"But why?"

"I am the messenger of the Outer Gods, existing to enact their will. Their will is incomprehensible to you with your fragile psyche. Do not try to understand."

"You say that you are bringing me somewhere to witness and learn, so I may one day teach what I have learned to other humans, but then say that everything is incomprehensible, and I should not even try. You are contradicting yourself."

"Yes," he said with a smile.

"Which is it?"

"Both. And neither. Your role is essential and of no consequence at once."

"You make no sense!"

"Oh, but I do. Just not to you."

"I must be here, but it doesn't matter?"

"Exactly. You are learning."

"Who are you?"

"As I said, I am the messenger of the Outer Gods. I go by many names on a multitude of worlds. Your planet is just one of them. I enact their collective will, even when their intentions go at cross purposes. I am all and nothing at once. I am the Stalker

Among the Stars, the Crawling Chaos, the God of a Thousand Forms."

"Why have you chosen me?"

"I could have chosen anyone. It might have been Sergeant Ivalu here."

"No. You chose me."

He smiled a smile that did not reach his eyes. "You're right. I wanted Sergeant Ivalu to think in his last moments he had a chance to survive. It has always been you. I chose you long ago. My presence has guided you long before you ever reached Gallou Cove. I watched you eons ago, having been shown you by one of the Great Race of Yith. This path you are on is no mistake. It is your destiny to observe what I am about to show you."

"What? Yith? What is that?"

"The Great Race of Yith escaped their planet to find safety on your planet before your kind's primordial ancestors had evolved. They possess the ability to see through time and space and travel through it as well. I sat with them, and they showed me you."

"Why am I important?"

"You are not."

"Then why have you been watching me for eons if I am unimportant?"

"Because I have a task for you."

"A task that must be done, but is not important."

"Correct. Your race has had its prophets in the past, to prepare your kind for their place in the glorious future if they are required. The greatest of these prophets was Abdul Alhazred, and his work has been preparing the way for generations of your short-lived race. He studied in the nameless city and worshipped Yog-Sothoth and Cthulhu. His writings are the greatest collection of truth your pathetic people have ever produced. And he learned what he learned without leaving your planet, only through his worship of beings lesser than my father. Yog-Sothoth knows all, sees all, is all, and he imparted his wisdom to Alhazred. But you have the chance to witness the glory of all, to learn not through the dreams of Yog-Sothoth, but at the seat of great Azathoth himself. You have transcended your earthly prison to bear witness, to be the greatest prophet your world has ever known. Your glory and knowledge will prepare the way for the future, unless upon awakening Cthulhu deems you unnecessary or Azathoth awakes. We have arrived."

Adele looked at the scene in front of them. A monstrous indistinct form sat in the centre. Around this form, a horde of beings writhed in a chaotic dance, each keeping its own time to a monotonous pipping sound that reverberated from everywhere and nowhere at once. The ominous beating of drums joined the thin flutes making the sound.

"So lies my father, Azathoth. He has slumbered for millennia and will continue to do so as long as the pipes and drums lull him to sleep. Should he awake, everything that is will cease to exist. You are to watch his slumber."

"For how long?"

"Eternity. Or until you are called upon."

"To be a prophet?"

"No. You have no purpose."

"So why am I here?"

"It has been willed that you observe."

"But why am I observing if I have no purpose?"

"It has been willed."

"By who?"

"All and none. You must do it, but have no purpose."

"This is madness!"

"Yes, it is. I will leave you now to your inconsequential function. Watch the slumber of Azathoth. Listen to the pipes. The truth will find its way. I have other matters that require my attention." His hand released hers, and he began to drift away in the direction they had come. Adele made to follow but found herself unable to move, left floating in space.

The thing that was William Akeley left. Adele was alone with Azathoth. But as she looked around, she realized she was not alone. Around her stretched countless beings, some human but most not, floating, close enough to see but not close enough to communicate. It became clear as she floated there that what she assumed was the monotonous sounds of a flute were something different. The piping was a cacophony of screams coming from the beings surrounding the sleeping giant. Her mind succumbed and torn asunder by the scene unfolding. From deep within her, a cry began to build, and her sounds joined the others in an orchestra of madness. The great being slept.

#

"Joe's body washed up on the beach, in the same location where we found the original sea creature," said Molly. "We found Pete's body in the remnants of the town without a mark on him. Adele is alive but in a coma. I have transferred her to a hospital in Halifax."

"I'll arrange for her transfer to our secure medical centre," said Harjit over the phone. "We'll want to monitor her cognitive functions, to see what we can learn from her. I'll have the bodies of the other two retrieved for study."

"Joe was covered with bite marks and scratches, but the local coroner said the cause of death was drowning."

"The assumption is that they found the way to Daisy's cavern?"

"Yes. The three of them were gone a significant amount of time, and we found the entrance that they uncovered. Colonel Jeffers has two soldiers on guard with orders to shoot anything that crawls out of it."

"I'll send you assets to do a proper search. Do you have anything else to add?"

"Not at this time, sir. I'll finish my formal report and email it to you by the end of the day tomorrow."

"Ok. We'll be in touch. You know, I had high hopes for the three of them. I thought they were special, especially Dr. Kramer. I figured they'd be with me a long time."

"Frankly, I noticed nothing special out of them during our brief interaction."

"You and I look for different things. Keep holding down the fort Molly."

"Thank you, sir."

Harjit hung up the phone and sat back in his chair, his steepled fingers resting on his chin. His sojourn did not last long before he pulled up three files on his computer. The images of Pete, Joe and Adele looked back at him. Opening Pete and Joe's records, he typed the word 'deceased' on them. They moved to a different folder on his server upon closing them. Harjit stared at Adele's photo, contemplating it for a moment, before typing 'incapacitated' on her record. It transferred to another part of the server.

The phone on the desk trilled. Harjit hit the speakerphone button. "Harjit here. What's the news?"

"Boss, we got a report of a 911 call for a medical emergency to a home in Regina. Paramedics were first on the scene. It was a real shit show. There were signs of the Other in the place. Something in the home attacked one of the first responders; they don't think he will make it. His partner came out unharmed. He might be a candidate."

"Email me his profile. I'll take a look. I have a few positions that I need to fill. Thanks for the heads up."

"Just doing my job." The line went dead.

Harjit waited for the email to arrive. Once it did, he opened up the attachment and scanned the profile of the paramedic from Regina. Liking what he saw, he picked up the phone. "Tabitha, I need you to make travel arrangements for me. I'm off to Regina this time." Pause. "Yes. And then I must go to Cape Breton. Make sure we have a meritorious service plaque made up for Joe Mills; I must visit his wife." Another pause. "Yes, word came in this morning — the worst part of the job. I almost passed on him due to his marriage, but we are so short-staffed right now. Pete Ivalu is dead, but I have no one to tell." Pause. "Thanks, Tabitha, I will." He hung up.

Turning his attention back to his computer, he looked again at the paramedic's file and began to compile his notes.

Troy Young

The Happenings of December 13, 2012

Memo #1

Author: Harjit Singh
Written: May 19, 2013

Subject: The Happenings of December 13, 2012, Fort McMurray, AB

My name is Harjit Singh. I am a member of the Department of Extraordinary Phenomena for the Federal Government of Canada. My employment with the Department started six months ago. Director Jim Norton asked me to write this memo regarding the circumstances of my coming to work for the Department. The Director asks every employee who makes it to the six-month mark to document their story.

I was employed at the Charlton Oil Field in the Athabasca Oil Sands near Fort McMurray, Alberta. My wife Neha and I had both taken jobs there; she in the payroll office and me working out in the mines. The high pay attracted us to Northern Alberta. Not much other reason to go somewhere that far north and remote. It took time for us to fit in; Canada's a diverse country, but Alberta has an (unfair) reputation for being backwards and racist. Alberta was no worse than other parts of the country. I've been getting "Go back to your own country!" all my life, to which I respond, "I'm from Brampton!"

At last, they accepted us in Alberta. Yeah, there was good-natured (racist) ribbing from the guys in my crew at first, but we bonded over Molson Canadian, Hockey Night in Canada, and making fun of the Americans that came to work on the fields. Work hard, find common interests, and put up with the crap, and eventually, you'll be able to fit in anywhere. The world has changed a lot in the past six years. They'd probably be written up today for their comments.

I don't want to leave the impression that my crew were bad guys. They weren't. They were like brothers to me, and I miss them every day. I want to enter their names here for the record because they deserve to be honoured. I knew their wives, their kids. They welcomed us into their homes, their lives, and made us feel part of the community. Doug Grayden. Vince Dorlan. Mike Kloves. John White. Dave Leonard. Part of what I do now, I do for them.

I remember the night like it was yesterday. It was Thursday. It hadn't snowed that day, but we were already buried under forty centimetres of the stuff. It was cold but not as severe as some days; it got to a low of negative twenty Celsius that day. We'd just got off our shift, and we headed to get out of our work gear, grab a shower and go to Cheever's, our local bar for a quick beer before going home to our families. We'd been talking about having a pre-Christmas gathering, getting our families together that Saturday, the kids playing together, you know, the kinds of things that people close to one another do, especially when you live somewhere isolated.

We were almost back to the main admin building and were passing by one of the power shovels we used to excavate the oil sands when something dropped from above us. A large black glob hit the ground in front of us with such force it disintegrated, splashing us. We figured it was a deposit of heavy crude that had been stuck to the digger and had dislodged.

As I was standing at the back of the pack, the splash missed me. Big Mike, he was in the front; he took the worst of it. Big Mike lived up to his nickname. He was a former centre with the BC Lions football team, six foot five and three hundred pounds. But he was your stereotypical gentle giant. I feel the need to stress this now before I write about what happened later. I think if his bulk hadn't been in front, I might have gotten hit with it.

Initially, we were stunned and started cursing the idiot that had left their machine in such a condition. If it had landed directly on one of us, it could have killed us. But as we stood there, things started to get weird. The first thing was the smell. It didn't smell of bitumen. It smelled more of fresh-picked mushrooms, that earthy wet smell that they have. And the scent was strong, far stronger than you'd expect. It stopped Vince in mid-bitch, and nothing could stop Vince once he got started on something.

Next was the colour. The light was dim; the sun set at a quarter to four that day, and the lights from the admin building didn't make it that far. But whatever was on the guys had a tinge of purple. We could see hints of purple on the snow.

And that's when the weirdest thing of all happened. The purple started to contract as if it was sucking in on itself. The splatter zone was shrinking right before our eyes. It pooled in a uniform circle and then seeped into the ground in front of us. At that time of the year, there should have been four metres of frost under our feet. No liquid should penetrate it. And it disappeared into the frozen ground.

The snow showed the impact of whatever it had been, but it left no other trace, just what was over us. Dave brushed the snow away from the ground where we had last seen the pool, think there must be a deposit or something. He dug to the dirt underneath, hard as cement, without a crack or any other visible disturbance.

We were freaked out by then and walked to the admin building in silence. Everyone took an extra long shower to get the stuff off. No one felt like going to grab that beer anymore.

Mike called in sick the next day, which was unlike him. Everyone else was melancholy, and we did our work without the jovial camaraderie that we usually had. During the break, Doug called Mike's house to check on him. Mike said he was fine, just a headache that he couldn't shake, and promised to be at the family gathering the next day.

The families came together as planned at Doug's place. Mike made it as promised, but he did not look himself. His eyes were bloodshot, and he had heavy purple bags under his eyes. A loud talker usually, Mike was quiet that day, agitated. While the kids played and the wives were in the kitchen, we headed to the garage. Doug opened his fridge and passed out beers, which Mike refused. This was so unlike Mike; I've seen him polish off six at lunch and not even have a slight buzz. He kept rubbing his face and pacing back and forth. He confided in us he hadn't slept since our encounter, that he had intense dreams about floating in space, and had a constant strange piping sound in his ears that no one else could hear. He hurt all over, even his teeth; one of his molars had fallen out. We urged him to go to the doctor. He said his wife had been nagging him to go too. He had an appointment for Monday morning.

Mike never made it to the doctor. We don't know what happened after he left the party, but the police were called to his home on Monday morning when the neighbours heard screams from inside his house. It was terrible. Mike was sitting on the front step, crying and rocking back and forth, muttering gibberish. Inside they found the bodies of Eileen, his wife and Jessica and Billy, his two kids. Little Jessie was only four. She was everything to Big Mike. Billy, well, they had a good relationship too, but Jessie was special. Nothing made him prouder. They found her with every bone in her body crushed. Eileen was lying at the bottom of the stairs like someone had pushed her down them. Billy, who was seven, it looked as if he had tried to protect his sister from her father. I can't imagine the terror that must have been present in their final moments. Mike didn't resist the police when they arrested him; he just let them lead him away. I hear one cop at the scene quit the force the very next day over what he saw in that house. Someone later burned it down, as no one would ever want to live in it again.

Our bosses gave us the day off, so we met at Cheevers. Doug was a mess. He had the same drawn-out appearance that Mike had at his house that weekend. He'd started to have similar dreams, the same symptoms that Mike described. John grabbed him and pulled him out of the bar, telling him he was going to the doctor right away. We agreed we should go and get checked too.

Of course, the doctors couldn't diagnose anything. They had no idea what they were dealing with. Luckily someone did.

Jim Norton showed up in Fort McMurray on Wednesday morning with a small team. They secured the wing of the hospital, and his medical staff gave us a going over. He never told us what was affecting the guys, but everyone had whatever it was in their systems except me. They would stay under his care until the danger had passed. I was free to go.

I never saw any of my friends again. Jim told me he had taken them to a secure facility, and that the very best care had been given to them, but that there was nothing they could do but make their final days as peaceful as possible. He assured me their families would receive generous pensions from Charlton and the federal government.

Jim asked me to go with him and his team to the oil field, to show him where it had happened. His team tested the hard soil, and we found the power shovel we had walked past. They recovered residue from it. Later that day, he asked me if I would join the Department.

This is how I first found out about the Other. In the past six months, I have seen things I never thought possible. The threat it poses is real, and one we need to be diligent in stopping.

I left Neha and our daughter Julie. It was a few weeks after I joined. I couldn't shake the story of Mike and what he had done to his family. Later, Jim told me that Mike had said it was the darkness. "The darkness made me do it!" he kept screaming right until the end. What if I had an episode like Mike's? I couldn't risk harming them, so I left.

Neha and Julie moved back to Brampton to be around family (hers and mine). I haven't been in contact with them, and no one knows where I have gone. Jim has them monitored at all times, lets me see photos and videos of them both from time to time; Julie has lost her first tooth and looks so much like her mother. Every time I see these photos, it tears my heart out all over again, but it reminds me of why I do this. I'm doing this for Mike and John and Dave and Vince and Doug. For their families. I'm doing this to keep my wife safe from me. But mostly I'm doing it for Julie, making this world a better place for her. The Other needs to be stopped. I doubt we can do that, but we have to try. Those of us that know about it owe it to everyone else to protect them from it as best we can. I will do whatever it takes to do that, no matter where it takes me. I dedicate the rest of my life to make this a reality. On the memories of my friends, and the lives of my wife and daughter, I promise you this. I love you all too much ever to stop this quest and will do what it takes to succeed. By any means necessary.